CRYSTAL MOON

Book 4

ADDISON CARMICHAEL

ISBN: 9798725951547

"You know what the issue is in this world?

Everyone wants a magical solution to their problem,

And everyone refuses to believe in magic."

--Lewis Carroll/ALICE IN WONDERLAND

Crystal Moon

Prologue

"You knew about him? All along?" I rasped.

"Oh course, I did, Jillian. Who do you think ordered me to train you?"

The wind punched from my gut at the ultimate betrayal, having fit that last piece of information confirming the dark mystery behind my abilities.

How could I have been so naïve, so stupid?

All this time.

"I told him he shouldn't waste his time, that you'd never join us. You're too noble. You don't have the stomach or soul to rule a beautifully darkened world. But trust me, Jillian, it will happen, and soon. We just have to clean up a few loose ends. Unfortunately, now one of them is you. Apologies, dear heart."

Suddenly the driver's seat of the car was empty.

Screaming, I reflexively grabbed the steering wheel from the passenger's side.

Just as I heard the blaring horn of an oncoming semi-truck and was blinded by its flashing headlights in the midnight darkness.

Crystal Moon

Chapter 1

I opened my eyes to a room that was strange and unfamiliar. The walls were an ugly mint green. The two framed pictures on the walls were generic landscapes. Cream colored blinds covered the single window to my right, and I couldn't be certain, but I thought I hated blinds, that they reminded me of being in…

That's when I noticed the retractable rail on the side of my bed, then the blinking machine attached to wires and tubes that led back to me.

"Oh God, Jillian, you're awake!"

My eyes shifted to the brown-haired man halting by the open door.

He dropped a bouquet of daisies, then called down the corridor, "She's awake! Get Dr. Lewski quick!"

The man then ran up to my bedside and grabbed my hand that I noticed had an I.V. tube taped to it. He was nondescript enough, but there was something repellant about him and his too serious gray eyes that made me yank my hand away.

"I'm sorry, Jilly. I didn't mean to hurt you," he said, pressing a light hand on top of my head. "I'm just so damn glad to see you back with us."

I tried to apologize for my rude reaction, but for some reason my voice wouldn't work.

"No, don't try to talk. The doctor will be in…Dr. Lewski, she just woke up!"

A pudgy man with dark rimmed glasses and white lab coat entered the room. The brown-haired man stepped aside, so that the doctor could take my pulse and go through a cursory exam.

"Whaa..?"

"Don't strain your voice, Ms. Azure," the doctor said. "It should return in good time."

In good time?

Where was I? What happened to me?

"W-whar.?"

"You're here at Denver Grace Hospital," he answered. "You were in a car accident and were seriously hurt. It was touch and go there for a while, but thankfully you pulled through."

I tried to speak again, but my throat was too dry. I weakly gestured for the plastic cup and straw on a rolling side table. The doctor helped me take a couple of sips, and the stale water wet my larynx enough to open it a bit.

That's when I noticed several greeting cards, vases and baskets of flowers placed around the room, more than a dozen—daisies and tulips and carnations, palm plants and succulents. But it was the lavender roses in a lead crystal vase on the windowsill that caught my eye and made my heart skip in anxious hope. They were long-stemmed and surrounded by fern leaves and puffs of babies' breath. They were also dead.

That's when I realized for someone who had been in such a critical auto accident that left me "touch and go", I had no plaster casts, no bandages or stitches or bandages on my body anywhere. In fact, other than being stiff and achy, I felt no real pain of any kind.

"II-how…long?"

The doctor and the man exchanged an anxious look, but it was the man who stepped up then and gently folded my hand into his.

"Jillian, sweetheart. You've been in a coma for more than seven weeks."

Coma!

Seven weeks?

Logic and reason told me that he probably spoke the truth, but there was something else, something deeper that screamed this was all a lie.

"W-who..?" I swallowed hard to gather saliva, then tried again, "Who are…you?"

He dropped his smile and my hand simultaneously, then looked accusingly at the doctor whose own expression wasn't happy with my question.

"Not to worry," the doctor reassured him. "It's natural for a coma patient to experience dissociative fugue—temporary memory loss. Just talk to her as you normally would."

"Jillian," the man tried again. "It's me, Doug. Your fiancé."

I frowned at him, searched his lean face for any recognition, any hint that I would even be attracted to him in any way. It all came up blank.

"Do you know who you are?" the doctor questioned me.

"Jillian…Azure?"

Truthfully, I only repeated what they had said moments ago. I couldn't make the connection between myself and this name. In fact, I couldn't remember any of my personal history at all.

"That's right," he said with a broad smile, then turned to the man, Doug. "You see, it's all coming back. Just be patient with her for a while yet, Mr. Hayden. Give it time."

"Time?" he ground out. "She's already been out for almost two months! How much longer do I have to wait?"

"Patience, as I said. For now, she needs rest. I'll send the nurse in to attend to her. In the meantime, you should go on home."

"What if she slips back into the coma?"

"Unlikely at this point. Honestly, Mr. Hayden, the best thing you can do for Jillian now is to give her a little space to regain her bearings. I'm certain you'll see a significant improvement with her on your next visit."

I hated that these men were talking about me as if I wasn't there. Still, if that meant they would both leave, I would gladly tolerate it.

Doug Hayden stepped up to me and took my left hand that didn't sport a diamond ring and kissed it, smiling down at me.

"I'll be back first thing tomorrow, Jill. I promise."

I twitched a cheerless smile, mostly to satisfy him enough so that he would go away. Hayden kissed the top of my head, then followed the doctor out into the corridor as they continued their discussion of my wellbeing and the prognosis of my future stay there at the hospital.

With both gone now, I quickly took inventory of all that I had just been told. I had been in a major car accident that almost killed me, and I had been in a coma for seven weeks. My name was Jillian Azure, and I had an unappealing fiancé by the name of Doug Hayden. I hated mint green walls and window blinds, and I loved lavender roses, even if they were dead.

Not a lot to go on, but at least it was a start.

* * *

"Jillian, love. Don't leave me. Please. Fight it and come back to me. Fight with all your strength!"

It was a vicious battle, but the caramel warm voice called me to the surface from the watery depths that again tried to suck me down and drown me, this time for good. I knew this voice, loved this voice. It had miraculously rescued me from the black quagmire that had trapped me before, and was fighting desperately for me again.

After viciously thrashing about in sheer panic for hours, my soul finally spotted the glimmer of light above, and I frantically swam up to it. Gratefully I broke the surface from my dark, watery grave and sucked in a deep, cleansing breath of mental oxygen.

I was alive. Again.

Taking real, physical, ragged breaths, I became suddenly aware of my true surroundings and the hospital bed I slept in.

It had just been a dream, a nightmare of sorts.

Or was it?

"Jillian, love, wake now. You need to come back to me now. Please. I don't have much time left."

My eyes cracked open, and I saw a darkly handsome man with amazing green eyes and a kissable smile that curved up at one corner as if he was hiding a delicious secret. His wavy black hair was just long enough that a few rakish strands hung over one eye and the ends curled up slightly at his neckline. He wore a midnight blue shirt and black slacks that suited him very well.

"Hi, beautiful," he said with a widening smile. "Thanks for coming back to me. You nearly slipped away again, and I'd be lost without you."

"Sorry."

He pressed a gentle hand on top of my head, and my entire heart and body instinctively eased as if stepping into a warm bath. "It was a tough one, but you did it. The death-sleep curse is completely broken this time. You'll be fine now."

I sighed deeply, knowing he spoke the truth, even though I wasn't sure what that truth was.

"Purple…roses," I rasped.

He rubbed tiny, comforting circles across my forehead with his thumb. "They're your favorite. I really think they just remind you of an amethyst geode."

That was right, too. I didn't know how I knew, but I knew that I would think this.

"They're…dead."

He quirked a playful grin. "I suppose I should do something about that then, yeah?"

He checked the open door behind him, then raised his forefinger to his lips for me to keep silent. Then he twirled his hand, creating misty looking gold sparkles, then flicked his fingers, sending the line of twirling sparks in the direction of the vase. Instantly the drooping roses plumped out and bloomed with bright color and vitality as if they were freshly picked.

"Better?" he remarked.

I nodded, smiled.

"Who…are you?" I asked.

He was about to answer, but a nurse stopped by the opened door and gave the man a disapproving look. He flicked his fingers at her, and she straightened, blinked hard, then robotically walked away.

"Don't...go."

He leaned down and kissed my forehead. "My time is almost up, so I have to go now, but I'll still come back to you once more."

"Promise?"

"I do. I love you, Jillian. Rest now and be well."

With that, he left the room. A few minutes later, the same nurse returned with a food tray, beaming at me as she set it down on the rolling table.

"Wonderful, you're awake now," she said brightly. "Just in time for dinner."

"Who was...that man?" I asked, desperate to know his name.

Her smile twisted. "Man?"

"The one who was...just here."

The nurse checked over her shoulder, then turned back with shaking head. "No one's been here for the last three hours, dear. You must be mistaken."

"No. He was here. You saw him."

"I didn't—"

"You saw him! Where is he? I need him!"

She pressed me back on the bed as I started to rise, going into her nurse-restraining-agitated-patient mode. "You're confused. It's alright. It will just take some time."

I relaxed against her grip, knowing to fight her would do no good. I didn't have the strength yet to overpower anyone, and right now I was acting like a maniacal mental patient. It was best to weakly comply to their requests and suggestions if I didn't want to be strapped down or transferred to the psyche ward, extending my prison sentence here.

"Sorry, I thought...sorry."

"Nothing to worry about," she said, relaxing her hold. "This has all been disorienting for you, I'm sure."

She rolled the table across my lap. "Have some dinner and get your strength up. I'll come back to check on you in a little bit."

I forced a cheerless smile, and she left to attend to her other patients. Turning to the window again, I spotted sun rays shining through the sleek crystal vase, throwing rainbows against the sill. The roses were a pale violet now, some in full bloom, others in awakening buds.

They had been dead, but now they were alive, vibrant.

He did come into my room and magically restore them to life. I saw the gold sparkles fly from his fingertips. I still felt his soft lips on my forehead.

I didn't imagine him. I wasn't crazy.

The lavender roses. They were my proof.

I pushed the tray table away, then carefully swung my legs over the side of the mattress. I didn't know if I had the ability or strength yet to stand upright, but I had to try.

Inch by inch, I lowered my bare feet to the ground and shakily stood like a newborn colt, holding onto the rolling I.V. pole that had its hooks in me.

Miraculously I was up. Now was the much harder part.

Slowly I shuffled one foot in front of the other, again, then again, and again. One step, another step, all the while hanging onto the rolling I.V. pole for support.

It seemed to take forever, but at last I made it to the window. I reached towards the crystal vase of fragrant roses and searched for a card amongst the blooms. I needed to know his name. It was important that I knew who he was, that he really existed.

Deep inside, I found a small notecard that simply read:

Get well quickly—Love, M

That wasn't a lot of help.

I sucked through my teeth at the sharp stitch in my side, my stiff legs aching and trembling from even this small exertion. Gripping the card in one fist and the I.V. pole in the other, I shuffled back across the room and collapsed onto the bed, huffing hard as if I had just hiked up Pikes Peak.

It had been worth it though. I now had proof that my magical man was real and not just a delicious figment of my fantasies. I smelled and touched his lavender roses. I still held his card in my fist, my lifeline, my anchor. Maybe I only had the first initial of his name, but it was written with an artistic flare in his own hand.

Did Doug Hayden know of him?

I looked at my ringless left hand.

Probably not, I reasoned. I sensed that it was vital he not know as well, that no one learned of my mysterious visitor.

Laying my head back on the pillow, I closed my eyes and breathed with relief.

He said he would return. He promised. I needed him to, counted on that. He was the one who woke me from my black sleep with just the call of his seductive voice. And he was the only one who could ever help me see the light of day again.

* * *

"Make sure she takes these three times a day with meals," the doctor instructed Doug Hayden. "She'll need to finish the entire bottle."

"Thank you and your staff here for all that you have done for us," he said, placing a protective hand on my shoulder.

The doctor smiled down at me sitting in a wheelchair now wearing black slacks and a long sleeve pink blouse. "We'll miss our star patient around here. Your physical therapy this last week has gone remarkably well. I'll see you next week for your follow up exam?"

I smiled and nodded. I was well practiced doing that this past week.

"Thank you again, Dr. Lewski," Doug said, shaking the physician's hand. "Thank all the staff here for us too."

Being overly pleasant and cooperative the past eight days had paid off, and I was now being discharged early from my hospital prison. Few memories had returned to me, fragmented images at best, but I was definitely getting better at lying about them.

Actually, it was easy. People typically gave me prompts at my pauses, and their expressions most times told me what they expected to hear.

The nurse wheeled me down the busy corridors, then took the elevator down to the lobby and rolled me out through the parting glass double doors into the fresh air.

"I'll bring the car around," Doug told her. "It'll just take a second."

I took advantage of his absence and stood to scan the parking lot and area around it. "M" wasn't there, anywhere. Instantly I deflated with disappointment.

After an entire week, I was now beginning to question if my magical stranger had really been a wishful delusion from my confused coma dreams. I would have believed it too, if it weren't for the lavender rose in my hand and the notecard wadded in my fist.

With the anticipation of my discharge this afternoon, Doug had taken the cards, balloons, bouquets and baskets home last night. Apparently we lived together in a small house rented in the small town of Oakwood forty minutes north of Denver where he grew up. He explained that my parents Rachel and Bill Azure had moved to Florida three years ago after they retired and I graduated Colorado State University where Doug and I first met. They sent their love and planned to visit next week when I was feeling better.

"I like geodes, don't I?" I asked Doug the day after M's visit.

He gaped at me a moment before saying, "You're finally remembering, Jillian! And yes, I think you prefer rocks to any living thing. That's why you teach earth science at Lawndale Community College. They're holding your job for whenever you want to return, but they said no rush, to take your time to recover fully."

I had braided back my long ash blond hair today, something I must not normally do by the surprised look on Doug's face when he first picked me up. Listening to a recitation from Dr. Lewski to a small group of interns during his rounds, I learned that I just turned twenty-six years old and was in relatively good health with the exception of my memory loss and the slight limp due to some damaged ligament on my right leg that hadn't healed.

A dark blue Lexus pulled up to the curb, and Doug jumped out and rounded the car to assist the nurse helping me into the passenger's seat. We left the bustling city behind and was driving quietly up the rural forested highway before anymore was said between us.

"You look different today," Doug said. "Especially your hair."

Self-consciously I touched the braid slung over one shoulder. I thought wearing street clothes, I would be able to look into the bathroom mirror and remember the young woman with glacial blue eyes staring back, but she was still a stranger.

"I could pull the braid out, if you'd rather," I remarked.

"No, it's looks good. Different, but good."

There was more awkward silence before Doug added, "I should warn you."

I shot a look to him. "What?"

"Dove insisted on throwing you a welcome home party. You know Dove. She went all out, and now half the town will be there. You remember Dove Trevor, don't you, sweetheart?"

"Of course," I lied. "Dove. She's our…neighbor."

Doug grinned, facing the highway. "A few streets over, but that's as far as I would be able to live within the proximity of any of your friends on the town events committee, especially Dove. Ever since we moved to Oakwood ten months ago, you both have been inseparable. And no offense, but she never knows when the party's over and it's time to go home."

"How long do you think everyone will stay tonight?"

"Not long, I'm sure." He glanced at me with drawn brows. "If it gets to be too much, Jill, just say the word and I'll boot everyone out the door. It's just that Dr. Lewski thought seeing a few familiar faces might help break up your mental logjam."

I nodded, then turned to the passenger's window to gaze out at the endless pine trees, red rock hills and boulders racing by. I tightened my right fist in my lap, feeling the sharp edges of the folded notecard.

Something was off.

I shouldn't be heading in this direction. I knew it somehow.

Soon we drove by the Oakwood city limits sign and entered the bucolic mountain town that was straight from a vacation postcard. I recognized none of the new or historical buildings or any of the people who waved or raised hands at us.

We turned onto a clean suburban street, and as forewarned a dozen cars were parked along the curb. The two-story house we parked in front of was decorated with balloons and banners. Immediately our car was bombarded by a mass of greeting, welcoming, chattering strangers, opening my door, touching and clinging and ushering me towards the house. I felt like I was caught in a deadly human riptide that was washing me out to the open ocean.

Once inside, a squirrel-like woman with puffed, freckled cheeks and curly red hair squealed and embraced me with a suffocating bearhug.

"Welcome home, Jill-Pill! They said you wouldn't pull through, but I knew you would. No one can ever keep our girl down for long, right?"

"Dove?"

"You remember! Chuck said you wouldn't, but I told him you couldn't forget your partner in crime here back home. Hey, the Aurora Lights Festival is coming up, and if you're up to helping out…"

She chattered on, but I merely grinned and nodded and tuned her out. She was just one of the many noisy drones that bombarded me the entire evening, each one with new interrogation questions of their own. I was getting good at the "Oh, rights" and "Of course I remembers" when pummeled with the Q&A of my alleged past life.

I was agreeing to a neighbor's recollection of our block party barbeque last fall and the fact that I loved Susan's garlic red potatoes when Doug came up from behind and touched my shoulder.

"Sue, Tim, you don't mind if I steal my fiancée from you for a few minutes?"

They happily agreed, and he led me away to the gratefully quiet office in the next room.

"Thanks," I said with a long breath. "Five seconds more, and the woman would've been in our kitchen whipping up my favorite side dish."

"How're you holding up?" he asked. "You look a little overwhelmed."

I had been overwhelmed since the moment I stepped out the car, but I politely passed it off.

"I'm fine."

"Really? You don't look it. Damn, this was a bad idea, I'm sorry."

"It's all fine. Thank you again for arranging all this."

"It was Dove's doing mostly. I should've known she'd go overboard. You know Dove."

"Of course."

The door opened, and a blond man about our age wearing tan slacks and green button-down shirt walked into the office. He was tall and athletically built with looks that would turn any female's head a few times.

"Great, you made it," Doug said, gesturing him over. "Jill, you remember my cousin from New York, James Nolan."

"James?"

"We took him river fishing last month when he was here last," Doug coaxed.

The man studied me hard, his quicksilver eyes narrowing, and I swear I could feel him probing through my mind. Quickly I broke the intense connection and plastered on my well-practiced plastic smile.

"Of course. Nice to see you again, James."

He gave me a gentle hug, saying quietly in my ear, "Glad to have you back, Jillian. For a while we were afraid that we had lost you for good."

An icy shiver raced up my spine, and I reflexively stepped back.

"Can't get rid of me that easily," I said with a nervous chuckle.

"Apparently not."

I shot a wide look at him, and he flashed a charming, handsome smile.

"James is out here on business," Doug explained.

"Here in Oakwood?" I asked, surprised that he would have any dealings in this small town.

"In Denver," James corrected. "Good timing too. Gave me a chance to swing by and make sure Doug and you were doing okay."

We fixed stares, and my gut gripped.

He was lying. It was a casual, innocuous thing for him to say, but I knew in my bones the man's comment wasn't true. Or at least not completely.

"That's kind of you," I said.

"Not at all," he answered. "We do for family, Jillian. And you're family."

A crack of thunder startled me. Seconds later, hard rain battered the roof and windows, and several people squealed and headed outside for their cars.

"Looks like the party's over," Doug said. "I'd better make the rounds to say goodbye to everyone."

James pulled his silver stare from mine, then turned to Doug. "I should head out too. I'll try and stop by again before I fly home tomorrow."

"Sounds great," Doug said. "It'll give us a chance to grab some coffee before you leave."

He gave me a quick hug and Doug a manly shoulder slap, then left the room.

"You okay, hon?"

I jumped again at the next quick flash outside and thunder rumble, then turned a twitching smile to Doug's tight expression.

"Fine. It's just the storm. Let's both say goodbye to everyone."

Within twenty minutes the last partygoer headed outside into the now misting rain. Doug closed the door, and I grimaced at the mess, the place looking like the aftermath of a frat house kegger.

College!

That's right. I still needed to…

"Don't worry about cleaning up," Doug said. "Gretta will be by first thing tomorrow to take care of it. Head up to bed, and I'll be up in a few minutes."

I shot a wide look at him, and my stomach dropped. Did he expect us to sleep together tonight? That would be a reasonable thing, of course. After all, we were engaged to be married.

"Doug, I…I can't…"

"Oh. Of course," he said, disappointment dropping his expression. "No pressure, really."

"I'm sorry, it's just that…"

You're a stranger to me. And a repellant one, at that.

His hand shot up to stop me. "It's okay. You're still recovering, getting used to everything again. You take the bed tonight, and I'll sleep in the guestroom. Then we'll figure all this out tomorrow."

"Doug, I'm sorry, really. It's not—"

"Don't worry, I understand," he cut in. "Or I'm trying to. Dr. Lewski said that you're making remarkable progress, and that all your memories will fully return soon. We just have to be patient."

He stood there awkwardly a long moment, then finally said, "Well, goodnight, Jill. Let me know if you need anything."

"Thanks for everything, Doug. You're a good man."

He gave me a stiff nod, kissed my forehead, then made his way towards the kitchen. I heard the clink of glass and knew he was pouring himself something much stronger than an iced tea. Once again, my gut gripped with deep guilt.

Although I was relieved that I wouldn't have to share a bed with the man, I was too keyed up to manage any sleep right then myself. The rain had completely stopped now, so I headed outside to the front yard for some fresh air.

Crickets and frogs sang their night songs as I wandered around the front lawn. I breathed in the comforting aroma of wet grass and pine resin from the freshly spritzed trees, and rosemary and lavender from the flower garden edging the side fence.

I sat on the park bench underneath an aspen tree and gazed up at the moon and stars breaking through the remnants of storm clouds. It was a beautiful night, but I still felt like I was walking through some bizarre dream, that nothing here was real and would dissolve with the misty fog rising and curling from the ground. Worse, I feared that I would always feel this way, as if I was locked in some mental prison I could never escape from.

"Jillian, love."

My breath caught at M's voice, and I jumped up and frantically looked around. He stepped from behind the fir tree and walked up to me. I reached up and pressed my hand to his firm chest to make sure that I wasn't imagining him this time, easing when I felt his steady heartbeat.

"You're real."

"I am," he said, folding his warm hand over mine.

My entire mind and body settled peacefully. Of everything I had experienced and learned and listened to these past eight days, he was the only thing that felt utterly right.

"I love you," I said, stating this more as a fact than expressing an emotion.

He smiled. "You do."

"And you love me."

"With all my heart and soul."

"Then why didn't you come back for me?" I accused, pulling from his grasp. "You promised."

His smile melted. "I'm here now. This is me keeping my promise."

Technically this was true. Still, I wanted to beat his chest that he should have returned sooner to take me away before these strangers who I didn't want to be with drove me to this unknown place and force me into a life that I didn't recognize or want in any way.

"What's your name? Who are you?"

"Marc Zander," he said. "I'm the love of your life. Or will be."

"What's that supposed to mean?"

"It means that you haven't met me yet," he said. "But you will."

I took a step back, my fractured memories wreaking havoc inside my brain, all spinning and fighting to surface and fit together.

"I don't understand. What are you talking about?"

"That I was able to pierce the veil of time in order to come back to you," Marc Zander said.

"What? You're crazy!"

"I know this will be hard for you to understand or accept, Jillian, but I'm from the future. Your future," he said. "And that you're the one who sent me back."

I pressed a hand to my forehead. "That's…No, that's impossible."

"Not for you. You're a very powerful mage. Or will become one anyhow."

"This is insane," I reasoned with shaking head.

"It's true," he said. "You had no choice but to send me back here. I was the only one who could break the death-sleep curse chaining you into a coma after they tried to kill you. Then when you woke, they tried again, and very nearly succeeded. They'll do anything to stop the Red Moon Prophecy from happening."

"Red…You're not making any sense!" I said, rubbing my forehead hard.

"Please listen, love. The spell threads are breaking, and this is the last time I can come back to warn you. You need to find the present me and convince me to train you in your gift of sorcery, or all will be lost. I'm so sorry this enormous burden has been placed on your shoulders, Jillian, but if you don't succeed, the entire world will be lost to darkness."

"Find you? You're here now. Take me with you, please. Let's just get out of here now and go—"

"You don't know how much I wish that." Marc then took my palm and placed a rose quartz crystal stick into it. "Follow the bread crumbs. Go to the university and find me, as soon as you can. Don't wait."

He placed both hands on my face and leaned down to gently touch his lips with mine. I'm sure he only meant it as a quick parting gesture, but the hot electricity between us heated to a fiery flame, and I was desperately kissing him back, clinging hard to him, refusing to let go and break the connection and lose him forever.

Then as suddenly as it started, his frame began to grow liquid and translucent. My fingers gripped harder around him, but I was soon only grasping at a fading ghost.

"Marc, don't go! Please!"

"Find me. I love you, Jillian Azure. Always," he said, the sound as thin as the wispy fog sucking the last vestiges of him inside the swirling vortex like a whirlwind.

With that, the shimmering image of my mysterious, magical man completely disappeared, and I stood in the dark, foggy garden alone.

Crystal Moon

Chapter 2

A young woman whose name I couldn't remember was cleaning the remnants of last night's party in the living room when I walked downstairs. She dumped a few plastic cups into the filled garbage sack, then twisted and tied the ends, tossing the bundle towards two more by the front door.

"Jillian, good morning!" she said, wiping her brow with the back of her arm. "Hope I didn't wake you. I tried to do this as quietly as possible. Doug said you had a hard time sleeping last night."

A condition that was true enough, but how he knew was a mystery since we had slept in separate rooms. He was probably covering potential gossip. Kind of him.

"Thanks," I said, looking around. "Where is he, by the way?"

She gestured towards the hallway. "In the kitchen fixing you breakfast. Honestly, you really hit the jackpot landing that one. If Frank so much as tossed a Pop Tart into the toaster for me, snowballs would be flying in hades."

I grinned. "Thanks for cleaning up, but you really didn't have to do this."

"My pleasure, really. Just returning the favor for when you arranged the neighborhood to bring in dinner for me and the family the entire week after having Benjamin three months ago. We all help each other where we can, right?"

I nodded. "Thanks again. Well, I'd better see what Doug is cooking up."

"Should be awesome. You always rave about his culinary skills. That reminds me, old man Ellis at the bakery sent over some muffins and donuts this morning. I put them in the frig. He said he was sorry he couldn't make it to the party last night, but welcome home."

I smiled my continued thanks, then padded down the carpeted hallway towards the country sized kitchen just as Doug dressed in jeans and blue polo shirt set a stack of wheat toast on the dining table. His expression lit up at first sight of me.

"Hope you're hungry," he said. "I didn't know what you'd want, so I made some of your favorites to be on the safe side."

"I am, thanks." Sitting down, I grabbed two toast slices, then dished out some berries from another bowl.

"Did you sleep okay?" he asked, sitting across from me.

I studied his expression to gauge what he wanted to hear. It was painfully obvious he hoped I would say that I had a difficult time sleeping without him and would I please share our king bed with him tonight, if not this afternoon.

"Well enough," I answered, nibbling on the toast. "Is there coffee made?"

Disappointment shadowed Doug's face as he poured a mug for me, passing the sugar and cream my way. I used only the cream after testing my preferences the past week and decided I didn't like sweet coffee. He frowned at me as I took a sip.

There was the distant sound of the front door opening and closing.

"Gretta must be finished cleaning then," he said, digging into his own food. "I tried helping, but she shooed me away."

"Nice of her to do that for us."

"Mainly for you," he remarked. "Everyone around the neighborhood has bent over backwards to help you out. It's their opportunity to pay you back for all the things you do for everyone else. You always say that it was just the way you were raised, but you really just have a heart of gold."

"That's kind of you to say."

"Just stating simple fact. Any more memories coming back?" he asked.

"Some," I lied. "Everything's still sluggish. Please be patient."

He raised storm-gray eyes that fixed hard with mine. "I have been. It's about damn time some of that paid off."

I flushed, lowered my gaze, whispering, "I know. I'm sorry."

He eased then. "No, I'm the one who's sorry. This isn't your fault. I know you're trying your hardest to remember everything."

"I am. Very hard."

"You're even remembering things about us, right?"

"Of course," I lied again.

I was about to list a few things I had overheard about us last night, then decided it was better if I kept silent since I couldn't be sure if any of those details were true.

Doug reached across the table to take my hand, but I reflexively retracted it. His fingers curled into a fist, and I saw by his renewed fury that he had reached his tolerance limit of my avoidance.

"Is this the way it's going to be from now on, Jill?"

"I'm not sure what you mean."

"Bull crap. You know exactly what I mean. Backing away from me when I try to hold you or touch you or kiss you. Covering yourself when I walk into the room."

"Sleeping with you," I added testily. "Isn't that what you really mean?"

The best defense was always a stronger offense, after all.

Where did I hear that?

He shot to his feet. "You think I'm pissed off because you won't have sex with me?"

"Aren't you?"

"Yes, dammit, of course I am! But I more furious that you say you remember me and all that we share together, but you won't frigging touch me. You act like you don't even know me. No, you act as if I *disgust* you. Tell me that you don't feel that way, Jillian, that I'm imagining everything."

I opened my mouth, then closed it again. There comes a point when all the lies and half-truths reveal themselves in the blinding light, and that time was apparently now.

"I just need time, Doug."

He raked a hand through his brown hair. "Time? That's your answer."

"That's all I can give you right now, I'm sorry."

He tossed his napkin on his plate. "Fine. Then by all means, take all the time you need today, Jill. I won't be in your way."

"Where are you going?"

"To the gym, then the office, then I don't know," he said, stalking away. "Call you later. If I have time."

Guilt warred with relief at his departure. Doug was right in all that he said, and I didn't blame him for his frustration, but I couldn't give him what I didn't have.

I would have to try harder. Find a way to remember him, love him, feel anything at all for the man. He had been patient for eight long, rollercoaster weeks. He deserved that much.

After finishing breakfast, I washed the dishes and hunted for their proper places in the cabinets. Even this task seemed odd and unfamiliar.

"Knock, knock."

Closing the utensils drawer, I turned around to see Doug's cousin James standing in the kitchen doorway.

"Apologies that I let myself in," he said. "No one answered the door."

I plastered on my practiced smile. "Sorry, I must have not heard the bell. I've been distracted this morning. Come on in."

He looked around. "Where's that stogy cousin of mine? More importantly, why did he leave his lovely wife alone here to fend for herself?"

"You just missed him. He went to the gym before he heads to the office."

"Working on a Sunday?" James studied my flushed expression, lifting his chin. "Oh. Sorry, someone should have warned you about that childish temper of his."

"It's hard for him."

"Because you still don't remember him." James raised a hand to stop my protest. "I guessed last night, Jill. You're a very good actress, but I'm a better detective."

"You're a police detective?" I asked, shocked by this, then realized that I had just given myself away while confirming his theory.

"No," he said with a chuckle. "I'm an account executive, but I'm gifted at profiling people and situations."

"I really want to remember him, all of you, all of this," I said, gesturing to the house.

"You can't force it, Jill. I know you think you're being kind by telling everyone, including Doug, what they want to hear, but in the end, it only hurts them worse."

"Then what do I do?"

James cracked a sexy smile and shrugged. "I have no idea."

"I thought you were the man with all the answers."

Now where did that come from?

He laughed. "Hardly. If I did, I would have double-downed on the Tesla stock when it was at eight." James stepped closer, then took my hand. "Seriously though, don't beat yourself up. Doug's been through the wringer the past couple of months wondering whether you would live or die. He's still a bit of a mess right now. Give him some time."

That seemed to be the thin echo of everyone—more time. Yet, something inside of me said that I was in danger of losing time completely, that I had to act now, today, before all was lost.

"How long are you staying in Denver, James?" I asked.

"My business here is taking longer than I anticipated, so at least another day or so," he said. "I'll go see if Doug has cooled off enough to grab some coffee. It'll give me a chance to talk some sense into that thick skull of his."

I gave a nod.

He laid a hand on my arm adding, "Don't worry, he'll come around. I'll make sure of it."

I waited until he walked away before I let go of the breath I was holding. There was something about the too attractive, charming man that reminded me of a dangerous angelic being like Gabrielle or Michael. Or Lucifer.

Alone now, I pulled the rose quartz crystal stick from my jeans pocket and studied it.

Follow the bread crumbs, Marc Zander said.

Pocketing the crystal, I headed into the downstairs office and surveyed the small room, spotting a tan leather purse on the back credenza. Must be mine. Strange that it should just be sitting here as if waiting for me.

Taking inventory of the contents, I found a hodgepodge of typical purse items, including car keys and a red wallet with my Colorado driver's license, credit cards and forty dollars in cash.

Replacing everything back into the purse, I sat down at the desk and switched on the computer. It was password protected, and I had no clue what that might be. I opened up the top drawer and rifled through the pens, sticky notes and general supplies, but it wasn't written down anywhere.

"Dang it."

I could call Doug and ask him, of course. It wasn't a suspicious thing just to use the home computer. But even this ordinary task seemed like something I shouldn't let him know about. Not until…

What?

Why didn't I want Doug to know what I was doing today?

The second drawer didn't provide the password either, but there were several bills with either my name or Doug's, a checking account that we shared, and one that was mine alone. I also found my passport with stamps from Canada, Mexico, Argentina, Angola, Peru, Italy, Egypt, Borneo.

Wow, I was a prolific world traveler. An odd collection of places to visit though, not your typical tourist spots.

I stuffed the checkbook and passport into my purse, then opened the bottom drawer.

Amongst the files, I spotted a large manila envelope with my name labeled on the front. Inside was a blank application for temporary employment to the Colorado State University in Fort Collins. A yellow sticky note was paperclipped to the application with the phone number and name of Helene Hornsby. On impulse, I called the number, not knowing what I was going to say.

"You've reached the voicemail of Dr. Helene Hornsby," the recording said. *"Please leave your name, number, and a detailed message, and I will get back to you as soon as possible. If you are a student..."*

I hung up before the recording finished. I had no idea who this woman was, or why I had her name and number on a blank employment application, which could be years old anyhow. I didn't even know what I was really searching for, or if this was connected in any way.

Future Marc did instruct me to go to the university to find him, but which one? And what was I supposed to do once I got there?

Follow the breadcrumbs.

"That's a big help," I muttered.

I peeled off the sticky note, then stared at the logo on the top of the application. I grabbed my cellphone and pulled up the university's website, entering the name into the search bar. Instantly there were a few hits, and I clicked onto the staff profile of Dr. Helene K. Hornsby, professor of geological and earth sciences.

The woman was fairly young looking with short cropped red hair, a slightly crooked nose, and a wide overly friendly mouth. My heart picked up speed, because besides Marc Zander, she was the only other person since I woke up who looked in any way familiar. From where, I didn't know. I just knew that I knew her.

It was something. A step.

A breadcrumb to follow.

I picked up my cellphone and hit the "redial" button.

* * *

"This is insane, Jill," Doug said as I packed clothes into a small suitcase. "You can't just leave like this! Do you have any idea where you're even going?"

I grabbed two more blouses from the closet. "Just up to Fort Collins, not too far. I'm meeting with Dr. Helene Hornsby at the university tomorrow morning."

"What the hell for?" he asked warily.

"Honestly, this is just a personal fact-finding mission. I spoke with Helene at CSU this afternoon and found out that we had planned to get together before my accident."

"Really? That's news to me."

For me, too.

It all happened so fast. After impulsively calling Dr. Hornsby again, she answered on the second ring.

"Helene Hornsby?" I asked, wincing.

"You got her. Who is this, and how can I *not* help you?" she grumbled.

I shifted the cellphone to my other ear. "This is Jillian Azure. I'm not sure if you know—"

"Jilly? Oh God, where have you been, rocker-girl?" she rushed out. "I've been trying to get a hold of you for weeks! Then when your phone was disconnected, I really freaked and just gave up all hope of ever talking to you again. I thought maybe I had offended you or something."

I gaped for a moment. "No, I'm sorry. I was…indisposed."

"Does this mean you're in then? It's not too late," she said. "Our team doesn't leave for another month. I know, I know. It's taking me a lot longer than I anticipated to get the grant money for the dig."

"Dig?" I swallowed dry saliva, then started again, "I'm sorry, Dr. Hornsby—"

"You can knock off the 'doctor' crap. I'm still the same old Mount Saint Helene that I was in college."

"There at CSU," I guessed.

"Of course, num-nuts. After we graduated, I leveled up and stayed here, while you struck out for parts unknown," she said. "I was shocked when we even reconnected three months ago. Anyhow, you still didn't answer my question. Are you going to join the team or what? I have another guy slated, a pain-in-my-ass, egomaniacal chemistry prof here who wants to test out a new theory in applied sciences, but I'd rather it be my geology bud. Please say yes."

"I'm…not sure."

"Okay, then at least come up here and see what started this whole thing," she said. "Give me a chance to talk you into coming with us."

I pulled out my pink crystal, unconsciously rubbing the sharp edges. I swore I saw tiny lights dance inside it.

"What is it?" I asked.

"Uh, uh. Come here and see for yourself," she said with whispered excitement. "Call it a tempting sample of things to come. I promise you won't be disappointed."

"Maybe I hadn't talked it over with you yet," I told Doug as I zipped up my stuffed suitcase. "Helene and I are old college friends. She's a geoscience professor there now."

"Really? I don't remember any Helene Hornsby," he remarked suspiciously.

Oh, right. Allegedly, he and I met and dated in college. He would have known all of my friends.

Then why didn't he know her?

"She was a classmate. You can't know everyone I knew back then, Doug. In any case, I think it would help me remember more if I met and talked with her face-to-face."

Doug raked a hand through his hair, trying to compose himself and process what I was saying, doing. I had blindsided him, but I had to go. I knew I did.

"This is totally nuts, Jill. At least let me drive you there myself. I'll take some time off and we'll meet this professor friend of yours together."

"I don't need a babysitter, Doug."

"I'm not trying to be," he said. "I'm just worried. You're going off half-cocked here."

"Well, I'll be fine on my own. I'm sorry, I have to go. I'll call you this evening when I get to my hotel room."

"Jill!"

I grabbed my suitcase and headed downstairs and out the front door, Doug racing after me.

"Jillian, stop!"

I halted on the porch and turned to face him. "Please understand, Doug. I have to do this, and I have to do this alone. It's just for one week. We both could use the space from each other, regain our bearings. Afterwards…"

"Afterwards, what?"

"I don't know," I said honestly. "Doug, if I never regain my memory—"

"You will."

"If I don't, then you and I will have to start from scratch. Right now, I'm not sure that I want to start at all. I plan to use this time to find out. Maybe…you should do the same."

He frowned at me, clenched his right fist at his side, his jaw muscles bunching. Then at once he deflated in defeat. "I've waited eight weeks for you to wake up and remember me, Jillian Azure. I guess I can wait one more."

Tears stung my eyes. He was a good man, and I was breaking his heart. I hated myself for that.

I leaned up and gave him a quick kiss, then stiffened when he desperately tried to hold onto me and deepen the kiss. Breaking from his grasp, I dashed down the porch steps and over to the white Honda

Civic parked in the driveway, closed my suitcase in the trunk, then sat behind the wheel.

Doug stared at me with deep injury. I couldn't blame him. It was a thoughtless, careless, crazy thing I was doing, and I might very well be throwing away the best thing that had ever happened to me.

I turned the ignition, then backed out of the driveway and drove away.

* * *

It took me less than two hours to reach Fort Collins. It was a larger and more modern city than the quaint town of Oakwood, but smaller and more rural metropolitan Denver. It was a young mixture of both, a big city that hadn't grown up yet.

After settling into my hotel room, I decided to walk around the university campus to get my bearings, as well as erase the guilty memory of Doug's look of betrayal.

It was a beautiful campus, all the buildings contemporary, bright and open. According to my transcripts, I had spent four years here earning my bachelor's degree in earth sciences, and another two earning my master's in geology and getting my teaching credentials. I tried hard to pull any recollection of this place from my brain, but nothing appeared. Yet, I could see myself attending here, easily blending with the students I passed along the scenic walkways.

The sun was setting and the walkway security lamps were snapping on, so I decided to head back to the hotel. Tomorrow morning I would meet with my college friend, Helene Hornsby, and with any luck strike some memory sparks.

It was twilight by the time I finally reached my car parked at the other end of campus. I had been second guessing my impulsive action in coming here all day, but for the first time I knew I was doing the right thing. This small assurance helped regain my lost appetite, and I drove to the bistro around the corner close to my hotel.

I parked along the curb and stepped out. Then took two steps and halted.

Tiny vibrations buzzed inside my jeans pocket. I pulled out the pink crystal stick, and it pulsed a dim light that immediately blinked out when I faced the bistro. When I turned, it flashed on again, very dim, brightening and dimming as I moved it back and forth, like a compass locating true north.

At its brightest, I looked up just as a car passed the quiet two-lane street. Directly across were a series of connected shops. The thing that caught my eye though was the wooden sign that read *Haut Coffee*.

I had to go there. I felt it in my bones.

In the end, it was sheer curiosity that finally moved my feet forward and across the empty street, until I was standing in front of the coffeehouse window. The light inside my quartz crystal then blinked out. I shook it as if it was a flashlight losing battery power, but nothing happened.

"This is stupid," I muttered, pocketing the crystal.

Annoyed with myself, I looked across the street at the bistro with full intension on heading back. I waited for a car to pass, then three and five. Just my luck, the lazy street that was empty of any vehicles only moments before suddenly filled with bumper-to-bumper traffic walling me off from crossing again.

Growling, I turned back to the coffeehouse.

Well, since I was here anyhow, a caramel latte with premade salad would be an easy meal to take back to the hotel.

I walked inside and over to the end of the order line.

While standing there, I ran through their menu items written on a board above the glass pastry counters. Deciding, I turned back and smiled at the hipster girl in front me who returned a generic nod. We all moved up one place, and my bored attention scanned the dining area, my sight halting at the man sitting at the far corner table.

"Marc?"

Afraid my eyes were tricking me, I focused harder.

There was no mistake. Dressed in black jeans and a green thermal shirt, Marc Zander was lounging back, reading a textbook while sipping coffee. He was real then, not some image or hologram or figment of my coma dreams after all.

He said to find him, and I did.

"Now what?"

"Excuse me?" the girl in line remarked.

"Nothing, sorry," I said.

Impulsively I dashed from the line, dodging tables and chairs and customers, until I stood in front of Marc, gaping like a fish.

He raised his incredible green eyes to mine, laying down his book. "Can I help you?"

"Marc Zander?"

"Yes. Did you need something?" he asked.

I stood there, still not believing my eyes. He was real. And he was here, really here.

"You," I said.

"Excuse me?"

"I need you. Now."

He warily eyed me as if I was some unbalanced mental patient. I couldn't blame him. This present Marc Zander wouldn't know me from Eve. So where should I go from here?

Cautiously he stood, looking to make his quick escape plan. "Uh, sorry, I think you're mistaken. Have a nice day now."

God, I was about to lose him again!

Possibly for good this time.

I couldn't let that happen. Fate only gave limited chances after all.

That's the only reasonable explanation I could give for impulsively planting both hands on his face and my lips on his for a long, desperate kiss in hope for some instinctive recognition of what we could be together.

It worked.

He gripped both of my wrists and started to push me away. Then something shifted, and the chemical energy between us ignited into crackling fireworks. I could feel it. He could feel it. I swore the entire room watching us could feel it.

Slowly his fingers relaxed and slid away, and he reached around my waist and pulled me against him. Then Marc Zander started to expertly, seductively kiss me back, and the pretty fireworks turned into an atomic bomb.

"You bastard!" a woman behind me yelled. "You swore never to cheat on me again!"

CRYSTAL MOON

CHAPTER 3

Marc broke the explosive kiss and staggered back just as I whipped around to see the red fury on a young brunette woman's face.

"Whoa, this is a big mistake!" Marc said. "I don't even know this woman. She just came up and kissed me."

"Marc—" I started to explain.

"Funny, she seems to know you," the brunette said with folded arms.

"Amber, it's not what you think," he tried again. "Someone must be pranking me. I swear that I've never seen this person in my entire life."

"You swear," she snorted. "Yeah, you've promised a lot of things, haven't you, *Magic Man*? Heather was right, and I am so done with you this time."

"Amber, wait!"

Marc started to chase after her, but she grabbed a random coffee cup off a table and threw it at him. Cursing, he jumped back, shaking off the steaming liquid dripping down the front of his shirt and jeans as the girl ran out the door weeping.

I started to discreetly leave myself, but Marc rounded on me faster, clamping his fingers on my wrist like a manacle.

"Not so fast. Who put you up to this?" he demanded. "Was it Epstein? Lenninger?"

"No!"

"Dan Wallace?"

"No! Nobody made me do anything," I said, trying to pull from his iron grasp. "I'm sorry. I didn't mean to cause you trouble. I just…"

"What?"

"I…I just wanted you to remember me."

"Not buying it, crazy lady. Never seen you before in my life. What's this really about?"

"Is there a problem?" a burly, older man came up to us and asked. By his nametag I saw that he was the manager.

"Yeah, this psycho blond here just pranked me and got me into a world of hurt by my girlfriend," Marc complained.

"I think you'd better release this young woman right now, sir," the manager said in no uncertain term.

"But I'm not—!"

"Let go of her now and leave. Before I call the cops."

Marc roughly released his grip, then stalked out, muttering black curses.

The manager then turned to me. "Are you okay, miss?"

I nodded, swallowed hard. "I'm fine. It really was my fault. He was someone I thought I knew, but I was mistaken. I'm sorry for the disruption."

"If you're sure," the manager remarked unconvinced.

"I am, thank you."

With the excitement over, the customers watching us grew disinterested and turned back to their own business. Marc's textbook still sat on the table, and I grabbed it and dashed out the door after him.

Outside on the sidewalk, I scanned the now darkened city street, but he was nowhere in sight. Inwardly I kicked myself for my impulsive actions.

What had I been thinking? In some remote way, I had hoped he would feel some connection between us. It had been a foolish expectation.

But he did feel something. He did kiss me back.

I shook off the heated memory of it. It didn't matter. He was gone now, and I had no clue where to look for him again.

At least now I knew that the man actually existed, that he wasn't some figment of my imagination. That was something.

Dang it, I had royally mucked up our first official meeting though. It should have gone so much better, more casual and friendly. I hoped it wasn't too late to repair the damage I caused. I swore the next time I met Marc Zander again…

If I did.

I needed to find him. Fast. Somehow.

I looked at the thick book in my hand—*Ireland's Land, History and Culture.* I opened it and flipped through the pages, but there was no name or notes or indication of any kind on who it belonged to. The only thing inside was a register receipt indicating that it was purchased today from the CSU bookstore.

I guessed Marc to be in his early thirties, so he was too old be a student. The brunette woman mentioned something about the other girls on campus, which meant there was a good chance then he was an instructor then.

If so, Helene Hornsby would know how to find him.

* * *

The modern glass and stone designed lobby of the earth sciences building seemed vaguely familiar when I walked inside the next morning, and I had such a sense of rightness that I knew I was on the correct track.

The geology lab was on the second floor, and I took the stairs, passing several students and staff. The door was open, but I still knocked on the door ledge before entering the empty room filled with desks and counters and shelves with every rock type imaginable.

"Helene?" I called.

"Back here by this demon Ficus plant," she shouted back.

I spotted the rustling leaves at the far end of the room and moved around the obstacles towards the corner window. The woman I recognized from the website profile photo stood from her crouched position, roughly brushing the tall plant's branches out of her way.

"Evil thing," she muttered, kicking its plastic base. It toppled over, and its branches knocked a few things off the nearby shelf. Helene growled and righted it again.

"I swear this thing grows legs on its own and moves just where it's the biggest pain in my backside. Jillian, hi! Man, it's great to see you again after all this time."

Not shy, she reached over and gave me a bearhug. This felt right too, and I gladly returned the warm embrace.

"Helene, thanks for making time for me this morning."

The redhead waved me off. "My next class isn't for another two hours anyhow. How has life in the small town been treating you? Bored out of your skull yet and ready to come work with me here at the college?"

She eagerly raced out all the typical catch-up gossip between two close friends. I was glad for it. If I was going to progress any further on this bizarre quest, I needed someone to help me, someone I could trust. That meant with every strange part about my new life, too.

"There is something else actually," I admitted. "The reason I never got back to you about the upcoming trip."

"I wondered about that. What happened?"

I rubbed my forehead roughly. "Apparently right after we last talked, I was in a car accident that left me in a coma for seven weeks."

She belly-laughed, her expression slowly sobering as she studied my serious face. "God, you're not kidding."

"No, I'm not."

"I'm so sorry, Jilly! I didn't know."

"That's okay, you wouldn't."

Helene leaned against the counter, gaping at me. "Wow, I knew something must've been up. You've never been one to pass on a dig. A coma, wow."

"And I only came out of it nine days ago."

"Wow."

"Without any memories whatsoever of my life, my home, my friends. My fiancé."

"Wow! Oh God, Jillian, how horrible! Wait, you're engaged?"

I shrugged. "So he and everyone else keeps telling me. Doug seems like a very nice guy, but he's having a hard time with me not remembering anything about him or us. I don't blame him. It's frustrating for me too."

"You don't remember anything at all?" Helene asked.

I shook my head. "Very little. It's all there though, I can feel it. It's like there's this dam of information that I can't break through. For some reason you seem familiar to me though. I'm hoping that spending time with you will help jog my memories more."

Helene touched my shoulder. "Anything I can do to help out, Jill. I've always got your back, you know that. Well, I guess you don't now, but trust me, you do. Hey, come over to my house for dinner tonight, and I'll break out the old photos and share some of our crazy exploits. We'll get those stubborn mental juices of yours flowing again."

"Sounds great actually. Yes, I'd really like that."

"If not, we'll just have to make some new ones, right?" she added.

I knew I liked this woman. I was glad to finally have at least one person on my side now, someone who wasn't going to pressure me to remember things I couldn't, whose life wouldn't be irrevocably altered if I never did.

"Speaking of making new memories, what's this dig you're wanting me join? Did you find something interesting?"

"Come look," Helene said with widening grin.

I followed her across the room to a closet that she unlocked and opened. Inside was another collection of rocks—no surprise there. But I was instantly intrigued when she pulled out a grapefruit sized geode.

"Ready?" she asked.

"Go for it."

The geode had been previously cut, and Helene spread both halves apart. Immediately my breath caught at the multicolored crystals inside.

A sunray reflected across one of the facets and flickered across my eye, and something inside my brain brightly flashed. Like a computer downloading information in seconds, suddenly I knew everything there was about the subject of geology. In fact, I realized that this was my burning passion in life. I adored rocks and crystals of every kind. To me, they held the mysteries of the universe.

I wanted to weep for joy. It felt so great just to remember something.

"What do you think?" Helene prodded.

I took the geode half from her hands and studied it closely. Again, my mental files gloriously burst with scientific information.

"A natural rainbow quartz," I said with slight awe. "Where did you find this?"

"It was sent to us from a carpenter in Dublin," Helene said. "He was going through his late father's belongings recently and found this."

"Where did his father find it?"

"Allegedly off the coast near Spanish Point in Ireland."

I frowned at her. "Ireland? Isn't this a little unusual for that area?"

She nodded quickly. "And this is just a sample. The man, Mike O'Halloran, said his father had been a history professor in Dublin and was always traveling doing field research, bringing home artifacts here and there. His son donated or sold most of his collection, but his father left a note with this geode, giving explicit instructions that at his demise, his son was to contact the geology department here at CSU and let us know of this rare finding."

"Here?" I remarked, handing it back. "No offense, but why Colorado State of all places? We're not exactly the British Museum or Smithsonian."

"O'Halloran didn't know why his father requested us specifically, but I've learned through the years never to question a true gift like this."

"So if you're getting a dig together, I take it there are more," I said.

"Lots more, according to O'Halloran's letter to his son. Some even boulder size."

"What?"

"But that's not even the best and strangest part," Helene said. "When we cracked this one open, we found this."

Helene reached behind another geode half on the shelf, and handed me a plastic baggy with what looked to be a tiny, aged parchment fragment with an inked symbol of a sunburst.

"Wait, you found this *inside* the geode?"

Helene hiked her amber brows. "I have video showing us making the original cut and everything. This is no hoax. O'Halloran said he has a map where his late father found them, which he'll only give to us in person when we come."

"Holy Smoking Joe," I said.

"I know, right? So of course, I went to Lester Packman—he's the head financial honcho here, if you don't remember—to see if he would approve to finance a team to dig out what other geological and archeological treasures we might find. Being the usual tightwad that he is, of course, he said no. So I've been trying to procure another source for grant money."

"Any luck?"

"I have one fish on the line," she said. "Some trust fund kid with a Marlin Perkins complex. We're meeting again at a charity function tomorrow night. You should come, Jill! I know you'll be able to talk the woman into green-lighting the funds."

"Me? No, I couldn't."

"Please. I desperately need your help, Obi-wan. You're my only hope."

I sent her a withering stare. "Hilarious. How formal is this charity function anyhow? I didn't bring much with me."

"Don't worry. I have you covered there. Please? Please, please, please?"

She clasped her hands under her chin and gave me a sad puppy dog pout, and I finally made a guttural noise of acquiescence. She was helping me with my personal factfinding mission. The least I could do was go to some charity dinner with her and be her wing-woman.

Helene bounced on her toes, clapping. "Awesome! And you'll come with us on the dig too, of course."

"That, I don't know yet," I said.

"Come on. It'll be super dirty and muddy and grueling with lots of hiking and backbreaking hammering and chiseling and bumps and scrapes and blisters and broken toes and fingers, then stale, warm ale afterwards at the local pub. It'll be a blast!"

"Well, it does sound fun."

The idea sounded more appealing by the minute, in fact. Not just in the new discoveries we might stumble upon, but the time away from my own personal amnesic dilemma.

"Tell you what," Helene said, closing and locking the closet. "After dinner tonight, you can try on this dress I have—"

"Hornsby! This had better be a bad rumor about you kicking me off next month's dig for some flunky rock student of yours!"

Helene muttered a mild curse, squeezing her eyes shut.

I sucked in a sharp breath at the black fury of Marc Zander's voice behind me as he stalked up to us.

"Is this her?" he demanded. "Tell me you're not dumping me for…"

I turned around with a wince. "Actually, I haven't decided if I'm going yet."

Marc's forest green eyes widened.

Then stormed with the fury of a category-five hurricane.

"You," he stated through gritted teeth. "Is this another sick joke then? Getting chewed out by my girlfriend and tossed on my ass by the store manager last night wasn't enough? You're making sure to ruin everything else in my life now?"

"Please, let me explain," I began.

"Whoa, what did you do to the guy, Jillian?" Helene chuckled. "Not that Magic Man here probably didn't deserve it."

Marc narrowed his eyes at her, pointing a warning finger. "That's one, Hornsby."

She rolled her eyes. "Please. You're not even a blip on my scare-o-meter."

"This is all a simple mistake," I broke in, flushing.

"Really? Well, lady, your simple mistake just cost me my girlfriend," he ground out.

Helene snorted, waving a hand. "A huge favor then, Zander. It's well rumored that Amber Martin is just another prof-hunter."

"Prof-hunter?" I asked.

"A female student who's hunting for a professor husband," she explained. "You're lucky that the girl didn't get herself knocked-up to seal the deal, Marc. That one was truly hardcore, from what I've heard, and you're not exactly the most responsible guy. I keep telling you to stop playing in your own backyard. It's not wise or professional. Not that it's ever stopped you before."

"That's two, Helene," he ground out.

Apparently, the man's nickname wasn't due to his ability to pull a rabbit out of a hat. As he glared at me, it was hard to imagine how I could ever fall in love with such a hotheaded, philandering jerk, now or in the future. This was not the same gentle man who visited me in my coma dreams, the one who woke me, who warned me, who loved me.

"You still didn't answer my question, Helene. Is she the one you're replacing me with on the team?" he demanded.

"Maybe."

"If she is, I swear—"

"Actually, *she* is standing right here," I said with folded arms. "And as a matter of fact, I am joining Helene's team."

He shifted his fiery green stare to mine. "Now you're doing this just to piss me off, aren't you?"

"No. Actually, that's just a bonus. I have my own personal reasons for going."

"Yeah, I'll bet."

"I do," I insisted. "This may be a new concept for you, but this isn't in any way about you."

I turned to Helene, saying, "Email me the necessary paperwork. I'll talk to you tonight at dinner."

With that, I stalked out of the room, hearing the volcanic argument blasting behind me.

* * *

"This is us in the Mojave Desert measuring the latest seismic reading at the San Andreas Fault," Helene said, pulling up yet another photo from her laptop computer. "We were getting field credit by interning at the U.S. Geological Survey our senior year. Fascinating as hell. I still have the rock I found with the tiny vein of gold in it."

While sitting next to her on the couch and eating mint Oreo cookies, I studied photo after photo Helene scrolled through and listened to all of her stories. We obviously spent a lot of time together in college and even roomed together that last year, but lost touch after going in separate directions after graduation.

Sad actually. Helene was upbeat and fun and someone I even now enjoyed being with. I could see why we shared a close friendship back in college.

"Jogging any memories?" she asked, seeing my expression.

I shrugged. "Not many. A few fragmented images, and only after you've already told the story and showed me the picture, echoing that yes, it probably did happen, but that's all."

Helene touched my shoulder. "Well, that's something. Give it time. Everything will come back eventually."

"That's what everyone keeps saying," I said. "Hey, don't say anything about this to anyone, okay? Me being in a coma and all, I mean."

"Yeah, sure."

"Or about my life in general back in Oakwood."

"Of course," she said. "Everything between us has always been confidential."

"Thank you," I said, feeling a huge relief by it. "Helene, we were pretty close friends back then, right?"

"The best."

"Then don't you think it's odd that I dated a guy here who you didn't even know about? Or at least make mention of him when we reconnected?"

One who I was serious enough with to accept his marriage proposal and move to his hometown.

Yet, I still wore no engagement ring. When I questioned Doug about it in the hospital, he told me I was extremely picky and hadn't decided on anything yet.

"A little strange, I suppose," Helene admitted. "But that was just you."

"How do you mean?" I asked.

Helene puckered her expression, trying to choose her words.

"There was always an element of mystery about you, Azure. You always held back…something. Especially that last year. It's okay, I never pushed. Your business and love life were your own. We all have own secrets, right? That was the symbiotic part of our friendship, trusting and respecting our silence whatever that was."

She shrugged, adding, "Then when we reconnected a few months ago, there wasn't a lot of time to catch up on our personal lives. We only talked on the phone two short times."

"What did I say to you?" I asked.

Helene absently scrolled through a few more photos of us together. "Just career stuff. I didn't even know you moved away from Denver until you told me yesterday."

"But you did say I was ready to join your summer dig?"

She lifted a shoulder. "It didn't take much for you to agree to join. You were even in the process of filling out the paperwork. When I didn't hear back from you, I called and left messages. The last time I tried, your number was disconnected. I just took that to mean you had changed your mind and…Damn, I should've driven out to your place to check things out."

"That's fine, Helene, really. How could you know?"

Doug disconnected my cellphone?

After several weeks in a coma, maybe my faithful fiancé didn't expect me to ever wake up again and was dismantling my life from his piece by piece. Then when I did wake up, he bought a new phone to cover his tracks.

Maybe I wasn't the only guilty party in our tenuous relationship.

"Can I tell you something?" I remarked.

"Always," Helene said.

"I think Doug and I were having issues before my accident. We might have even been on the verge of breaking up."

"Why would you say that?" she asked.

I shrugged. "Little things. Like the fact that I'm not wearing any ring or hadn't made any wedding plans. Then there are big things like me eager to run off on this trip that I didn't even tell him about. The tension between us now is unbearable, and I'm beginning to think that it has nothing to do with my amnesia."

"Another reason you're here, and he's not," she added for me.

I nodded. "Doug's seems like a nice, decent guy, but he's still a complete stranger to me no matter how hard I try to remember him."

"What's his name again?" Helene asked.

"Douglas Hayden. He graduated here a year before us with a business degree. He's now a C.P.A. in his own accounting firm back in Oakwood."

"Hayden," she said, trying the name out, then shook her head. "Nope, don't remember the guy. Not that our kind and his would've ran in the same circles. Anyhow I wouldn't sweat it, Jill. If you really love the guy, then I'm sure you'll find your way back to him again. If not, maybe you should part ways. No one should stay together out of obligation or false nobility.”

“Maybe.”

There was a slight pause, then Helene asked, “Can I ask you something nonrelated?”

“Shoot.”

“What happened between you and Marc Zander yesterday? I didn’t even know you knew the guy.”

My cheeks heated as I looked down at my fingers laced tightly in my lap. How could I tell the only friend I had now that he was allegedly my boyfriend from the future? Not to mention that he miraculously woke me from my coma and restored dead flowers to life with the flick of his sparking fingers and said that I would be the savior of the world someday.

“Mistaken identity,” I answered.

Helene arched a brow. “If there was tongue, there was no mistake.”

I narrowed a stare at her. “I forgot what a crude person you could be.”

“See, you’re remembering. Seriously though, whether or not you and your fiancé get back together, Marc Zander is not the sort of man you want to…rekindle old memories with. You’d do best to stay far away from him.”

That roused my curiosity.

“Yes, I’m getting that,” I said. “Do you think there was something between me and him in the past? Did he go to college here with us?”

Helene’s expression tightened then as she closed her laptop, and I began to wonder if there was some sensitive history of her own there.

“No, he only came to CSU three years ago from somewhere back east.”

“Tell me about him then,” I said, more than intrigued now.

Helene bit into a cookie, frowning. “I’d rather not, but since it’s you…Well, the first month he was here, Zander’s unorthodox experiments caused the fire department to come out and the chem lab to be remodeled.”

“Seriously?”

I bit down a smile, imagining him as some young mad scientist who's experiment literally blew up in his face. Not a great start for a new professor trying to prove himself.

"Hate to admit that he's brilliant though," Helene continued. "Knows it, too. You just have to listen to him lecture for ten minutes to know that he thinks on an entirely different plane than the rest of us mere mortals.

"I sat in on one of his classes when he first applied to join our team this summer. It was so weird. All of his students listened to him completely mesmerized, as if they were all under some magic spell. Even I was transfixed by every charming word that came out of that sensuous mouth of his. Learned a lot about how physics and earth's elements aligned…"

She shook her head, adding, "Anyhow, that's what really started his nickname. The man seems to captivate and hold everyone in place with the sheer power of his brilliance and charisma."

"I take it that his pet name spread to other extracurricular activities as well," I said.

Helene snorted. "You aren't blind and know what the guy looks like. Add that to his magnetic personality and utter genius, and you have the perfect man-trifecta. No, his nights are rarely spent alone pouring over some physics textbook. He can charm the pants off the most frigid virgin and make her thankful she's a woman. I have on good authority," she added that past statement quietly.

She didn't seem wrong. I squirmed uncomfortably at the hot memory of our kiss last night, unwillingly craving more.

This was the future love of my life—a self-centered, hot-tempered, philandering creep?

No, something had to be wrong. I would never dump a decent, honorable man like Doug Hayden for a jerk like Marc Zander.

"You want to know the truth about me and Zander?" I asked.

Helene's eyes went wide, and she quickly scooted closer. "Don't tease me now, Azure."

"I had dreams about him when I was in my coma," I began.

"Whoa. You do know Marc then?"

I shook my head. "Never met the man before."

"Then how..?"

"Like I said, I dreamed about him while I was in my coma. Then I swore that I woke up in the hospital to see him standing there in the living flesh. Only this Marc Zander wasn't anywhere near like the one I met this morning in your science lab. Or yesterday at the coffeehouse where I kissed him."

CRYSTAL MOON

CHAPTER 4

"I've been thinking about what you said last night about Marc Zander," Helene said as I squirmed my way into the cocktail dress that she loaned me.

It was a sparkling silver-white with long sleeves, but was formfitting and hit mid-thighs, making me feel a bit self-conscious. With my hair waved and free-flowing down my back and my makeup a little more dramatic than normal, I finally passed Helene's muster to attend the charity function and make our case before her rich potential grant donor.

"Please forget everything," I said, assessing my appearance in the dresser mirror. "I haven't exactly been myself the past week. Whoever that is. Or was. It was just crazy talk."

"Maybe you're not wrong," Helene said, plopping down on the edge of her mattress. "It all makes perfect sense, except for one thing."

"Only one?"

"You said that this future Marc Zander visited you in your coma. What if it was really the other way around?"

I froze, looked at her reflection in the mirror. "What?"

"Since you were the one in the coma, maybe your disembodied soul did a flyby at the same time that Marc was sleeping, and both of your souls connected."

I sent her reflection a disparaging stare. "Please. I've thought about what I told you last night too and finally figured out what really happened."

"Okay, smart lady, what's your theory?"

"Simple. Since I was considering joining the dig before the accident, I must have been pouring over the college's website and accidentally came across Marc Zander's profile photo. My brain subconsciously recorded his image, then made up the entire insane story while I was in my coma."

"But you were awake when you saw him that first day in the hospital," Helene said.

"I was slipping back into my coma," I countered. "It was just my brain bringing me out of it again using the same fictional character I made up. It obviously worked too. The brain's mechanisms are a bizarre wonder."

"Doesn't explain the magical resurrecting roses."

"They were probably in full bloom all along, and my eyes and mind were playing tricks on me."

Helene crossed her legs, scrunching up her face as she considered.

"How about the first night you came home?" she said, her gesturing with her hand. "When you saw future Marc again in your garden."

"You mean when I saw him *disappear* into thin air?" I remarked with arched brow.

"Your crystal."

"That I could have had all along," I added. "I found a dozen more in my house the next day. Rocker-girl, remember?"

Helene deflated, disappointed with my logical and reasonable explanations. She wanted a mysterious science fiction story that I couldn't provide her. Personally, I was glad to have voiced the apparition of Marc Zander aloud, so I could then rationalize what really happened.

"You're not being very fun about this," Helene said.

I grabbed up my purse. "Sorry that I even brought it up. Do both of us a favor and ignore anything remotely crazy coming out of my mouth for the next week or so until I can get my head fully together again."

"Spoiled sport. Still, I guess it's better than falling in love with CSU's man-jerk of the year." She groaned, then stood up, brushing down her own jungle printed, green dress. "Ready to go charm some money out of rich people's tight fists?"

"Lead the way."

Helena drove us to a local hotel near the lakefront. The charity buffet dinner was to help raise funds for the Children's Hospital in Denver. The function itself was in full swing by the time we walked inside the crowded, elegant ballroom. Helene introduced me around to a few of her colleagues, then finally led me across the floor towards the linen covered tables.

"Okay, do your own magic, rocker-girl," Helene whispered in my ear. "Mama needs a big wad of cash to finance her trip next month."

"I'll do my best," I said.

"FYI—this woman is a Green Peace, save-the-owls, tree hugger kind of person, if that helps."

"Really?" I remarked with a soured expression.

She waved me off. "Most bored rich kids grow up to be either narcissistic shopaholics or over-zealous activists with too much time and money on their manicured hands."

"Terrific," I muttered, then plastered on a pleasant smile when Helene drew us up to an elegant redhaired woman wearing a burgundy colored pantsuit.

"Roz, hi! So nice to see you again," Helene sang out, air-kissing the woman's cheek. "This is my colleague, Jillian Azure, the one I've been talking to you about. Jilly, this is Rosalyn Callaghan of Callaghan Enterprises."

We greeted each other, and I was impressed with the woman's strong, assertive handshake. I was also surprised to see that she didn't wear excessive jewelry or have an expensive manicure either.

I did a quick mental profile on the woman then. If Rosalyn Callaghan came from big money, it didn't show in any visible way other than her designer dress and Jimmy Choo heels. By the way she wobbled, I'd bet ten-to-one odds she didn't pick them out for herself either.

No, she looked to be more of the Jungle-Jane type who would go around in jeans, tee-shirt and muddy hiking boots.

"Helene tells me that you're in charge of your family's main company?" I commented.

"Just a parttime apprentice to learn the biz," Rosalyn said. "My mother and older brother handle the actual running of it. Not my thing. Most of my time is spent running our local wildlife refuge."

"Very altruistic of you," I said. "Must be a lot of work."

"It is," she said. "The work, not being altruistic. I love being one of the handlers there, so it's a true joy for me. My fiancé has a hard time pulling me away from the place every night."

"Sounds interesting," I remarked. "Tell me more about the place."

Rosalyn Callaghan instantly brightened and went into a full litany of the big game animals their nature reserve rescued and protected. She had been recently promoted to director of the park itself and spent nearly every waking hour there. It was her passion, and the animals were her children.

This woman wasn't some pampered heiress then. Made sense. There was a rough wildness about her that said she would never allow herself to be caged up by anything, including her family's wealth and social status.

"It must be killing you to be away from the refuge right now," I said.

Rosalyn nodded. "In a big way. But it was my turn to attend a few charity functions for the family. We all switch off doing the circuit. Part of being a Callaghan."

I nodded. "Can't be easy for someone like you who prefers everyday action to schmoozing snobby socialites."

"You have no idea," the woman said, grimacing at the fancy crowd.

"Then I won't waste your time or schmooze you in any way," I said. "Rosalyn, we need the funds to help finance an expedition of the upmost importance. If we're right, this will change the entire natural world for the better, especially the wildlife."

Helene gaped at my outspoken request without so much as a warmup after a several drinks and a couple of private dinners. She kicked my ankle for me to shut the hell up, and I kicked her back that I knew what I was doing. After less than fifteen minutes with Rosalyn Callaghan, I knew she was an upfront, direct person who despised being wined and dined and pandered to. I also guessed where her true priorities lied, and targeted that.

"Jillian," Helene hissed through teeth, gripping my arm. "Maybe we shouldn't take up so much Rosalyn's time and go say hello to a few more people."

I stood my ground, meeting Rosalyn's stare with my own, allowing her to process what I had told her.

"Okay, Jillian, you have my attention," she said finally. "In what way will this trip of yours change the natural world so dramatically?"

"We found something," I said. "Something amazing. Something that shouldn't exist."

Her brows hiked. "What did you find?"

I shook my head. "You have to see it for yourself, like I did. Come to the university's geology lab tomorrow, and we'll show you. Then I'll tell you why it will help you, your kids, and all the natural world."

"Intriguing." Rosalyn sniffed, studying my even expression, then said, "Okay, I suppose it couldn't hurt to swing by and see what you've got. When do you want me?"

"About eleven o'clock in the geology lab in the geosciences building," I said. "You can arrange that, can't you, Helene?"

"Y-yeah. Sure, anytime. I can always get someone to cover my classes."

"Great. We'll see you tomorrow then."

"I'll be there," Rosalyn said, then sneered when glancing over my shoulder. "Sorry, I'd love to hear more, but I'm being beckoned by my aunt who came with me. Aunt Rhiona's been researching another income stream for the company and truly believes I care an iota about any of it. I'll see you both tomorrow at eleven."

With that, the amber haired heiress pressed through the crowd as if she was Moses parting the Red Sea towards the other end of the room. Helene blinked hard after her, then turned her widening eyes to me.

"You did it, you creepazoid! How in the holy heckles did you manage to swing that gig in record time?"

"Guess she was easy to read," I said.

"Easy, my fat fanny. You didn't even have to mention that you're a card-carrying member of Green Peace and spend your weekends embracing redwoods."

"She wouldn't be into Green Peace, and she's no bored, tree hugging heiress. No, she'll be ready to finance our fieldtrip to Ireland as long as you…"

My mouth popped open when I spotted Marc Zander unbelievably moving through the crowd looking lethally gorgeous in black tux and red silk shirt and tie.

What was he doing here? From what Helene told me, this event was strictly invitation only to those of a high income stream, and he was a low paid college professor.

"As long as I what?" Helene added at my pause.

My mouth snapped shut into a tight line as I watched him head straight to Rosalyn Callaghan and the older woman next to her. Both women brightened instantly as he smiled and chatted with them, obviously charming the pants off both.

And doing a very good job of it.

"Oh, hell no," I muttered, then barreled through the crowd towards them.

"Jillian, wait!" Helene called.

But I was hellbent on a mission not to let that manipulative, egotistical man thwart my perfect efforts to land Helene's grant financing.

Smiling wide at something he said to Rosalyn, Marc shifted his stare to see me furiously stalking towards them. His smile turned wickedly amused as he snapped his fingers in my direction.

Suddenly my right heel broke, and my legs came out from under me. Gasping, I barreled into the back of a stick-thin man who then fell forward, the tumbling domino effect continuing until six people were scattered across the floor, squeals and champagne glasses flying.

Helene scrambled over and helped me up.

"God, Jillian, what happened? Are you okay?"

Limping on my sore ankle, I narrowed my stare at Marc Zander chuckling darkly, then led Rosalyn Callaghan and her aunt out of the ballroom, one woman hooked on each arm.

"Not in the least," I spat, shaking the champagne that dripped off my arm. "But I will be. You can count on that."

* * *

When Rosalyn Callaghan walked into the geo lab the next morning wearing a khaki logo tee-shirt and camouflage pants, I knew that had profiled her correctly. Doing my own homework late last night, I saw how active she was in her wildlife refuge and her passion to return the big game animals she cared for back into the wild if at all possible.

"I hope you don't mind me bringing my fiancé, Brian Lochlan," she said touching the arm of the tall, attractive man beside her. "He just flew in this morning, and I promised to show him the sights today."

Helene happily introduced us all around, then went into her well-rehearsed needs and objectives and wish list for the geode dig. Both Rosalyn and Brian appeared politely interested, but halfway through the tedious speech, I could see we were losing the battle. Animals were their passion, not inanimate rocks. If I didn't step in, we could kiss our financing goodbye.

Funny how fate sometimes intervenes in the least likely places. After returning to my hotel that first night with Marc's textbook, I read the entire thing and learned all I needed to know to convince this woman to finance our project.

"Rosalyn," I began, "did you know that wolves in the wild are now extinct in Ireland?"

That caught her and her fiancé's attention. Helene looked warily at me, suspicious on where I was going with this.

"No, I didn't know that actually," Rosalyn said.

"Sad really," I added. "At one time they were once such an intrinsic part of the Irish landscape that the country was once referred to as 'wolf-land'. That's why Irish folklore is filled with them, particularly the legends of the talking wolf and shapeshifting humans into wolves."

"Werewolves, you mean," Brian remarked with a quick look to his fiancée.

"Yes, you could call them that," I said. "Silly, I know, but it just describes how common these animals were on the island."

I went into a couple of stories that vividly described this fact.

"How did they die out then?" Rosalyn asked.

"They were literally hunted and slaughtered into extinction by humans," I said. "The very last recorded wolf was killed in 1786, over two hundred years now."

"That's so criminal," Rosalyn remarked.

I nodded. "I agree. Ireland is an ancient land, but modern man has ravaged it beyond its original recognition. Now the countryside is a shadow of her former self. And this is only one place, one example of how man has destroyed natural wildlife into extinction. If we're not careful, there won't be any animals left on this planet."

"That's what my mother Brenna Callaghan says as well," she said. "But what can we really do about it?"

"That's the perfect question to ask. The answer is that there's still hope of restoring the land and its creatures like the wolf back to its original and natural habitat. And I believe these rare crystals are the key."

"How so?" Rosalyn asked, tilting her head.

Honestly, I couldn't tell you what then took control of my mouth. It was unbelievable the science and history I recited between animals and their environment that's been impacted by human interference, listing dates and incidences as if I was downloading all this information directly from the computer.

"That's been the worst problem of all," I continued. "It doesn't matter what we try to do now to repair the damage caused by human beings, it won't make a bit of difference if we don't stop the destructive domino effect we started.

"In 2019, Ireland tried to reintroduce wolves back into the wild in their country, but it was unsuccessful. Why? Because the land itself is no longer the same. These geodes show that the iron and minerals in this area shouldn't be here, but they do. How? What caused this incredible land transformation?"

"So what did happen?" she asked.

I shook my head. "We don't know. That's our mission. To find out why landmasses just like this are changing so dramatically that it won't sustain its natural, native life. Once we find out, we can then take the steps necessary to reverse the process. Only then can we successfully reintroduce those animals like the wolf that were once native to Ireland and have them again thrive and be a part of its self-sustaining ecological environment."

"You're absolutely right. And you've definitely sold me," Rosalyn said, nodding. "You have your trip funding, Jillian. I'll make the recommendation to my mother tonight when I talk to her, since she has the final say."

Helene covered her mouth to contain her squeal of glee.

"That's excellent, Rosalyn, thank you," I said happily but calmly.

"I'm so intrigued, in fact, that I'd love to tag along on the trip too, if you have no objections. Brian and I are getting married a week before you leave, and it would be a fantastic place to spend our honeymoon. What do you think, hon?"

Brian Lochlan touched her shoulder, smiling. "Sounds great. Anything that will get you away from the refuge for a couple of weeks."

"We'd love to have you," I said. "The more, the merrier."

"Great. I'll call mom today and make it official," Rosalyn said, then glanced at the wall clock. "If you'll excuse us now, we promised to meet one more person here before Brian and I head to the lake to go sailing."

I frowned. "Another person?"

"Dr. Marc Zander, professor of applied physics," she said. "I believe you and he are colleagues? He's going to make his case for becoming the lead on the team. He claims to have the necessary leadership experience and more sophisticated methods to extract your geodes. It has something to do with lasers? Anyhow, he says he can cut the costs in half, and extract the rocks much faster."

"Does he now?" I muttered, my face burning at his underhanded takeover plans.

Helene gripped my arm to remind me that now wasn't the time to lose my temper. Reluctantly I relaxed my expression and forced a toothy smile.

"I hope Professor Zander shows you everything that he's capable of doing, Rosalyn," I stated. "I wouldn't want the wrong person leading this important project."

We went through polite goodbyes, and I waited a few minutes after the Callaghan couple left before I stalked across the room.

"Jill, where are you going?" Helene demanded, chasing after me as I dodged counters and tables and chairs.

"To cut the manipulative Professor Zander himself in half," I stated through gritted teeth.

"Just stop!" Helene said, grabbing my wrist and halting me halfway down the corridor.

"Why?"

"Because for one thing, you're going the wrong way, num-nuts," she said. "Zander's in the applied science lab, which is in the other direction."

I turned and stalked down the opposite corridor. Helene growled and ran to catch up to me.

"For another," she continued as she chased after me, "this is still my gig, not Zander's. There's nothing to worry about."

"Not if he razzle-dazzles the Callaghans, and they give *him* the financing," I countered.

Helene bit her bottom lip. "Good point. Maybe we should hijack Rosalyn on her way out of the meeting."

"That will be too late. No, we have to counterattack now."

"Actually, that's not the way things are done around here," Helene said. "Bad form, and all that. Administration would have my butt, then my job."

"Marc Zander crossed *bad form* last night and went straight to selfish, egocentric machinations when he crashed the charity event last night to purposely steal your donors out from under you."

We pulled up in front of the closed door of the applied science laboratory. I peeked through the small door window. The man was already successfully charming the couple by the amazed look on their faces as they watched him split a rock into two pieces with the help of a thin red laser.

"You're right though," I admitted.

"Finally," Helene breathed with relief.

"You should stay here and keep your nose clean from any backlash from administration. However, I don't have a teaching position here to worry about."

"Jillian!"

Ignoring her, I barged into the science lab, and Marc turned to me with a sneer.

"I'm sorry, but this is a private session," he called. "You'll have to leave now, Ms. Azure."

"Not on my life. Or yours," I muttered.

Fury coupled with some bizarre, primal instinct took over, and I reached into my pocket to pull out and point my now glowing pink quartz crystal stick at him. Within seconds, I felt an inner boil in my gut roil and rise up through my torso and down my arm. Then a white light blasted through my fingers, the crystal directing this strange power towards the laser and bent the red diagonal light skyward.

The fluorescent lights directly above exploded in a shower of sparks. Brian reflexively covered Rosalyn with his body as the sparks and embers rained down and more fluorescents popped and burst into sparks.

I sucked in a sharp breath at what just happened. Somehow, someway, I made this happen. Me and my rose quartz crystal.

Marc gaped at me for five seconds. Then he glared with dark green fury and raised his right hand and flicked his fingers at me.

Suddenly I was knocked back hard on my backside. Then alarms sounded and automatic fire sprinklers opened overhead, raining water down in several sprays, drenching me from head to toe.

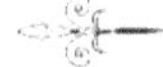

CRYSTAL MOON

CHAPTER 5

Fire alarms blared and emergency lights strobed. People were shouting and running chaotically up and down the corridor. The Callaghan couple rushed out of the raining, sparking room and into the screaming crowd, while Helene chased after them.

Thoroughly drenched myself, I tried to stand, but slipped on the wet floor and landed painfully on my hip again. When I finally managed to scramble to my feet, Marc Zander reached me and clamped his hand onto my wrist.

"Nice try," he stated through clenched teeth.

"Let go of me!" I yelled over the ear-blasting alarms while the sprinklers continued to spray us both.

"Uh, uh," he said, tightening his hold as water dripped from his chin and jaw. "You're not going anywhere, Ms. Azure. You and I are going to have a chat about what just happened."

"I didn't do anything!" I yelled, trying to twist from his iron grip.

"Liar."

"Let go of me now, or I'll scream!"

"Go ahead. No one who is still around will hear you above these alarms."

I let out a blood-curdling scream.

Marc touched his fingers to my neck, and suddenly my larynx tightened, cutting off my voice. I gripped my throat and tried to say something, but no sound came out. Glaring at him, I mouthed my sentiment of him and whatever dirty trick he was pulling, and he arched a brow and tsked.

And where the hell was Helene, the big coward?

With the jerk of Marc's hand, all of the automatic sprinklers stopped, the fire alarms silenced, and the door to his science lab closed. I widened my stare at him.

How? I mouthed.

"Ready to talk now?" he asked me.

I lifted my dripping chin, glaring at him. I tried once more to pull from his grip, but he was too strong. My face heated with fury, but I reluctantly gave him a tight nod.

"You will answer my questions," he ordered hard. "All of them."

When he gave me a little shake at my refusal to answer, I gave another grudging nod.

"Okay, then. And watch your language. I have tender ears."

I snorted, not amused. He twitched a smile, then released my wrist and gently touched my neck. Suddenly my larynx relaxed and opened. I coughed and sputtered, holding my throat, then tested my voice.

"H-how did you d-do that?" I rasped, then coughed again. "And the fire alarm? And sprinklers? And the door closed by itself!"

"Very amusing, little trickster," he said. "Who sent you?"

"Excuse me?"

"Who's your master?" he demanded.

"My *what*?"

"Don't play innocent. I saw you bend that laser with your conductor."

"My..? Look, don't blame me for your failed experiment. Something that happens quite often anyhow, I hear."

"Sarcasm noted." Marc picked up my rose quartz crystal from the water pooled near my feet. "Here, you dropped this."

"Thanks." I pocketed it, then roughly raked the wet strands of hair off my face with my fingers.

"A little amateurish, but well played. The Callaghans won't give me a dime of their grant money now after that stunt, you conniving brat."

"What stunt?"

"Drop the pretenses," he stated. "Now tell me, who's your master? He must know about the geodes then. How did he find out?"

"Are you insane? I'm no slave, you freak."

He rolled his eyes saying, "Not a master as in a slave owner. A master as in your instructor, your superior. Is it LeCroix? Martinelli? Sandoval?"

"Instructor for what? I have absolutely no idea what you're talking about and it's driving me crazy!"

"Not a far stretch for you."

"Oh, you're such a riot," I spat.

Marc growled quietly, looking around at the destruction of his classroom lab. "Dean Ryker is going to blow a gasket again at this cleanup cost. I don't suppose you have five grand laying around your bank account doing nothing."

"No."

He nodded in resignation, then arched a brow at me as I stood shivering and hugging myself tightly. "Better get you into some dry clothes before you catch pneumonia. Then you and I are going to talk."

I was about to vehemently decline and leave, then decided that walking through the building and across campus looking like a drowned alley cat wasn't that appealing. Reluctantly I followed him across the dripping, sparking room to the door at the far corner. It led to another classroom and adjoining office. Marc went inside and returned with a CSU sweatshirt and what looked to be surgical scrub pants.

"Here," he said, handing them to me. "You can change in the office."

"You keep extra clothes around?"

"Mishaps happen," he said. "Too often, in my case, as you so ungraciously reminded me. Make it quick."

Testily I snatched the clothes from him, then closed myself in the office to change. After pulling and tying my hair into a wet ponytail, I exited with my wet bundle in a plastic sack I found to see that Marc himself had changed into a red tee shirt and jeans.

"Better?" he asked.

"Some," I grumbled, rubbing my arms briskly.

He frowned. "You're still cold. Let's grab some coffee and get you warmed up."

Reluctantly I accepted the temporary truce and followed him out the door and building and across the lawn to a student café. He ordered two coffees, then gestured for us to head back outside to sit on a bench in the warming sun.

He took a sip, groaned in relief, then asked, "So what rank are you? Probably not very high if you're still using your conductor."

"Rank? Why would you think that I was in the military? And what's a conductor?"

He studied me hard, frowning. "You really don't know what I'm talking about, do you?"

"No shock, Sherlock. Do you want to explain yourself?"

Marc picked up my right hand and examined it like a physician. He then placed it between both of his own.

"Do you feel anything?" he asked.

"No, of course…wait, your hands are getting so warm and are starting to…Ow!"

I sucked in sharp breath, retracting it at the electrical zap.

"You felt that?" he questioned.

"Of course I felt it, you jerk! What did you just do?"

Cursing, Marc raked a hand through his wet, wavy black hair. "And you still think you didn't bend my laser with your crystal."

"How could I do that? Besides, I was clear across the room, so if you think you're going to blame me for your accident, bucko, think again. Helene was watching through the door window the whole time and will vouch for me, if you try to sue me for damages."

He studied my expression, saying, "Forget the damage. You seriously don't know that your magic shifted my laser's direction?"

I shook my head. "I still don't…wait, did you just say *magic*?"

"God, you are an ignorant novice, aren't you? Yes, magic. Real elemental magic. Which apparently you have."

"Are you completely insane? Never mind, you are. And I'm out of here."

"Wait, Jillian," he said, grabbing my arm as I started to get up and leave. "Back in the lab, did you feel a strong power inside you that worked to blast out right before the accident?"

I opened my mouth to deny it or anything as ridiculous as what he was suggesting, then closed it again. I knew what had happened and what I felt. I don't know what it was or how I did it, but I couldn't deny that it took place.

He studied me hard, then widened his eyes. "God, that was your first time, wasn't it?"

"First time for what?"

"To call up your magic. We have to get you tested, verify you even have the gene. If you do, then we'll need to get you certified and have a master assigned to you." He stood and tossed his cup into the nearby trashcan. "Let's go. There's a lot to do and no time to waste."

"No!" I said, standing and facing him. "I'm not going anywhere with you, crazy man, until you tell me what just happened and what the hell is going on!"

Marc dragged a hand down his face, then explained, "Jillian, you may not believe this yet, but elemental magic in this world really exists. And you, my dear girl, are one of the few fortunate people who can call it up and manipulate it at will."

I fixed my widening stare with his. "You're crazy. Magic doesn't…"

Marc snapped his fingers and handed me a red rose that unbelievably appeared out of thin air. I frowned at the red rose in my trembling fingers, remembering my coma dream of another Marc shooting golden sparks from his fingers across the room to resurrect a crystal vase of dead roses.

But I wasn't unconscious or dreaming now. This Marc, present and live Marc, just performed this same miracle in front of my waking, lucid eyes.

I wasn't imagining it.

Which meant that everything that happened in my coma wasn't a dream and really took place.

"I prefer purple."

He smirked and snapped his fingers again, and the rose changed to a lavender color. "I'll keep that in mind for the future. Now go retrieve your things from Helene's classroom. Then I'll take you to my private working lab outside the city, and we'll see what you've got."

* * *

Helene gaped at my appearance when I returned to her office. "I'll refrain from asking where you got the interesting change of clothes. My imagination is already running rampant."

"Just temporary," I muttered, grabbing my purse off her desk. "Did you take care of the Callaghans?"

She nodded. "All is well on the financing front again. With the bonus that Rosalyn Callaghan won't let Zander lead our team for all the fancy lasers in his arsenal now. Let's go out and celebrate."

"I can't. I have…an appointment elsewhere."

Helene eyed me suspiciously. "With whom?" At my pause, she groaned. "Jillian, the guy's dynamite. You don't want to go near Marc Zander, trust me."

"I can take care of myself," I said, slinging my purse strap over my shoulder. "Trust me, this is important. For the dig."

She grunted her doubt. "Are we still on for dinner later?"

"I'll meet you at the restaurant at six," I confirmed. "I promise."

I drove back to my hotel, changed into street clothes, then headed down to the lobby just as Marc walked inside. He must have gone home himself, since he was now wearing black jeans and an untucked, dark blue shirt.

Then again, he was a magician and could have snapped his fingers and reclothed himself in five seconds.

"Good timing," he said. "We'll take my car."

"Where are we going?" I asked as I followed him to the front lot where his black sedan was parked.

"To a defunct glass factory I'm renting," he said. "It's about twelve miles north of here near the tiny, depressed town of Silverdale. It's far enough away from any civilization, the ideal place for my more experimental spells."

"Remote then."

"Very remote. I can test you there without human interference. They tend to block several electromagnetic frequencies. Or call the police or fire department when things get out of hand. Or their local journalist. The last thing any of us needs is to call attention to ourselves."

Marc didn't say another word until we driving out of the lot and towards the rural highway interchange.

"So you're a real magician then," I remarked. "I didn't just imagine that back there."

"A mage," he corrected dryly as if insulted.

I shook my head. "You've lost me again."

"You'll have to learn the lingo. There are two distinctions between our kind—mage and sorcerer."

"You mean wizards?"

"No, not wizards or magicians," he grumbled irritably. "Mage and sorcerer, like I said. Listen and learn."

"What's the difference?"

"It's all based on genetics," Marc explained. "You're either born one or other. Being a sorcerer is rather common, but so is their magic. They can manipulate the natural elements of this world, transforming things as they will. It's all an advanced form of applied science really. Sorcerers have just been able to tap into that side of their brain and abilities."

Along the way, Marc explained the basics of those who could perform this "natural magic". It was a genetic, elemental ability inside the person, usually discovered in their late teens, although there were late-bloomers who's magical inclination didn't show itself until young adulthood. Never past twenty-one, so I would be an anomaly if I tested positive for magic.

"What's the difference about being a mage then?" I asked.

"There are no limits to the amount of magic a mage can develop," Marc explained, parking in front of the small, abandoned factory building surrounded by acres of field and forest. "We have the ability to do more than just manipulate nature. We can tap into the human mind, the world, the cosmos itself. And whatever comes after that."

"That sounds…ominous."

"It is, so the status itself is never taken lightly. Once a new mage or sorcerer is discovered, they are immediately certified and counted by the high mage council, then assigned a teacher and mentor."

"Who was yours?"

"An incredibly old and power master mage, Maximus Valerian."

"When you say 'old'?" I asked.

"Two thousand and twenty-one," he said, unlocking the front double doors of the building.

"Two..? Uh, how old are you then?"

He shook his head. "Thirty-four. Mages and sorcerers typically live the same length as any other human being. Master Valerian is one of the exceptions, having discovered and achieved the ability to extend his lifespan. Many have tried. Very few have succeeded. He's the only one still alive who has been able to achieve this."

"He sounds like a real live Merlin," I remarked instead.

Marc smiled wide, as he led me inside and through the bowels of the old glass factory. "He is, for the most part. As old and wise and dangerous as Merlin too."

"Can I meet him?"

"No. Master Valerian doesn't like conversing with sorcerers of any level."

"Only the mage elite then, huh?"

"Actually, yes. Don't take offense."

"I'll try not to."

We stopped in a large room that looked like a makeshift science laboratory. I frowned at the various experiments laid out on a long metal table.

"What if I don't pass your test?" I asked.

"If I find that you don't have any actual elemental magic in your system, then I'll give you a thought-eraser spell, and you'll return to your normal life without any memory of what I am or all that I just told you. Like I said, we need to keep our existence secret from the rest of the human world for everyone's protection, ours and theirs. It's one of the many rules you'll have to learn."

"Whoa, you are not going to do any head-scrambling spell on me," I said.

"The term is *cast*, and you would never know if I did or didn't." He smirked, saying, "Don't worry, it won't hurt."

That wasn't the point. I had already lost too many memories, and I wasn't about to let him or any person take any more of them away.

"Okay, time to get this done," Marc said. "Do you still have your crystal?"

I pulled the quartz stick out of my pocket. He took it from me and set it on the table.

"You can't have any conductor on your person during this test, or it will give a false positive," he said.

"Conductor?"

"Something that pulls out and directs your magic. You'll use it a lot at first, but eventually you won't even need it. By the way, where did you get it, since you knew nothing about your magical genetics?"

I shot a wide look to him. How could I tell him that he was the one who gave it to me? His future self, anyhow. The future love of my life.

"Just a friend," I said. "I'm a geologist. People are always giving me rocks and crystals. That one is just my favorite."

"Interesting. You must have sensed something about it to keep it with you. That's good. You'll need to learn how to rely on your emotions and instincts. That's where your true power lies."

"If I have any magic," I reminded.

He arched a brow at me as he measured and mixed various colored liquids from bottles and tubes. "There's something inside you. I'm not sure what it is yet, but it's there. My laser didn't bend itself and destroy my lab."

"Sorry about that. If it was me."

"Forgiven. And that won't be the last catastrophe you'll create, I'm afraid," he remarked. "Magic is all trial and error for the most part. Unfortunately, we tend to have a lot more error in the process. Okay, drink up."

He handed me a glass cup of revolting colored liquid, and I soured my expression.

"You're kidding," I remarked, taking a sniff, then winced at the even more disgusting smell of vinegar, manure and moldy boot. "No way."

"Drink it, Jillian. It won't kill you."

"Uh, uh. You're the magician. Turn it into a Cherry Coke or something first."

"Don't be so squeamish."

"I'm not squeamish."

"A coward then."

My eyes shot to his, then narrowed. He looked amused at my reaction to his challenge, and probably knew it would get me to cooperate.

I pinched my nose and drank up. Then sputtered and coughed and wanted to wash my mouth out with lye soap.

"Ugh, that was disgusting! I swear, if I start acting like some dancing monkey…"

My stomach started roiling, and I gripped it and doubled over.

Oh God, had he just poisoned me?

Was he really some psycho killer who had lured me out in the middle of nowhere to murder me and bury my bones in the nearby field?

"What did you give me to drink, you ba—!"

"Don't fight it, Jillian. Roll with it. Give over to your inner power."

I doubled over again, then suddenly straightened and felt like my entire body was on fire.

"There we go," Marc said, looking pleased. "I knew it."

"What?"

"Look at your hands," he said.

I raised my right hand, then yelped to see that it was glowing. The other one too. In fact, my entire body was glowing like a firefly.

"What did you do to me?" I squealed.

"Nothing permanent," Marc said. "It'll wear off in about five more seconds. Then I'll test your blood. The potion will react with it and give us the final results."

I felt like a human torch, ready to bolt out of there and dive into the nearest river. Then as fast as it happened, the fire inside of me began to fizzle out, along with the glow around my body, and I was gratefully back to normal.

"That was unpleasant," I remarked. "Don't you ever do that to me again!"

"Stick out your finger," Marc instructed, holding a small lancet and glass microscope slide.

"What? No! Get that thing away from me," I said, pulling my hands behind my back.

"Or you'll scream? Maybe a wandering racoon will hear you."

"Very funny. I mean it, Zander. Back it up."

He eyed me with annoyance. "Don't tell me that you're afraid of a little finger prick."

"I'm not…Ow!"

Marc had grabbed my right hand and pricked my forefinger faster than I realized what had happened. He pressed the tip hard, and a thick drop of blood immerged that he smeared onto the glass slide, placing another over it.

I ripped my hand from his and looked around for something to staunch the blood. Not finding anything with its sterility in question, I brushed it against my jeans leg.

Distracted and ignoring me now, Marc walked over to the far end of the long industrial table, then slid the test slide into the microscope and looked into the eyepiece. He straightened, pinched his eyes closed and blinked hard a couple of times, then looked again.

"What is it?" I asked, curious at his reaction.

He adjusted the eyepiece, then looked down at it yet again, then up to me with parting mouth.

"What's wrong?" I asked again, now becoming concerned. "Am I not a magic person then?"

"No, you have magic in your blood all right," he said, frowning deeply.

"Really? That's…are you sure?"

"Come here and look."

Warily I walked over and looked into the eyepiece for myself. I had viewed my blood under a microscope before in basic science labs, the ones everyone did in school. It always appeared normal before. This time, however, it was like looking at sparkling ladybugs dancing and sliding around each other.

"What is that?" I asked. "My blood cells are all lit up and so active."

"Very much so."

"So what does that mean?" I asked.

"That I'll definitely need a second opinion." At my obvious confusion, he explained, "You only need one dimly lit cell to verify any magical genetics. Yours are all lit up like a Fourth of July fireworks display. And they're moving. Every single one of them."

I frowned at him. "Which means?"

"Which means, I'm contacting Maximus Valerian and having him verify this for himself. Now."

CRYSTAL MOON

CHAPTER 6

"You're going to tell my future now, oh swamy?" I remarked with twitching lips.

In the adjoining office, Marc pulled the softball sized, red glass ball from a locked cabinet and placed it on a black ornate stand on an old desk.

"In a matter of speaking."

I frowned. "I was just kidding."

"I'm sure you were. Now hush. For this I need to fully concentrate. Max's barriers are extremely hard for me to penetrate. No wisecracks at that, Azure."

"So you can read minds too?"

"I can read the adolescent smirk on your face. Now quiet. Please."

Marc flattened both palms on the red crystal ball and closed his eyes. I didn't hear him mutter any words, but saw his lips moving. Within seconds, the ball began to pulse and glow a dark crimson. I reflexively stepped back as it increased in speed and intensity.

A burgundy mist suddenly appeared and moved from the glowing ball, then fanned out and curled along the ground, rising and rising until it disappeared, and suddenly a very attractive man with platinum hair wearing a charcoal colored business suit appeared. Whatever I expected was not this male model from some fashion magazine.

He checked his gold wristwatch, then raised bored blue eyes up to Marc. "This had better be important, Zander. I have a dinner meeting in less than an hour."

"It is important Master Valerian," he answered. "I need to show you something."

Heaving an annoyed breath, the man followed Marc into the main room and over to the microscope on the table.

"Have a look."

Valerian impatiently eyed him, then looked into the eyepiece. He straightened, frowned, then looked again.

"Where did you get this?" he asked, looking up at Marc.

"From her," Marc answered, touching my shoulder. "Max Valerian, let me introduce you to Jillian Azure."

"Impossible," Valerian said. "She's a woman."

"Hey!"

"I know," Marc said, ignoring me. "But this test doesn't lie. She has actual mage blood inside her. And something more I can't identify."

"You mixed the potion incorrectly."

"I didn't. I was very careful. The test is accurate, and this woman definitely has mage blood in her."

"Master? Rank?" the man asked me.

I shook my head, backing slightly behind Marc.

"Tell me now, young woman," Valerian demanded darkly.

"She doesn't have either," Marc said. "She's a novice, not yet declared. In fact, she just experienced her first conductor flash today. That's how I found her."

I wanted to correct the fact that I actually found him, not the other way around, but there was no need to go into the whole time-traveling future boyfriend thing. The two men were already eying me as if I were the prized cow at the county fair.

Valerian walked up and gave me a thorough up-down that made me more than a little uncomfortable, then startled me by pressing my right hand between both of his, closing his eyes and concentrating.

Seconds later, he raised his stare to mine with disbelief. "Yes, I can feel her raw mage power. It's very strong. And strangely familiar."

I yanked my hand from his.

"You say you discovered her yourself?" he asked Marc.

"She used a quartz conductor to bend a laser I was working with, having no idea what she was doing. Destroyed my lab in seconds."

"I said I was sorry," I muttered to him.

Valerian's brows hiked. "Light bending as a novice. Impressive. Where did you find her?"

"She's a friend of a colleague at the college I currently work for."

"Stop talking about me as if I'm not here," I ground out. It was too reminiscent of the way everyone had treated me at the hospital.

"I'm sorry, that was rude," Marc said, touching my shoulder. "It's just you're somewhat of a phenomenon. You, a female mage, shouldn't exist. It's like…seeing an aurora borealis near the equator during the middle of a cloudless, sunny day."

"I'm a freak?"

Marc smiled wide. "No—a question, and a wonder. A rare one. Do you plan to certify her yourself, Master Valerian?"

"Hey, what if I don't want to be certified or anything?" I commented.

"You wouldn't have a choice, my dear," Valerian said coldly. "It's the way we keep our kind in balance and check. I'll have Marc explain the rules, after I make my own evaluation. You will permit me?"

It sounded more of an order than a request. Regardless, I gave a reluctant nod, anxious to be done with it all.

Valerian's hand raised and glowed a cobalt blue. Then he closed his eyes and touched my forehead.

It didn't hurt an iota, but the sensation was uncomfortable and invasive, as if he were literally snaking through my brain, searching through my mental files. It lasted for more than a minute before he opened his eyes and retracted his hand.

"By all the powers, I had no idea there was a third," he said, eyeing me with disbelief.

"A third what?" I said, then turned to Marc who shook his head that he didn't know.

"Three then, not two," Valerian went on as if to himself, then looked at me again with faintly curved lips. "That explains the exception and familiarity. Yes, that would complete the prophecy in the most perfect way. I had assumed the third star meant your parents together, but I was wrong."

"What do my parents have to do with any of this?" I remarked.

"I must pull up the image again to verify it. Then I'll need to consult the texts with this new information." The mage turned to Marc with grave seriousness adding, "She can't be officially counted. No one must know of her or her abilities."

"Excuse me?" I remarked.

"Why?" Marc said at the same time.

"Others will hunt her if they learn of her existence," he continued to Marc, while ignoring me. "There will be many who will do anything to stop the prophecy from taking place, or manipulating it for their own purposes. There will be one in particular—Mars."

"Are you saying that she's a key to the Red Moon Prophecy?" Marc asked.

Valerian nodded. "Yes, the third star. She must come into her full power before it can all take place. Master Zander, I leave her in your hands for protection until then."

"What?" he and I both said simultaneously.

"And training," Valerian added.

"You want me to apprentice her?" Marc said with disbelief. "No, I can't do that, Master Valerian. I've never trained anyone before."

"You discovered her," Valerian said. "You are a mage of the seventh power. She will become your first apprentice. And hopefully not your last."

"No!" we both said again at the same time.

"I have decided. Master Zander, claim her and begin her training tomorrow at dawn. If my assumptions are correct, it won't take long for her to develop her full power. I must go. Preparations must be made now that the third key has been identified. The countdown has begun."

He turned to me, adding, "Learn your lessons from Master Zander well, Apprentice Azure. The world is depending upon you and your sisters to stop the darkness from descending on us all. Do not fail us."

"Are you totally wacko? I'm no key or savior of the world. I don't even have any sisters!"

"I rely on you, Master Zander, to protect her. With your life, if necessary."

With that, the man's image dimmed and disappeared into a cloud of red fog. Marc looked at me with awe and disbelief. Then with decision and determination.

"Whatever you have in mind, forget it," I ground out, stalking towards the entrance.

Marc ran up and blocked my path. "You heard Master Valerian. I must claim and apprentice you."

"I heard a crazy man in an Armani suit announce that I'm some magical superhero who's task it is to save the world. Yeah, good luck with that. Send me a postcard. I'm out of here."

"Whether you are or not, Jillian, you still must be trained. You can't learn to control your new magic on your own. Every mage must learn from a master. It's how it's done."

"Forget it."

"You're not leaving here," he insisted.

"That's where you're dead wrong, Magic Man. I'm completely finished with this bad Harry Potter movie. I'm going back to my hotel, take a hot shower, a long nap and sleep off this bizarre day. In fact, I'm sure I'm already dead asleep and am dreaming this entire crazy thing as we speak."

I walked around him, stalking towards the entrance.

"Jillian, wait! You forgot your crystal."

I halted, turned slightly. Marc grabbed it off the table, then held it out to me.

I eyed it and him suspiciously. He sent me a sly, charming smile, offering it to me, but didn't move an inch.

"You're not going to give it to me? Childish, don't you think?"

"Come get it," he said with a devious smile.

Cautiously I walked up and took hold of it, but he didn't let go of his end.

"Let go of it," I stated through gritted teeth. I tugged harder, but he held tightly. "What are you doing, Zander? Let go of my crystal!"

I yanked again, but he wouldn't let go.

Fed up, I decided to leave without it. I tried to let go of the crystal stick myself, but couldn't, strangely glued to it for some reason. I tugged again and again, but it held fast to my hand.

"What're you doing, Zander? Why can't I..?"

Marc then began muttering ancient words in an unfamiliar language. The crystal glowed, heated, vibrated between us. Panicking, I frantically tried to yank away with all of my strength, but couldn't.

His green eyes glowed and fixed with mine, and some strange invisible, unbreakable bond linked our souls. I felt it. He felt it. The only thing I could equate this sensation was the intense kiss we shared in the coffeeshop a few nights ago.

Ending the incantation, Marc solemnly stated, "It is finished. You, Jillian Azure, are claimed as my apprentice. I, Marcus Collin Zander, mage of the seventh power, seventh son of the seventh son, Master Mage Elias Zander, vow and declare it."

He released his end of the crystal, and I staggered backwards, the quartz stick ungluing from my fingers and dropping to the floor. I gaped up at Marc who was watching me intensely, waiting for my next reaction.

"You tricked me!"

"A cheap shot, I admit," he said unashamedly. "It was the only way you would cooperate. Sorry."

"What did you just do?" I accused with horror.

"You've been claimed and declared by me, Jillian. It's your first step towards becoming a true mage. It's your birthright and gift and privilege. I will teach you, and you will learn. I will not go easy on you, and at times you will hate and curse me to my face. That is a promise and a warning. But what I will do, I do for your benefit. Never forget that."

"You forget it! I'm not having any part of this."

"We begin tomorrow at dawn," he said, ignoring my protests. "I'll pick you up at your hotel. Make sure to have a good breakfast."

* * *

The car ride back was silent and hostile, mostly on my part. As I watched the forested highway race by, I tried to process everything that had happened, everything I discovered. Magic was real, not some fairytale nonsense I had come to believe. That much was fact. I was no longer in any coma or dream, and I witnessed it for myself.

Strangely, that part wasn't very difficult to believe, as if I had sensed it all along. Maybe I even knew about it before I lost my memories. It made me wonder why I so calmly accepted this unbelievable fact.

After some thinking, I came up with only three explanations. First, I was literally insane and was probably at this moment locked away in some loony bin, playing this entire scenario out in some warped delusion. Second, these men were master illusionists who were expertly deceiving me—for whatever purpose I had no idea, another unanswerable question. Or third, everything they did was in fact true magic, and I now possessed this same ability.

This last option was the least logical. Yet, I felt the harsh truth of it in my bones.

True elemental magic existed, and I, Jillian Azure, somehow possessed its supernatural ability to…

What?

The idea and possibilities were terrifying.

No. I didn't want this, any of this. I just wanted my own normal, unexceptional life back.

Doug flashed through my mind then. I pictured him impatiently waiting for me back in the house we rented in our small, friendly town. I was allegedly happy there, and why wouldn't I be? We were getting married. I had a teaching job that I liked at a local community college. I had friends, family. Everything I wanted.

Then why did I leave?

More importantly, why didn't I want to go back?

The hard truth was that I knew from the moment I woke from my coma that I wasn't in love with Douglas Hayden, and I didn't want to build a life and future with him. Even now I was hoping to find some way out.

Well, I had found it. In magical spades.

"Still trying to decide whether all of this is real or not?" Marc finally remarked, then glanced at me.

I folded my arms tightly and faced the passenger's window.

"So what have you decided?" he asked.

"I've decided that you have completely lost your marbles. Or I have."

He laughed, facing the highway. "Sorry, no mental illnesses in my family or yours."

"What do you know of my family?" I muttered.

"I know your father must be some powerful mage to create you," he said.

"That's where you're dead wrong. Dad's a retired plumber, nothing more, certainly no wizard."

"Mage," Marc corrected. "Were you adopted by human parents then?"

"Of course not."

One just had to look at my family to see the resemblances.

Or was that something I was convinced to see after a lifetime of coaching by the Azures? Did my parents really deceive me into thinking..?

No, not possible. I would have found out the truth by now if they had been lying about my birth.

Marc lifted a shoulder. "I'll have to check into your lineage. There's something off there to produce someone like you anyhow."

There was silence for another five minutes, before he spoke again, "I know how angry and confused you feel right now, Jillian. I remember the first time I discovered my ability. I was only sixteen and like you had no clue about the magical realm and my true background. Not to mention the timing was about as bad as it could get for a boy that age."

This distracted me from my own miserable reality, and I unwillingly turned to him.

"What happened?" I asked.

I could see the tiny curve of his lips, knowing he had sparked my furious curiosity to get me talking again.

"Linda Mardusi," he said with a lazy, faraway look. "Ahh, she was the girl of every teenage boy's fantasies. Somehow I impressed her enough to accept a date from me, although agreeing to do her science project for her definitely helped."

"Cheating to get a girl. Nice."

Marc lifted a shoulder. "All's fair in love and war, at least to a hormonal teenager. Our evening out was uneventful at first—pizza, movies, the usual. I was just thrilled she was with me and that my friends witnessed it, even if it was only for the one night."

"What happened?" I asked at his pause.

"The date was over, and I fully expected to take Linda home. She shocked the hell out of me when she wanted to go up to the lake to…stargaze."

I arched a brow. "Astronomy aficionado, huh?"

He chuckled darkly. "A passionate expert, too."

"Hmm. I take it you obliged her then."

"Hey, I may have been an inexperienced science geek, but I wasn't a fool," he said with another chuckle. "I learned a whole lot about…the wonders of the cosmos."

"A definite magical night for you then."

"Oh, yeah. That is, until I got so worked up that my dormant magical abilities unexpectedly blasted out of me, shooting sparks and fireballs everywhere inside the car. Burned part of her hair off and both my eyebrows."

I snickered, and he smiled wider.

"Yeah, not my finest hour," he added. "Or it was, too much. At least up until then."

"What happened after that?" I asked.

"She ran screaming from the car, of course," he said. "Hitched a ride with one of her friends parked next to us, and she refused to so much as look at me ever again."

"Poor guy. And you had no idea that you had this magical ability?" I asked.

"None. My mother was human, and I never knew my father. I was told that he was a Marine sniper who was killed in Afghanistan right before I was born. Only when I finally admitted to her about what happened at the lake did she contact my father, Elias Zander. That was the first time I met him, and he explained what we were. It still took some getting used to."

"I'll bet," I said. "Still, it doesn't make sense in my case. Both of my parents are completely human. Are you sure your test was accurate? Maybe it was just a freak thing that happened to me being so close to you. Maybe this is all a mistake."

"It's no mistake, Jillian, as difficult as it is for you to accept. You can feel the power inside of you. Don't you?"

I did. And it did feel rather good, if I was honest.

I recalled the thrilling sensation of the power blasting through me that shifted Marc's laser, and I craved to feel that again.

So okay, I did want to at least explore the possibilities. But why did it have to be Marc Zander of all people have to be the one assigned to train me?

"Seventh son, huh?" I remarked.

Marc twitched a smile as he focused on the highway. "Yes."

"Brothers or sisters?"

"All brothers. Mages only have sons."

"Really? Then where do mommy mages come from?"

"There aren't any," he said. "All mages are conceived by mage fathers and human females. We're particularly attracted to human women because…well, I'm not sure why. Females can be born with magic, but they come from sorcerers and only become sorceresses."

"Sexist, don't you think?" I remarked dryly.

"I didn't make the genetic rules, Jillian."

"Do you know your brothers?"

"No."

"Do you want to know them?"

"No. Nor do they want to know me. Mages don't have the same family dynamics that you're familiar with. We're all…"

"Egocentric players too lazy to buy condoms at the local drugstore?"

He sliced me a dark stare. "Solitary people. This is not a life you want to offer someone you truly care about."

My cellphone chimed, and I looked at the caller I.D. and grimaced. Then hit the *Ignore* button.

"That's twice he's called since we left the factory," Marc remarked, glancing at me. "Who is he? Boss? Boyfriend? Overly protective brother?"

"Mind your own business," I grumbled.

"You are my business now, Jillian. Look, I know you're not exactly thrilled with me training you, but if you want to learn and develop your gift, then I'm the best man for the job. And if I'm to do this and be effective, I'll need to know all there is about you. So who's the guy?"

I faced the passenger's window, refusing to look at his dark scrutiny.

"Doug Hayden," I said finally. "My fiancé."

"You're engaged? That complicates things a bit, but we'll manage, I guess. Where does he live?"

"In our house. Back in Oakwood."

"You're only visiting here in Fort Collins then."

"I'm leaving in five days, yes, so you'll need to accelerate your teaching program. I do have a life to go back to."

Marc shook his head, facing the highway. "You can't leave here, Jillian. You have too much to learn. Five days isn't nearly enough time."

"How much will I need?"

"Years. Decades."

I snorted. "Absolutely not. I'll let you show me a few tricks and stuff, but I'm not sticking around here or you for the next month, much less decade."

"You don't have a choice, Jillian. It's who you are, and the commitment you and I made together."

"*I* didn't commit to anything," I stated through clenched teeth.

"You did, during the claiming ceremony. We both felt the connection. It was a commitment of body, soul and mind, if not in words."

I couldn't deny that something strange and supernatural had passed between us during his weird ritual and recitation. Even now I could feel the invisible bond gluing us together with every minute that passed.

This was insane! I couldn't have any supernatural commitment to this man. No matter what I felt at the time of his sick ceremony. Or now. Or that first night at the coffeehouse.

My cellphone chimed again. I checked the name, then turned off the power.

"You'll have to extend your time here," Marc said. "You should tell him."

"Really? And what should I say exactly?"

He lifted a shoulder. "You know the man, I don't. Either way, he needs to hear that you're not coming home for a long while. It's what you really want, Jillian, and deep down you know it."

"Why on earth would you believe that?" I ground out.

Marc smirked as he faced the highway again. "Call it man's intuition."

"And what do you mean by *that*?"

He arched a brow at me. "Your kiss, for one thing. No woman kisses with that much heat if she's pining away for her future husband back home."

"A lot you know," I spat, hugging myself tightly and facing the passenger's window again. "And for the record, you kissed me back."

"Not denying that. But it can't happen again, no matter how attracted we are to each other. We're teacher and student now."

I was going to debate the issue, but decided against it.

"Sorry about your girlfriend," I said instead. "I really didn't mean for her to breakup with you."

Marc grunted. "It was bound to happen anyhow. I can't have any long term relationships due to what I am. You'll understand that more later."

"That sounds daunting, and lonely."

"It's the cost we pay for what we are." He glanced at me, then turned back to the highway. "You should probably break up with your fiancé as soon as you can manage it."

"What if I don't want to?" I challenged.

"Your choice, of course. It's just a recommendation. Human relationships with mages never end well. They can't know of our kind and our abilities, and we can't tell them. You'll find yourself lying to him, hiding things, constantly. If there is no complete trust in any relationship, it will eventually and bitterly end. You saw what happened between me and Amber Martin."

"She said she caught you cheating on her. Before me, I mean."

Marc frowned. "I didn't, actually. That was just her perception triggered by a suggestion I planted into her mind should she come close to discovering my abilities. A failsafe incantation, so to speak."

"She came close then?" I asked, curious now.

"Yes, unfortunately. Last week she walked in on me in my lab while I was experimenting with a new image spell. The safeguard trigger kept her from seeing the dragon I accidentally conjured and was tangling with, the nasty, smelly beast."

"By making it look like some woman," I guessed, trying to hide my smirk at the scene it created in my own imagination.

"Yes. Quite compromising."

"Then I come into the coffeehouse out of nowhere and kiss you."

He bit down a smile. "Didn't exactly help convince her of my innocence."

There was a moment of silence before Marc added, "Why did you do it?"

"Kiss you?"

"No, take a physics exam. Yes, kiss me. You didn't know me from Adam. Do you always make a habit of walking up and kissing strangers out of the blue like that? I know you're no former student of mine. I would have definitely remembered you."

My face heated as I frowned down at my fingers lacing and unlacing in my lap. How could I truthfully explain why I did it?

"Why won't you tell me?" he asked.

"I'm not sure you'll believe me."

"Try me."

I looked up at him, suddenly wanting him to know everything about me, as least as much as I could safely share without causing some time warp paradox.

"I was in a car accident two months ago that left me in a coma for several weeks," I said.

"A coma? No, that's impossible," he said.

Okay, not exactly the response I expected.

"I was. You can check the hospital records. It's not impossible. It happens to people all the time. Well, not often, but it does."

"It would be impossible for you, Jillian, because you're not genetically human. Our minds and senses and nervous systems work on a completely different realm. It takes unbelievably strong magic—high level mage magic—to even put one of us into a semblance of what would be considered a comatose state."

"But I was. For seven weeks. That much is medically verified. In fact, I almost slipped back into it again if it hadn't been for…"

"Hadn't been for what?" Marc asked at my silence.

"A man. He brought me out of it."

Marc shot a wide look at me. "How?"

"I don't know exactly. He…called to me, and I responded. That's the only way that I can describe it."

"Hmm, I wonder if he was a mage who knew of you then. Who was he?"

I bit my bottom lip, before saying, "I never saw him before."

"Oh. I'll ask Max if he knows then. He might have heard something during a council meeting. What did he look like?"

I winced. "A lot like you actually. That's why I was so surprised when I saw you in the coffeehouse the other night. I thought…"

"I was the man who woke you up," he added for me. "So you kissed me from, what, gratitude?"

"You might say that. Look, I know it sounds ludicrous. I told you that you wouldn't believe me."

He shook his head. "No, that explains a lot actually. You were confused. It was a case of mistaken identity."

"That's what I told the store manager after you left."

He grunted. "Wish Amber would have heard that."

"I could go to her and explain it. Apologize."

He shook his head. "No, don't bother. She was just a minor distraction for me the past few months anyhow, a temporary way to salve the lonely…well, you get the picture. It was coming to a close anyhow. She wanted a permanent commitment, something I could never give her, being what I am. Helene wasn't wrong when she said you did me a favor by helping me break things off with the girl now, before more time elapsed. I shouldn't have let it go on so long. It wasn't fair to her."

"Helene! Ugh, I completely forgot that I'm meeting her for dinner in…twenty minutes ago. Dang it."

I powered on my cellphone just as it rang, and this time the caller I.D. indicated my friend in question.

"Tell her you'll be there in ten minutes," Marc said. "I'll drop you off myself."

"Did you…want to join us?"

He smirked at the reluctance on my face and shook his head. "No need for pretenses around me anymore, Apprentice Azure. I'm your teacher, not your boyfriend. And since you're my first student, I have a lot of studying up to do myself tonight before we begin tomorrow."

"Fine. But I'm not calling you master. Ever."

CRYSTAL MOON

CHAPTER 7

There was a painted star in the middle of the concrete floor of the old factory warehouse, but nothing else except for three softballs sitting in the middle of it.

"Now you try," Marc instructed, standing behind me.

"Shouldn't I be wearing a catcher's mask?" I asked warily.

"Not if you do it correctly. Go on. Like I showed you."

Letting out a cleansing breath and shaking out my arms, I then raised my quartz stick and pointed it at the three softballs.

"Now concentrate," Marc instructed close to my ear. "Work to feel the power rolling and burning inside your gut."

I tried.

"Nothing's happening," I stated through gritted teeth.

"You're still using your head, not your emotions."

A full minute. Even my teeth ground with the effort.

"Nada," I said, deflating.

"Let's try something else," Marc suggested. He reached around and pressed his hand flat on my abdomen, his body pressing against mine. "Relax. Feel the power spark and glow inside you, Jillian."

I felt something all right, but it wasn't the sparking power he was describing. His body molded and moved against mine as if trying to will the vibrations into me through his own skin. His other hand smoothed down my arm and gently clasped my wrist and lifted my hand holding the crystal.

"Do you feel the electrostatic sensations inside of you?" he spoke quietly into my ear that he nuzzled, his hot breath tickling the back of my neck.

"Mmm, hmm," I said with eyes closed.

"Feel it build. Feel it boil up into a tight, fiery ball that just needs to be released or it's going to explode out of you."

Oh, God.

"Good," he said, his hand releasing my wrist and pressing against my hip and thigh. "Now fan that spark into a flame, then work it up through your body and into your limbs. When you feel it in your hand, push it out with all your strength, like you're blowing—"

Without warning, white light shot up from my raging body and into my hand. The crystal grabbed hold and directed it into a fiery beam that exploded in the middle of three softballs, blasting them in all directions.

"Whoa!" I said, then turned to see that Marc was not pleased by the result.

"You were supposed to levitate the baseballs, Jillian, not blast them to smithereens. You lack focus and control."

"Hey, a little encouragement please," I grumbled.

"There's no time to coddle you. From what Master Valerian told me about the prophecy last night, we need to get you up to full power as fast as humanly possible."

Marc grabbed another softball from the filled crate next to us, then placed it in the middle of the star again.

"We'll try just one ball this time," he said walking back to me. "Maybe three was too many." This time he stood to the side, not touching me. "Now try again. Concentrate. Focus. Build the power inside you. Remember that you want to lift the balls, not destroy them."

"Fine," I spat.

Building and pushing the fiery light inside me into the crystal stick, the single baseball twitched, then slowly levitated off the ground for five seconds before bursting into a dove that flapped and flew away.

"Whoo-hoo, I did it!" I remarked with amazement. "Did you see that? I did that."

Marc heaved another frustrated breath. "Better, but don't pat yourself on the back."

"Hey, I not only made the ball float in the air, but turned it into a bird too. Not bad for a rookie, I'd say."

"That was promising, but your powers are still out of control. Your magic should never go renegade on you. Another thing, Jillian. Never overestimate your abilities. Overconfidence and arrogance are the main weaknesses of all sorcerers and mages. Never forget that. No matter how much magic you learn, there's always someone out there who knows more. And they don't always have your best interest at heart."

I nodded at the sage advice.

"Now again," he said after shoving the entire crate of softballs into the middle of the star. "One at a time. Keep doing it until the ability becomes second nature, like driving a car. No doves this time."

After three grueling hours and several hits and misses, I couldn't hold my aching arm up any longer. Marc massaged my sore muscles, but didn't let me quit, and I continued my basic training another two hours after that. All through the lessons he explained more and more of our kind's history, laws and regulations.

"There are spells that border on the forbidden, like physical attraction spells," he explained while I was levitating several objects at a time.

"Are you saying that it's not allowed for me to make you fall in love with me?" I said, almost losing my focus and dropping the chair and table I was holding in midair.

Marc snapped his fingers, and a vase of flowers appeared on the table, making it more of a challenge for me to balance the whole thing.

"Creating physical attraction is not too hard, but is against the law," he said. "A person's perception can be altered or a glamor can be cast either way. But creating love itself is impossible. No mage, no matter how powerful, can manipulate freewill."

I bit my bottom lip, trying to focus on the task at hand, but I was still curious.

"How about something like, I don't know…time travel?"

He snorted. "Whatever made you think of that?"

"Just a movie I watched last night. Has any sorcerer or mage ever gone back in time? Or forward even."

There was a beat of silence that made me turn to see Marc's tight, dark expression. I lost focus, and all the items came crashing down. He eyed me with irritation.

"What's wrong?" I asked.

"You still lack focus."

"I know," I waved him off. "I'm talking about the ability to time travel. Why won't you answer the question?"

"Because it's strictly forbidden, Jillian. It's a capital offense."

"To ask the question?" I asked with amazement.

"No, to attempt the spell." He reflexively checked around, then stepped closer, lowering his voice. "It's one of the most dangerous and criminal feats a mage can attempt. If convicted, you would be stripped of your powers and sentenced to the Dark Dimension."

"Dark Dimension? What's that?"

"A place you don't want to go, trust me. We'll save that conversation for another time."

"Hmm. And trying to find a way to travel through time will get you sent there."

"Undoubtedly," he said.

"It's a stupid law."

"Not really. In my opinion, no one should be able to travel to the past or the future. It gives this individual the theoretical ability to change events, to change fate itself, which could have disastrous effects. No one should attempt it. Ever."

That made me squirm. After all, that's exactly what happened when Marc himself traveled back in time to wake me from my coma curse. If he hadn't, I would still be asleep in that hospital bed with no hope of ever waking.

"Yes, but think of all the good it could do if someone traveled back in time before Hitler or Mussolini or Stalin came into power and stopped them," I countered.

"That argument has been made before during mage council meetings," Marc said, picking up the debris left from the day's lessons. "It's always tempting to play God, but we never know the ramifications or domino effect through the generations caused by such actions. That's why it's forbidden to work on it."

I studied his still rigid expression as I helped clean the general area.

"There's something else you're not telling me, isn't there?"

"No. Drop it, Jillian. We're done with this conversation."

I halted, straightened. "Max Valerian is working on time travel now, isn't he?"

Not to mention, that he must have been successful, if he managed to send Marc back to me from the future.

Should I tell him this?

What would be the ramifications if I gave him such knowledge though? Could it somehow, as he said, have a domino effect that would actually prevent this discovery and keep Marc from coming back to wake me from my coma and set me on this journey to find him and learn of my own magic and…

God, the possibilities were giving me a spinning migraine.

Marc snapped his fingers, and the rest of the place was instantly straightened and cleaned. Then he stalked over to me, again lowering his voice.

"Possibly. I don't know."

Waiting a beat, he added, "About two years ago, I was helping Max in his personal lab and spotted some old texts that were open. There was another sheet of paper next to them in his own writing. To the untrained eye it looked nothing more than a physicist's worksheet, but I saw the added spells from the same ancient texts opened next to it. I did my own calculations alone later, and if my assumptions were right…"

He raked a hand through his hair roughly, shaking his head. "I probably should have reported him to the mage council, but I just couldn't."

"Why?"

Marc nudged a shoulder. "Out of loyalty, I suppose. He chose to teach and mentor me as a big favor to my father. I credit Max for everything I am and know today. He's beyond brilliant and thinks on an entirely different level than the rest of us. If he had his reasons to attempt time travel…Anyhow, he was never successful, so there was no need to press the issue further."

He pointed a warning finger at me adding, "But keep this quiet, or all of us will be in trouble for it."

"Okay."

"I mean it, Jillian. Not one word. You and I could be indicted with him just for knowing about it."

"Okay, I got it." I studied the tightening of his clenched jaw muscles. "Do you trust him?"

Marc frowned. "*Trust* would be an inaccurate term I would use for Max Valerian. I'm respectfully cautious of him, as a lion tamer would be walking into the cage of his lethal cats. I know what he can do, what he's capable of doing. At the heart of the man, he is very good. But I also know that he holds to the unsavory philosophy that the end justifies the means, which makes him dangerous."

The sun was setting, and I was exhausted with all the paces Marc had put me through. Not for the first time, I begged to end today's session, and this time he relented.

"Are you meeting Helene for dinner again tonight?" he asked as we drove away from the old glass factory.

I shook my head. "She has a lecture tomorrow that she needs to prep for, so I'm going solo."

"Same here," he said. "Prepping for a lecture tomorrow, I mean. We'll have to delay our next session until later in the afternoon."

"Fine by me," I said, grateful for the short reprieve from the brutal magic lessons. Then I remembered what Helene said of his lessons, and it made me curious. "Actually, would you mind if I sat in on your lecture?"

He snorted. "Interested in Advanced Physics, are you?"

"Maybe. I'm a little professionally curious too."

"That's right, you're a science teacher at some high school?"

"Hey, geoscience instructor at a community college. Don't be such a snob."

"Apologies." Marc glanced at me with a twitching smile, adding, "Sure, come sit in. But no heckling to disrupt the class, or to put me in my arrogant, snobby place."

"I'll be good. In fact, I could help you prep tonight, and even come help you out tomorrow. The infamous Magic Man needs a lovely assistant, right?"

He chuckled. "You might be very lovely, Jillian, but you're a sorcerer apprentice, not an assistant, and I'm no two-bit magician, thank you very much."

"Yes, you're a mage of the seventh power, blah, blah, blah. Come on, it'll be fun."

He looked at me as if I was nuts, then relaxed his expression. "We might end up working for hours tonight."

"I don't mind. It'd be better than channel surfing in my cramped hotel room. How about it?"

Marc considered it, then finally heaved a tired breath. "We'll pick up a pizza on the way home. There's a lot to prep tonight, so we'll have to eat our way through the evening."

"Sounds like total fun."

* * *

"You've been up there almost two weeks already, Jill," Doug remarked hotly over the phone. "When are you finally coming home?"

I squeezed my eyes shut as I held the cellphone to my ear while pacing the small space of the hotel room. I had dreaded this conversation with him all day. But both Marc and Helene were right. I needed to finally tell him.

"Okay, don't freak out."

"About what?" he questioned suspiciously.

"I've decided to go on Helene's dig in Ireland," I said, wincing. "It's only two weeks from now, and I shouldn't be any longer—"

"What? No! Absolutely not, Jill. I forbid it!"

My brows hiked. "You forbid? Excuse me, did I somehow wake up from my coma in the seventeenth century?"

Something banged and crashed over the other end of the connection, but when Doug came back on the line, his voice was at least semi-calm.

"Is this what you really want, Jillian?" he asked. "To go on this trip with your friend?"

"I do," I said. "This was something that I had planned to do before I was even in the car accident. Besides, the more I'm with Helene, the more I begin to remember things."

Another pause. I could have kicked myself, knowing what he would conclude.

"But not anything about us," he remarked darkly.

I frowned. "I'm trying. Really."

"Are you?"

"Yes, I am! Do you really think I like having a huge portion of my brain closed down for construction?"

"Fine, but why do you have to spend so much time there at the college? Why can't you come home and work to remember our life here?"

"I don't know. There's just something about this place. Maybe because I spent so much time here in the past. Anyhow, I've been helping out Helene and some of her fellow instructors here and there, and it feels good to do something productive. I promise to come home right after the trip."

"How long with that take?"

I bit my lip. "A couple of weeks maybe? The timeframe hasn't been firmed up yet."

Doug let go of a long breath. "I can't stop you from doing what you really want to do anyhow. If it's helping, then I guess that's something. Will you at least come home this weekend for a couple days? I really need to see you."

"Uh, not this weekend. Maybe the next?"

There was dead silence.

"Jill, is there something going on up there you're not telling me about?"

I chuckled nervously. "Why would you say that?"

"Is there?"

"Of course, not," I lied. "Everything's fine. Doug, I really have to go now. I'm helping one of the science professors with his class this morning, and I don't want to be late."

"Fine, we'll talk later then."

"You bet."

"I love you."

I was about to return the sentiment for his sake, but couldn't bring myself to voice this one particular black lie. Doug was a good man, and he didn't deserve false declarations.

"You're the absolute best man I've ever known, Doug. And the most patient. A woman would be crazy not to love you back. I'll call you tonight, okay? I should have more details about the field assignment then."

Quickly I hung up, my stomach gripping with the guilt of torturing this poor guy. Hopefully in time I would come to remember and care for him again. Still, if what Marc told me about being a sorcerer was true, I would have to eventually break it off with him anyhow.

There was a knock on my hotel room door. Quickly, I swiped the tears off my cheek, sucked in a cleansing breath, then walked over to answer it.

"Ready to go?" Marc asked, stepping inside.

It had been decided last night that he would pick me up before his lecture this morning in order to take just one car, since we planned to drive directly to the old glass factory for more practice afterwards.

"Let me slip my shoes on and grab my purse."

I wore a short summer dress today and decided on my matching pink flats. He frowned down at my bare legs as I walked to the closet to grab them.

"How'd you get the limp anyhow?" he asked.

Honestly, I forgot that I still favored my right leg after more than three weeks. The doctor said the torn ligaments might take weeks, even months to heal completely. Or they might even be permanently damaged, and I would have to accept the limp as my new reality.

"I'd say none of your beeswax, but you seem to believe everything about me is your business."

"You're not wrong," he said. "What happened?"

"I told you I was in a car accident a couple months ago," I answered, sliding my toes into my shoes. "I'm pretty much healed up, except for some stubborn torn ligaments. The doctor said I might have the limp all my life, if they don't heal. It is what it is. A little painful at times though."

"Sit down," he ordered.

"What? No, let's go already. I still need to grab something from the coffee stand in the lobby on our way out."

"Sit down, Jillian."

His tone brooked no argument, so I warily obeyed and sat on the edge of the mattress. Marc took a knee in front of me, then lifted my right leg and braced it on his upraised thigh.

"What are you doing?" I asked.

He shushed me and held my ankle between his warm palms that grew hotter with every second. A blast of fire shot into my ankle and up through my leg. Reflexively I yelped and tried to yank away, but his grip on it held fast.

Finally, he released his hold and stood.

"Try it now," he instructed.

"Did you just..?"

"Quit arguing and try it, Jillian. Healing isn't one of my stronger suits, but I can manage a few torn ligaments."

Strangely, the dull pain that had been in my ankle for three weeks was now gone. Tentatively I stood and took a few, much smoother steps.

"Better?" he asked.

I shot a look up to him. "It's perfect! Thanks, how did you do that?"

"Another lesson for another time. Right now, we have to get to campus for my lecture. Is my lovely assistant ready for our show?"

"Lead the way, Magic Man," I said, now having a definite spring in my healed instep.

Marc's lecture was mesmerizing, particularly with his incredible demonstrations that I helped with. Like Helene told me, the man had a true gift at breaking down the most complicated formulas and concepts and making them easy to understand and appreciate, and I was glad he was my own teacher on all things magic now.

"That was fun. Let's do it again," I said afterwards when we were driving to his private laboratory out of town.

"It was, but let's not," he said, facing the highway. "The less people who know about our association, the safer you'll be. Max warned that some unknown mage could be hunting you. Or will be, once he discovers your existence."

I snorted. "Max is a paranoid old man in a business suit."

Marc chuckled. "I'll tell him you said that."

"Please don't. I don't want to wake up one morning croaking on a Lily pad in some murky pond."

"Turning you into a bullfrog would be beneath the mage. A tiger cub, maybe."

I sent a cheerless smile, then turned to the passenger's window.

"What's up now?" Marc asked irritably.

"Nothing."

"Out with it, Azure." When I didn't respond, he added, "Whatever you're upset about will interfere with your abilities and make this afternoon's lessons twice as hard as they should be. What's going on?"

I frowned, then finally turned to him. "I told Doug this morning that I'm going on the dig in Ireland, and that I'm staying here until then. He wasn't happy."

"I'll bet not."

"He also wanted me to come home for the weekend," I added, wincing.

"Are you? I was planning on a full day tomorrow since it's Saturday and I won't have any classes, but I understand if you want to go see him instead."

I frowned. "I told him no."

"You didn't have to."

"Yes. I did."

There was silence for another long minute before Marc said, "Do you love him?"

"What? What kind of question is that?"

"A very simple one. Do you love the guy or not, Jillian?"

"That's none of your business, even if you are my mentor."

"The fact that you're not answering the question tells me a lot."

I narrowed a stare at him, but his expression remained cool and unintimidated. He also wasn't going to let me off the hook in answering the question.

"No. I don't know. Okay, no, I really don't love the man. How can I? I hardly know him since I woke from my coma-curse."

"Fine, but do you feel of spark of energy or chemistry that could lead to the possibility of it?" he posed.

I shook my head. "Nothing. I don't want to feel anything for him either. God, I'm such a slime."

He snorted. "You're not a slime. You're honest. But this passive-aggressive behavior of yours with him will only get you into deeper trouble."

"You think I should officially breakup with Doug then."

Marc lifted a shoulder. "Not for me to say. But it is for you. And you're not doing the man any courtesy by pretending to feel something for him that you don't, or stringing him along for weeks and months on end. Tell him how you feel now, and be done with it. Then both of you can finally move forward with your lives."

He was right, and I knew it.

"Sometimes I just hate you," I grumbled.

"I warned you that you would," he said. "I'm your mentor, not your buddy. I tell you what you need to know, not what you want to hear."

"Oh, I'm so privileged," I muttered.

He chuckled. "Just wait. It's going to get a whole lot worse."

"Wonderful."

"Now brace yourself," he said, parking in front of the abandoned warehouse. "We've got a lot of ground to cover this afternoon, and not a lot of time to do it in."

* * *

By the end of the next week, even Marc admitted the amazing progress I was making with the development of my abilities. As he first instructed, levitation and other minor magical abilities became easier with fewer mishaps, and eventually became second nature.

Transforming objects were more difficult. I did manage to turn an old glass bottle into a beautiful lead crystal vase that I took back to my hotel room and filled with wildflowers that I also zapped up, and his microscope into a telescope, then back again—a harder feat than it seemed.

All during the lessons and days, Marc interspersed the hands-on teaching to instructing me in the basic concepts of natural magic and incantations, sharing more about the history of magic itself and those who learned to harness its power, both the good and the bad.

"Remember that elemental magic isn't bad in itself," he reminded me, while we broke for lunch at a Chinese restaurant in the nearby small town. "It's just applied physics on a different level, a skill to be honed and a tool that can be used for good or for ill.

"You need to work on your conscience and character even more than your magic, Jillian, or the power itself will become your god and rule you with an iron fist, destroying you and everyone else in your path."

I nodded, sipping my egg drop soup. "So you're saying that black magic is only black, because the person wielding that power has bad intensions and a dark soul."

"Exactly. That's the most valuable lesson of all. Never forget that. Do you want that wonton?"

"No, take it," I said, allowing him to spear it with his chopstick. "What happens if one of us breaks a mage law then? You mentioned something before about a council of judges and some kind of magic jail?"

Marc halted eating then, and checked around before lowering his voice even further. It was a tick of is that I was learning whenever he spoke about something deadly serious.

"With great power comes greater responsibility, as the saying goes," he began. "So we have a council of seven of the wisest master mages to police and judge our people. If a sorcerer or mage breaks one of our laws, they're brought before the council. If convicted, a punishment is decided at that time. Depending on the level, a rebellious adolescent sorcerer could get off with a warning, if it's not too serious."

"And if it is?"

"Yes, there are stiffer punishments for higher leveled sorcerers and mages convicted of more serious crimes—limitations of power, magic abilities and power temporarily and sometimes permanently stripped, even exile to the Dark Dimension, at the very worst."

"Yes, that's the one—the Dark Dimension. You mentioned that before. What is it?"

Marc shook his head. "A place not even of this universe, but of a different dimension. It's a dark, evil realm filled with demons of mass destruction. An unequipped sorcerer sent there is always running from these monsters, day and night. No one survives long in that place, and their death when caught by these voracious beasts is long and torturous."

I scrunched my expression, imaging such a nightmarish place. As well as its current population.

"I can't accidently call up this place, can I?" I asked.

Marc's cracked a small smile, easing then. "No. Only a master mage on the council itself has the ability to open a crack between the dimensional veils to send a convicted criminal there before it snaps closed again."

"Oh, good. That's a relief." Then I frowned, adding, "Do you think Max can access this place? He's even older than those on the mage council."

"Maybe. Either way, he would have no desire or reason to, so it's not an issue. He only focuses on those things that are important, as you should be doing. You still lack focus."

"I swear, if you tell that to me one more time, I'm going to—"

"Scream?" he added for me.

"Launch a bunch of exploding softballs at your face!" I said instead.

He laughed, but personally I wasn't amused. I was frustrated with my life, my lack of progress, my entire spinning new world.

"I know it's all overwhelming, Jillian," he said, seeing it on my expression. "Look, you're a teacher. You know that student is always first confused with all the new information you impart onto them, but eventually it all clicks into place. I'm a hard instructor, but I'm not without empathy, having been there myself at one point. You will learn all that you need to know and become the powerful sorceress you're meant to be. I'm confident of that."

I grunted, nudging my empty soup bowl forward. "I'm not though."

"Remember when I told you that overconfidence is a mage's weakness? The opposite is also true. Lack of confidence cam be a major detriment and hinderance. You need to believe in yourself and trust in your magic before you can call it up, or it will fail you every time."

"Enough already, sensi. My head is going to split with information overload. Can we go home now?"

Marc wadded his napkin and tossing it on the half-empty plate. "Fine. Let's go, apprentice. You're done for the day. We'll start again tomorrow at nine."

"You're letting me sleep in on a Saturday? Yay," I said tiredly, getting up from the corner booth.

As he drove down the highway, Marc didn't bombard me with more information that was already crowding and shoving for space inside my brain, but turned on the radio and let soft classical music play. Gratefully, I relaxed back into the seat and enjoyed the rest of the ride home. I had almost drifted off, in fact, by the time he pulled up into my hotel parking lot and shut the engine.

"Coming up?" I asked, giving my drowsy head a quick shake.

He shook his head. "Not this time. You're beat, and I need to go home and grade essays. I still have to work for a living after all."

"Yeah, that's something else I've wondered about. Why don't you just zap a million dollars into your bank account?"

"Not ethical, and it's against one of our laws."

"Again with the magic laws." I frowned. "Sounds like I'd better get that list of rules and regs soon before I accidently break one of them out of ignorance."

He laughed. "No need. Until you graduate to mage-one, I'm responsible for your actions. It would be me paying the penalty for whatever crime you ignorantly committed."

"Sorry ahead of time then."

"It's all good," Marc said unconcerned. "Mostly it's a matter of knowing right from wrong and acting accordingly. You obviously know that it's wrong to counterfeit currency, if it's easy for us to do. Right?"

"Hmm, I suppose. So I guess that means that it's wrong for you to cast an attraction spell on some beautiful woman and compel her to follow you home one lonely night?"

His brows hiked. "Unequivocally. However, in my case, there's no need. I use my magnetic personality and brilliant wit."

"Look who's dreaming now."

We both laughed at that. Marc flicked his hand, and my passenger's door swung opened.

"Show off," I grumbled.

"Just being polite and gentlemanly. And maybe I was showing off a little to impress you."

"Why on earth would you want to impress me?"

"Because you're definitely a beautiful woman who I find myself wanting to show off for."

Our eyes fixed and held for a long moment. Then Marc frowned and looked away.

"Sorry, I shouldn't have said that. It was inappropriate. As your teacher, I shouldn't—"

"I feel it, too, Marc. I've always felt it. Why do you think I really kissed you that first night in the coffeehouse?"

He snapped his gaze back to fix with mine, his lips parting. Then without warning, Marc leaned over and kissed me.

He pulled back with slight alarm, braced for my violent, negative reaction. Instinct and need took over me then, and I leaned into him and desperately, passionately kissed him back, sliding my arms around his neck.

The heat intensified as we shifted and kissed again and again as if we couldn't get enough of each other, declaring ourselves and our intensions and feelings and hopes.

Until we broke apart at the pounding of his door window. And I gasped at the sight of Doug standing there, his face red with fiery rage.

CRYSTAL MOON

CHAPTER 8

"Doug! Oh, God."

I scrambled out of the car and rounded the back bumper just as Marc opened his door.

"What the hell are you doing with my fiancée?" Doug ground out, giving him a hard shove in the shoulder.

Marc stood his ground, lifting his chin. "If you don't know that much, no wonder she doesn't want to be with you."

Doug cursed and gave him a right cross to the jaw, knocking him down.

"Doug, no!" I screamed, crouching down to Marc. "Are you okay?"

Narrowing his eyes up at Doug, he spit a few drops of blood to the side. "No, but I will be."

Standing, he worked out his jaw, then like a cobra strike returned his own iron blow to Doug's gut, doubling him over.

"Stop it, both of you!" I yelled, pressing an arm back at both of them, just as Doug jumped up to throw another punch. "This is all my fault! I shouldn't…Marc, you need to leave. Doug, you and I need to talk. Right now."

"There's no way I'm leaving you alone with this guy, Jillian," Marc said.

I touched his chest. "Please. I'll be okay. Go, now."

He raised his fingers to trace my cheek and smiled softly. "I'll call you later. Make sure everything's okay."

"Get away from her!" Doug spat, shoving him away from me.

Marc viciously rounded on him again, but again I pressed between them. He pulled his glare from Doug, then gave me a nod and got back into his car. After revving the engine loudly twice, he gave one final warning glare to Doug, then backed up and drove away.

"So is he the reason you're still up here, Jill?"

I turned my focus from Marc, back to him. "No." *Well, not the only reason.*

"Really? That's why I found your faces plastered together here in the frigging parking lot in full public view?"

We were drawing a very concerned crowd from around the parking lot and sidewalk. I needed to diffuse the situation fast.

"I'm sorry. It was a dumb, impulsive thing. I'm not even sure how that happened. We just…got caught up in the moment."

"Give me one frigging break, Jill. I know what I saw."

"What you saw was a mistake," I said.

"Who is he?"

"Just a colleague of Helene's I've been working with. Really, nothing's going on. Look, come up to my room, so we can talk. There's a lot to be said either way."

Doug shot an onlooker who started to approach us a black glare, making the older man back up and go about his own business. Then he nodded and followed me into the hotel. I walked quickly with him in tow across the lobby to avoid further speculation and took the stairs to the second floor.

Alone with him inside my hotel room now, Doug began to pace, glaring accusingly at me all the while.

"What are you even doing here?" I asked.

"What? I can't even come up and see my fiancée for the weekend, since you won't come home yourself, *like you promised me last weekend*?"

"That's not what I meant."

"I know what you meant, Jillian. And I can see now why you didn't want me to come here. What's his name, and how long has that been going on? Since you got here? Even before that?"

I wanted to argue that before I came up here, I was in a coma for two months. Now wasn't the right time to point out the flaws in his furious reasoning though.

"It's not what you think," I said instead.

"Original."

"It isn't," I insisted. "Marc is just a colleague of Helene's, and nothing more. We've all been prepping for the upcoming trip to Ireland."

"I can see that," Doug ground out.

I rubbed my forehead roughly, getting nowhere. "It doesn't matter what I say, does it? You're just going to think the worst."

Doug gestured roughly with his arm. "I just saw you both swallowing each other's tongues and ready to head up here to your room, Jillian. What else should I think?"

"Not what you're thinking now, because he wasn't coming up here to my room with me. He was just dropping me off after…"

"After what?"

Marc was right about the complications of having a normal, honest relationship with a human man now. Since I couldn't explain to Doug that we had been working on developing my magic, I couldn't tell him the truth of my whereabouts.

Besides, I couldn't convince Doug that he didn't see what he saw. Marc kissed me, and I kissed him back, and I had no regrets. The truth was that I knew who I really wanted now, and I needed to tell Doug that it wasn't him. No more stalling and making half-excuses. He deserved that much.

Slowly I stood and touched his arm. "Doug, I have to tell you something."

His expression went stark, rigid. "Don't."

"I've tried, Doug. I've tried with all my power to remember you, us, what we once shared together. But it still comes up blank."

"Jill, please. I'm sorry if I jumped to conclusions just now. I was just being a jealous, immature ass. We can work this out."

I stepped back as he reached for me. "No, we can't. I can't do this anymore. I can't keep leading you on to hope for something I can't give you. It's not fair to you. Doug, I don't love you, and I don't believe I ever will. I'm so sorry."

All color drained from his face. He dragged a rough hand down his jaw and remained silent for more than a minute before he spoke again.

"Is it that guy?" he questioned with a dark, even tone.

I turned away from his accusing, stormy gray stare, feeling the flush in my face and neck. Yes, it had a lot to do with how I felt about Marc Zander, what I hoped we would become now and in the future. But it also had to do with so much more—my new abilities, new desires, my new altered view of the world and those around me in it. But none of these true reasons I could share with this injured, confused, innocent man who had unluckily been a casualty in all of this. Maybe it wouldn't have helped for him to know of it anyhow.

"Marc has nothing to do with this, at least not in the way you think. This has to do with the fact that I don't feel anything for you, good or bad. That's not what you deserve in the woman you intend to marry and build a life with."

Doug gripped my upper arms, clenching like a vice. "You just don't remember everything yet, Jillian, but you will. You need to give us time."

"I've given it time, Doug. Enough to know that you and I don't want the same things, at least not anymore."

His hands slid away. "What are you saying? You're breaking our engagement?"

I nodded. "I'm sorry. I'm so sorry."

"So that's it then?"

Again, I nodded, allowing him time to process everything.

The moment came when his expression hardened and eyes narrowed. "You'll live to regret this, Jillian. I swear you will."

"You might be right. I may wake up some morning and suddenly remember everything, including us, and deeply regret sending you away. Right now, though, it's the kindest thing I can do. For both of us."

Doug stood there for another ten seconds, then growled and upended the table, everything on it crashing to the floor, and stormed out the door.

Tensed fear melted to deep relief as it closed behind him, and for the first time since I woke up from my coma, I truly felt free. I just wished I didn't feel so guilty about it.

* * *

"You didn't call last night," I said to Marc when he picked me up the next morning at the hotel.

I was about to point out that I had also called him and left voicemail messages that he didn't return, but refrained. After our intense kiss last night and the cataclysmic aftermath with my now ex-fiancé, I didn't want to read too much into his silence.

"Sorry, no excuses," he muttered, facing the forested highway as he drove. Marc ventured a quick glance at me then faced the road again. "How did your talk go with ape man?"

I let go a heavy breath. "Not good. We broke up."

There was a long pause.

"I'm sorry," he said quietly, his jaw muscles bunching. "I hope I wasn't the cause of it. I could call and explain things to him, if it would help."

"No, don't. It was something I needed to do long before, well, us." Another pause.

"Yeah, about that last night," Marc began, squirming a bit in his seat. "I'm sorry that things go out of hand and I…"

"Kissed me hard enough to make my head spin off into outer space?" I added at his awkward pause.

He twitched a smile. "Yeah, that." He cleared his throat, adding, "For me, too."

"Glad to hear it. I was getting worried there." Then I figured turnabout is fair play. "Why did you do it?"

"Kiss you?"

"No, correct my physics exam," I echoed him from the day after we met.

"Honestly?" He snorted, shook his head. "The hell if I know."

"Please don't flatter me too much, Romeo. I may swoon."

"No, it's not…" Marc growled, raking a rough hand through his hair before he spoke again. "Jillian, you and I can't be together, as much as I might want it."

He wants to be with me?

My heart and mind sang joyous hymns at his declaration, but I kept myself in check, knowing that he also had a "but" at the end of his statement.

"But it's forbidden for a master and his apprentice to…get together. For good reason."

"Name one," I challenged.

He frowned, glanced at me. "Well, it's inappropriate."

"Why?"

"Because I'm your teacher and you're my student. As a college instructor yourself, you should at least agree with that."

"Not in our case, Marc. We're both single, educated, professional adults with a very small age gap between us. Just because you're teaching me something new, something *not* on the Colorado Board of Education's approved curriculum, doesn't mean that we can't have a personal relationship if we want one."

"That's *if* we want one," he countered.

"Don't you?"

He kept silent a long moment before saying, "That's not the point. My assignment is strictly to teach you the skills and art of elemental magic, nothing more. If Master Valerian found out I was…Well, let's just say you would wake up one morning to find *me* croaking on some nearby Lily pad. He's become very protective of you and gave me my marching orders in very descriptive and violent terms that first day."

I bit down a smile at the image of it. "No problem. You'd just need a beautiful princess to kiss you back to your princely form."

He chuckled, then sobered and looked at me with serious green eyes. "He's right. It's better that we don't push the boundaries, no matter how we feel about each other."

"Well, Max is not my father and not my warden, so I don't see where he has any say in what I do or how I feel."

"You don't want me, Jillian."

I pressed a hand to his bicep. "What if I do?"

Smiling sadly, he took and kissed my palm before releasing it. "You don't. Trust me on this. I'm not good for you. I never will be. Now let's table this discussion so that we can focus back on your training."

Sniffing my annoyance, I turned to face the road, seeing the turnout that led to the abandoned factory down the road another quarter mile.

So it was going to be like that, was it?

Looks like if I wanted this man, then I would have to take the lead in this pursuit and convince him that we were meant for each other. Not a happy prospect, since I had absolutely no idea how to go about it.

"So what's on tap today, oh wise Merlin?"

"Today you're going to learn a few glamor tricks and some incantations that go along with them," he said. "You'll always need both. One for the appearance, and the second and third for the sound and memory duplications."

"Hey, do you think I'd scare Helene if I came back looking and sounding like her?"

"I think you'd give the poor woman a coronary," he chuckled. "Would serve her right."

"Hey, now. She's my best friend, and right now my only one."

"I was kidding. Sort of."

I studied his tightening expression. More than once, I wondered what triggered their strained relationship. There was definitely no love lost between them, but Helene was strangely evasive whenever I brought up the subject.

"What is it between you two anyhow?" I asked.

Marc didn't respond, then parked in front of the building's entrance as usual, shutting down the engine.

"Marc?"

He turned to me, frowning. "I suppose I should tell you, or you'll never shut up about it."

"Please do."

He nodded. "When I first came here to CSU, I dated her younger sister, Elise."

That took me by surprise. Neither he, nor Helene, had mentioned this interesting fact before. I knew Helene had a much younger sister, but I had never personally met her.

Oh, God! I just remembered that I had never met her sister!

"Was it…serious?" I asked, distracting myself from the hammering heart that I remembered something, anything.

"Yes. Well, as much as I could allow it to be with any human woman. But yes, I cared for Elise very much."

"You obviously broke up at some point," I added.

After all, he had been recently dating the brunette who just broke up with him, so Helene's sister had to be out of the picture by then.

"Yes."

"And there's no way you're getting back together again?" I added at his awkward pause.

"No, definitely not," Marc said, gripping the top of the steering wheel with white knuckles.

The continued silence was now making me extremely nervous.

"Marc, what happened between you two?"

His mouth tightened into a straight line, his jaw muscles bunching before he finally said, "She was killed. During one of my worst failed experiments right here at the factory. Helene's never forgiven me. And I don't blame her."

* * *

Although Marc explained briefly what happened that day Helene's sister died, he wouldn't go into details, then dropped the subject altogether. I understood. Or at least I tried to. It was a burden that still weighed heavily on him, and Helene's continued anger and grief didn't help alleviate Marc's own confused guilt over the accident.

"That's it for today," he said, just as the setting sun shot amber beams through the western windows. "We'll start again tomorrow morning. I'll pick you up at ten, let you sleep in a bit."

Glamor spells weren't as easy and simple as one would think, but by the afternoon I was easily transforming myself into celebrity after celebrity, then from one animal to the next. I also learned that a living being couldn't be transformed into an inanimate object, or the other way around. That was logical, but surprising information.

"Sounds good," I said with a slight groan as I rounded out my stiff shoulders and shook out my wrists. "Hey, the hotel serves brunch on Sunday. Come by, and we can feed like there's no tomorrow."

"Tempting, but I'd better not."

"Come on. You can take an hour to eat a decent breakfast. My treat," I said.

"Will you stop asking if I keep saying no?"

"No."

"Then yes, I'd love to, Ms. Azure. I'll be at your hotel tomorrow for brunch at ten. But I'll expect extra focus and work from you after that. You still aren't getting teleportation correctly, and that's one of the final tests before graduating up to mage-one status. I want you to work on that."

"Deal," I said, grinning wide. "How about dinner when we get back to town?"

He grunted, slipping his hand behind my back to lead me out of the factory warehouse. "Not tonight. I have a lot to do if we're going to spend tomorrow working on your magic. And no negotiations."

"Fine. Guess I'll just eat all by my lonesome."

I sighed dramatically, and he sent me a withered stare. "It's not working, Azure. I'm not changing my mind."

"Apparently not," I grumbled, knowing both of us were talking about something else entirely. "You're as stubborn as a rock. You know that?"

"I do know that, which is why you should stop asking."

The ride back was lighthearted though, Marc definitely pleased with the progress I was making. I, on the other hand, was still irritated with his stubborn need to keep things strictly platonic between us. Throughout the entire day, he had successfully dodged all of my covert touches and any of my clumsy flirtation attempts to ignite that intimate, volcanic connection I knew was boiling just below the surface.

By the end of the day, I was ready to give up.

Ready, but still not willing. No doubt Marc felt something for me, but there was something holding him back from giving over to it. He might spout all the practical reasons a mentor and student shouldn't be together, or the fear of Valerian turning him into roadkill for messing with his new prized project, but I knew the truth. It had something to do with the accident that killed Helene's sister, something he wasn't admitting to, maybe not even to himself.

"Last offer," I offered hopefully.

"Thanks, but no," he said again. "Besides, you should get some rest."

"Care to join me?"

He sent me a narrowed stare. "You don't give up, do you?"

"Nope. Hey, I know what we felt for each other last night when we kissed, even if you won't admit it."

Marc's jaw muscles bunched as he focused on the highway, his finger gripping the steering wheel. "Yeah, about last night. That was a gross mistake. I let my libido get the better of me. Helene was right to warn you away from me. I'm a dog. Always have been, always will be. It's best we don't start anything that will just end up hurting you."

"I don't believe that, and deep down you don't believe that either. It was more than just sexual tension, and you know it."

He refused to look at me or even acknowledge what I said.

"Why won't you even open up to the possibility of something more between us?" I demanded.

"Drop it, Azure. It's not going to happen. Let's just focus on getting you up to speed with your magic."

"Think of all the advantages of two mages being together," I persisted. "We wouldn't have to hide or lie about who we are. We would understand and support each other. We could feel free to fall in love and have a family—"

"Yeah, I never said anything at all about love or family, Jillian. I'm not even sure if I'm capable of it."

"Of course, you're capable of it," I said.

He raked a rough hand through his hair. "You still don't get it, do you? No mage ever stays with one person for very long. It's not in our nature. You'll learn that."

"I don't believe you. I believe you're just scared because of what happened with Helene sister."

"You're damn right I'm scared!"

The blatant admission drained the blood from his face. There was silence for a tense minute before he collected himself and said, "I did fall in love. Once. I went against every bit of advice given to me by my father and mentor and allowed myself to fall for a human woman. And it got her killed."

"What really happened that day, Marc? You can tell me."

There was silence for so long that I thought he wouldn't. Then he growled low in his chest and pulled the car over to the side of the road and shut the engine. Then he turned to face me straight on.

"I'll tell you, so that you'll understand why there can never be anything more between us beyond teacher and student. Friends, at best. Then I never want to speak of it again. Is this understood?"

I nodded, bracing myself for the worst, and ready for my counterattack.

"Elise Hornsby was a student of mine," he began. "Bright, attractive, full of life and hope and passion for her future. It's a common thing for students to be enamored with their teachers. I'm sure you've experienced it many times. I've never acted on any of their overt invitations to move beyond the professional. But Elise was the exception."

Marc continued to share that Elise's stubborn persistence in asking him out finally broke down the well-enforced protective wall he built around his heart. Being a sorcerer in a human world is a lonely existence. Any relationship formed must be by necessity a shallow and temporary one at best.

But Elise wasn't content with just hooking-up. She worked hard to get under his emotional skin, never satisfied with having only a casual, superficial affair.

"In truth, neither did I," Marc continued. "Ever since I learned what I was as a teenager, I was instructed and forced to keep myself and new life secret and apart from everyone else. It's like...living your life in solitary confinement. Never being allowed to get close to anyone, to bear your heart and soul to that person, to have any hope for love and a family and a future together. Elise broke through all of those defenses and offered me a hope for all I had lost, for all that I really wanted deep down."

His master mage father, Elias Zander, learned of Marc's budding human relationship and paid him a rare, unscheduled visit.

"In short, my father told me to break it off with Elise or suffer the consequences. At first I thought he was threatening me, or her, but in truth he was just warning me once again that a relationship between a mage and human never ends well. And that it always painfully ends."

"You didn't break it off with her though, did you?" I asked at his long pause.

Marc shook his head. "I swore I would be the exception, that I would be careful and she wouldn't suffer the backlash of what I am.

That's why I found and rented the warehouse out of town, so that I could practice my magic without fear of her safety."

"I spent more and more time there," he continued. "Elise thought I was cheating on her, so one day she followed me to my lab. I was in the middle of a very experimental spell when she walked in and caught me. My shock and emotions effected my spell. I was only able to recite half of the incantation, and it inadvertently opened up a crack into the Dark Dimension."

"Oh, God!"

"A minor demon got through before it closed up," Marc explained. "Elise screamed and ran, but it killed her before I could destroy it."

Marc gazed out into the darkening forest beside us, adding, "My father was right. It didn't end well, and it did end her life. It's my fault for not believing him, and she paid the ultimate price for my ignorant and arrogant belief that I could be the exception."

There was silence for a long moment. I allowed Marc time to gather himself from reliving this painful, guilty memory.

"I'm sorry for what happened, Marc," I then said quietly. "Why would Helene believe her sister's death have anything to do with you, though? She couldn't know what really took place."

"She didn't, and still doesn't," he said. "I called my father. He helped to mask everything to make her death look like a mugging gone wrong in the park where we were planning to meet that day."

I felt sick at the thought of such a coverup. Yet another lie.

Still, to tell the truth would be unbelievable to Helene or her family or the authorities, and in the end didn't change its outcome.

"It's still not right that she blame you for her sister's death," I said.

"She has to blame someone," Marc said. "In her opinion, if we weren't together, if her sister hadn't met me there at the park that day, then she wouldn't have been killed by the mugger.

"In truth, if Elise hadn't loved me, then she wouldn't have come to my lab, and the demon wouldn't have escaped its prison and killed her. So even though the circumstances were changed slightly, I'm still the guilty party, and Elise Hornsby's death is my fault. All because she loved me."

CRYSTAL MOON

CHAPTER 9

"I can't do it," I growled, trying hard to levitate the Chinese food takeout box from the table without my crystal.

"Concentrate harder, Jillian," Marc instructed, standing beside me. "You can do it."

I had reached the point in my lessons that although I was generally doing well, I was frustrated with my own lack of progress. The physical repetition and practice had passed the point of infuriating, and I still could barely do the most basic things.

Shaking out my right wrist, I flexed my fingers, then pointed them in the direction of the tiny white box. The familiar fiery bubble of energy popped from my gut and flew down my arm and into my palm, but without my conductor, it refused to blast out of my fingertips.

Thirty grueling, straining seconds, and I dropped my arm in defeat. "Nothing."

"Yet," Marc added. "You've made great progress in the short amount of time you've been at this, Jillian. It will come."

"When?"

"When it will."

"Well, that's helpful advice," I grumbled.

"Okay, when you can teleport yourself easily and hit your intended mark, then you'll be up to the first level of sorcerer. Your abilities speed up fast after that. You just have to break through that first hard bubble. You're right at the cusp of that too, I feel it."

"How will I know when it happens?"

"Trust me, you'll know."

I grabbed my crystal stick off the table. "Maybe I should still use this for a while longer."

Marc snatched it out of my hand. "No, you have to learn to do magic without it, stretch your unworked muscles. Yes, it's sore and painful and tedious, but necessary for growth in your abilities."

He tossed my crystal on the table, then lightly massaged my wrist and pointed my hand towards the food container again.

"Once more," he instructed. "And concentrate."

I glared at the small white box, wishing I could blast the thing into the next county and never see it again. I knew I could, too, if I was holding my crystal conductor.

Maybe my crystal had become a crutch for me. But the thing I feared most was that I didn't have this powerful mage magic in my system at all like he and Max assumed. My parents were human after all, or at least I believed they were.

Yes, I'm sure they were. They would have told me, warned me at some point in my life if they had passed mage genes down to me. So whatever I had inside of me was probably diluted at best.

"I've tried," I insisted through clenched teeth. "I can't do it."

"You can. Try again."

I did. And again, I failed. By Marc's frustrated expression, even he could tell when I had enough.

"Let's take a break," he suggested, heaving a long breath.

"Great. Wait, is this a break like going into town and having lunch, or going into the back office here for more incantation memorization? I'm warning you now that my brain is on systems overload and can't take one more word."

Marc smiled. "A real break from all of this. I know it's all overwhelming."

"You have no idea."

"I do actually," he said. "Master Valerian was a demon with my studies and never let up, not even for a minute. Drill sergeants could take lessons from him. I wasn't sure if he was hellbent on me becoming a great mage someday, or in destroying my very life before I leveled up to mage-one status."

I chuckled tiredly. "Swim or drown then, huh?"

"*You* have no idea," he said, then checked around the warehouse with a tired breath. "Let's get out of here, get your mind off your lessons for a while."

We headed outside, and I gripped the small of my back as I painfully arched my spine. I took several cleansing breaths of the icy mountain air, and began to feel slightly better.

"This way," Marc said, waving me over as he headed towards a grassy foot trail at the edge of the nearby forest.

The hike over the rough terrain was invigorating and helped to stretch out several stiff, overworked muscles and limbs. I never realized how physically taxing magic itself could be. Even pulling a real rabbit out of truly empty hat was more grueling that one might think. Especially when that irritated bunny bit you on the hand.

Marc had pulled ahead by several yards, so I rushed to catch up with him. As I surveyed the old, thick trees and the underbrush on both sides, I wondered how old this place was. The thought humbled me, made me feel small and insignificant in its grander, ancient scheme. It also reminded me of my last conversation with future Marc, his dire warning of my ultimate destiny.

If he had been correct, of course. So far, very little had come to fruition to make me believe so, particularly with the lack of progress I was making with Marc himself. Present Marc, that it.

If I couldn't convince him that he could love me someday, how could I do any of the world altering things future Marc said I would?

Not for the first time, I was doubting everything, and ready to call the whole thing quits. Forget present and future Marc. Forget trying to develop magic and save the world. Who was I but a simple school teacher anyhow? What could I do that would make any difference in anyone's world?

After hiking and trudging through the forest and up and down rises and across streams and gulches, the foot trail ended at the edge of a clearing that held a small pond leading out to a running creek, fed by a cliffside waterfall. The pastoral setting was straight from a fairytale. I don't even think I would have been surprised to see fairies fly up from one of the wildflowers along the grassy bank.

"Wow, this place is beautiful," I said breathlessly. "When did you discover this?"

Marc laughed, taking my hand to lead me towards the waterfall. "Not long after I rented the factory. It's one of my favorite getaway places out of town when I need to mentally recharge."

He led me up a slippery, muddy footpath along the bank and a few feet up the hill. From there he led me directly behind the waterfall itself. I covered my ears against the noisy sound echoing off the short cavern cut into the hill.

"This is amazing!" I shouted.

Marc grinned wide and nodded. "I come here to yell out my frustrations," he shouted over the thunderous waterfall. "No one out there can hear anything in here. Not that there's anyone around anyhow. Go ahead. Try it."

I gave him a withering stare until he prodded me again. Then I sucked in a deep breath, and let out an ear-piercing, frustrated scream. I even added a couple of epithets for color, and the result was a very sore throat, but a much eased mind and spirit.

"Better?" he asked afterwards.

I nodded, holding my throat. It was raw and scratchy now, but definitely worth the temporary pain.

"Thanks. I did need that."

Marc led me back out and down to the flowery clearing by the calmer side of the pond and creek. We sat on the bank, both taking our shoes off and soaking our feet in the swirling, icy water and relaxing under the warm cloudless sky.

"I know you doubt yourself, Jillian," he said quietly, skipping a pebble across the water. "But you have more unharnessed power inside of you than any novice or apprentice I've ever come across, including myself. This is all just new to you. It'll take time."

Time. Why did it always come back to more time?

But time was quickly slipping away. I felt it somehow. Even though I no longer concerned myself with leaving Fort Collins and going back to a home and fiancé I didn't want, Helene's Ireland trip was only a week away. And after the trip itself, then what?

At this point I was certain of only one thing—the love I shared with Marc. Or will share. Or would share, if he would only stop stubbornly resisting any attempt of getting close to me.

I knew that he wanted to love me back, but his guilt over Elise Hornsby's accidental death kept him from allowing himself the opportunity at ever having another relationship again. If only I could convince him that it would be different with me, another mage. Or soon to be one anyhow.

While sitting peacefully, I slipped my hand into his. He started to retract his, but I held on tighter.

"Really? I can't even hold your hand?" I challenged with annoyance.

"Not when you want it to move towards more than just innocently holding hands, you evil temptress," he muttered.

But I also noted that instead of pulling away, he laced his fingers through mine.

"Just so that we're clear," he added. "Nothing more."

"No monkey business, scouts honor."

"Hmm, I would be more assured by that vow if you were in fact a scout."

I hiked my brows at him. "Afraid that I'm going to take advantage of your virtue?"

"Most definitely. You have a one track mind."

My smile widened slowly as the warmth of our simple connection flowed into me. This was so odd. I never thought I would ever take the lead in the pursuit of a romantic relationship. And I wouldn't have now, except that I knew the only reason for Marc's evasiveness was due to his belief of causing me harm should we take things to the next level.

"Tell me, do all sorcerers and mages remain single for life?" I asked.

"For the most part, yes," he said, scratching his nose with our clasped hands. "Some sorcerers get together, not many. Never mages, of course."

"Then how are baby mages born?"

He arched a brow at me. "Need the sex talk, do you?"

"I was referring to the fact that from what you've told me, there doesn't seem to be any mage marriages or families."

"There's not," he said.

"So you're saying that you've all come about through hit-and-run encounters?"

"Pretty much."

I shook my head, tossing a stone into the rolling water. "I'm not buying it."

"I told you several times that a mage's life is a solitary one," he said, his thumb absently rubbing circles on the back of my hand. "We're still human though, forgive the pun. There are times when the need to connect with another person overcomes our iron will, good sense and self-imposed celibacy, and things happen when we come across an attractive, willing human."

"What about fraternizing with a sorcerer then?"

"Sometimes a mage and sorceress get together," Marc said. "Not often. Too much social rivalry. Plus she tends to want to solidify the relationship and create a permanent bond, and a mage won't."

"Why not?"

He frowned, gazed out over the water. "It's not our way."

"Why not though?"

"Just because it's not, Jillian. There doesn't have to be a reason."

"In this case, there is though. Don't you see?"

Marc looked like he was about to counter my argument, then merely shook his head. "You're young in the craft and life, Jillian.

It's difficult to explain to someone who has only lived in the human world. You'll understand in time."

"I don't think I want to," I said. "I never want to lose my ability to fall in love with another person and hope for a future and family together."

He retracted his hand from mine. "You don't love me, Jillian. Get that notion out of your head right now. That can never happen with us."

"It can, if we both want it," I posed.

"It can't. I don't." Marc stood, then faced me straight on when I joined him. "Look, Jillian, I won't deny that there's definite chemistry between us, but I'm doing my level best not give into it, and you're not making it any easier. Whatever romantic notion you have in your mind, you need to let it go. Permanently. I'm your master-teacher, and you're my apprentice, and as soon as you learn enough to level up to official mage status, then my time with you will be finished. Then either you or I or both will be sent away from each other for good."

"What if I don't want that?"

"You won't have a choice. It's the law."

"It's a stupid law."

"But an unbreakable one nonetheless. Don't make me do something that will cause us both imprisonment, or punishment, or worse."

"I love you, Marc Zander. Why is it that you refuse to love me back? What is it that keeps you from even considering it?"

Because as I studied his tightening expression, I knew it had more to do than some dumb mage thing, or even the guilt he felt over his girlfriend's death. It went deeper. Someone had betrayed and injured him so deeply that he closed himself down to all future possibilities of truly caring for someone ever again. Someone…

"It was your father, wasn't it?" I finally figured out.

Elias Zander.

Marc was raised to believe his loving father died as a war hero before he was born. Then he discovered that his father was a philandering mage who just didn't want to stick around and raise his son, the accidental and unwanted byproduct of a typical mage one-night-stand.

"You're better than he is, Marc," I said. "You wouldn't do that to me."

"No. I would just inadvertently kill you in the process of one of failed experiments."

"That wasn't your fault. It was an accident."

"One that wouldn't have happened if I hadn't decided to stay around Elise too long," he added through clenched teeth. "Don't you understand yet, Jillian? I can't ever get close to another person without the fear of hurting them in some way—physically or emotionally. It's why my father left me and my mother before I was born. It's why I can't allow myself to love you now, as much as I want to."

I felt it then—the inner pop and glow of true magic. Brought on by nothing more than my deep, abiding love for this lonely man. It stretched out towards him, pulled his soul close to mine.

"I love you anyway, Marcus Zander. I love you with my whole heart. And there's not a thing you can do about it. It's my choice alone to make."

He growled, raking his fingers through his hair. "Dammit, woman! Didn't you hear a word I just said?"

I walked up to him and pressed my hands to his chest, pushing his back up against the tree, bracing him there with my own body. "Every word. Spoken and unspoken."

He lifted his chin, his chest rising and falling with every fast, heavy breath. "This won't work, Jillian."

"Not if you don't stop talking. Now do as I'm instructing for once, teacher. Kiss me until our heads spin into the comos. Maybe even farther than that."

His hands slid around my waist, drawing me against him. "You will be the death of me, Jillian Azure. I swear you will."

"Probably."

Marc narrowed a stare at me. Then his lips crashed down onto mine, his mouth shifting and claiming me desperately again and again until I couldn't reason.

Then with a flick of my hand we were in my hotel room with the *Do Not Disturb* sign firmly in place. I was just about to do another bit of magic, when Marc caught my wrist in mid-twirl.

Then he cracked a one-sided smile, while slowly unbuttoning my blouse, saying, "Let me do some of my own magic now."

CRYSTAL MOON

CHAPTER 10

I woke to the delicious sensation of Marc slowly kissing and licking my clavicle, moving to other more generous and sensitive areas. I smiled, stretched and arched for him like a lazy housecat that has dined on pure cream and that anticipated more coming her way. Marc did not disappoint.

His nickname was aptly attributed, I determined afterwards.

"You're shameless," I said breathlessly after making me beg for my final reward.

He grinned wickedly, answering, "And you're greedy. We're a perfect match."

We were indeed.

I suppose I knew that already, from the first moment I woke from my coma to see him. Well, future him.

We relaxed in each other's arms for a long time. In was morning now, and I checked the clock on the end table with a quiet groan.

"You'd better get up," I said. "You have classes to teach, professor."

"Hmm, later."

"It's Monday morning. Time for us both to rise and shine."

"I could cancel my classes," Marc muttered, beginning to kiss the length of my neck again.

I closed my eyes to the delicious sensation, but I needed to stop things before he regretted his actions later. "Common, teach. Up and at 'em."

I still had to nudge him away, and he narrowed a look at me.

"You're really going to make me leave?"

"I am," I said, sitting up to stop further progression. "One of us needs to be responsible anyhow."

He sat up, rubbed a rough hand through his mussed hair. "I can't go. My car is still back at the warehouse."

I waved off his lame excuse, getting up and slipping on a robe. "You can zap it back here in two seconds, and you know it. Now get up and get going, lazybones. I'm not going to be the one responsible for ruining your teaching career."

Marc made a disgruntled noise in his throat, then stood and made his way to the bathroom. When I heard the shower running, I couldn't help but grin at the thought of sneaking in and joining him. And I probably would have, if not for the knock at the door.

"Thanks, but I don't need…"

My statement cut off when I opened the door to see that it wasn't the floor housekeeper, but Helene.

"Oh. Hi."

"Hi yourself, stranger," she said.

"Uh, what are you doing here?" I asked nervously.

"If you'd answer your phone once in a while, then I wouldn't have to come here in person to see if you were still alive, would I?"

"Still living and breathing. Was there something you wanted?"

Helene gave me a twisted smile. "Only several dozen things we need to go over before the trip in less than a week. Can I come in already, or are you going to make me stand out here in the hallway?"

"Uh…" I checked behind me, biting my bottom lip. "It's kind of not a good time right now."

"No time seems to be good for you lately. What's the matter? You're as nervous as a flea on a poodle. If I didn't know any better, I'd…"

Helene glanced around me, gaping at the clothes laying on the floor near my feet, particularly those that didn't belong to me. Then her mouth did a small "o".

"You've got company," she remarked with a sly grin.

My face beaded hot and red. "I'll meet you downstairs for coffee, okay? Give me fifteen minutes."

"Hmm. Looks like you might need more than…Oh, crap."

Helene's expression went flat and pale, and I squeezed my eyes closed with dread hearing the bathroom door open. I glanced behind me briefly to see Marc walking out of the steamy room, dripping and wearing nothing but a bath towel around his lean hips. Then I turned back to Helene's tight, accusatory expression.

"I'd like to say that it's not what you think," I admitted sheepishly.

"And here I thought you *didn't* have rocks for brains," she ground out. "Guess I'll talk to you later. Sometime."

"Helene, wait!"

But she was already walking double-time down the hallway and disappeared around the corner, and I wasn't in the best attire to follow her. Not that I knew what I could tell her to let her know that she had it all wrong, that Marc and I were more than just having a fling. This was the real deal, true love, forever and ever.

"Who was that?" he asked, when I closed the door.

"Friend, now turned enemy, I suspect. You'd better get dressed and get out of here. I have some major damage control to attend to."

* * *

Twenty minutes later I kissed Marc goodbye in the hotel lobby, then braced myself and headed into the café still serving breakfast. Thankfully Helene was in a booth sipping coffee and nibbling on pastry, waiting for me. Swallowing hard, I headed over and sat across from her.

"You probably want to know about me and Marc," I began.

Helene raised her eyes up to me and sniffed. "Not particularly. That's the symbiotic part of our friendship, right? Don't ask, don't tell. Live and let live."

"Well, I'm changing the rules," I said. "We're not in college anymore, and I want a deeper friendship than that."

"What do you suggest then?"

I thanked away the waitress that came up for my order, not in the mood to eat or drink anything until I settled things between me and Helene.

"I consider you family now," I said. "And as family we should be able to talk and share about anything."

Helene took another sip from her mug, then nudged it aside and fixed her stare with mine.

"All right," she said. "Everything up for grabs then?"

"Everything," I agreed.

"Then I think you're making a monumental mistake with Marc Zander."

I nodded. "I know you do, but this isn't a casual thing between Marc and I. I love him. He loves me. This is the real thing for both of us."

Helene frowned down at her plate, then looked back up at me. "Where have I heard that before? Oh, that's right. From every single girl and woman he's come into contact with since the first day he came here to the university. That includes my innocent and trusting sister, Elise. Excuse me, my *late* sister, Elise."

My cheeks flushed at her reminder.

"Yes, Marc told me about your sister. I'm so sorry, Helene."

"Did he tell you that he was responsible for her death?"

"He does feel completely responsible, but that's just the guilt he placed on himself. He didn't kill her. You know he didn't."

"Not directly maybe," she admitted, "but if he hadn't blasted into her life, and she wouldn't have gone to the park that day to meet him where she was killed. She would've been safely inside her dorm room studying for her chem lab, like she should've been."

"Your sister's death wasn't Marc's fault," I insisted again. "Maybe she would have gone to the park that day on her own where she was killed. Or hit by a bus while crossing the street. Or developed some kind of terminal disease. None of knows when our time on this earth is up. We just have to live what time we do have to its fullest."

"Tell that to Francis Croger in the Philosophy department," she ground out. "All I know is that my sister was alive and well and had a bright, promising future, until the infamous Magic Man came to magically steal her heart and life away. And now instead of working at JPL solving the mysteries of the universe, she's sleeping the eternal slumber in Rose Garden Memorial Park."

"And now here you are," she continued, "plunging into those same dark, deadly waters that is Marc Zander. And you want me to simply sit here and watch while he systematically destroys your life?"

I reached across the table and grasped her hand. "I appreciate your concern, Helene. I really do. But I'll be fine. You need to trust me on this."

There was silence for a long moment.

Helene studied my expression hard. "It doesn't matter what I say about it, does it?"

"It matters a great deal. But Marc Zander is who I want, who I love. Nothing will ever change that."

She frowned deeper, gave a dry sniff. "He's not rooming with you on the trip."

* * *

"So Helene is happily onboard with us being together," Marc remarked skeptically as we ate dinner that night at the corner bistro.

Wincing, I picked at the last remnants of my salmon spring salad. "Well, I wouldn't say happily. She's accepted the situation, and let's leave it at that."

Marc made a doubtful grumble in his throat, his thumb absently caressing my fingers laced through his on the table. "She's the least of my concerns. Max is going to strangle my neck, and maybe some other more sensitive areas of my anatomy, when he finds out."

"Don't worry, I'll protect you if he tries anything. I do have some advantages being the master mage's pet."

"I don't know, Jillian. They both might be right. This thing between us may not be—"

"Do not say it," I said, touching his lips with my fingers. "We've already fought this battle, and I won. Fair is fair."

He smirked. "Yes, ma'am."

"That's better. Then no more negative talk." I downed my iced tea, adding, "After your class tomorrow, I want to head to the factory and have you test where I am now. Don't you think I might at least be up to mage-one now?"

Marc nodded. "Yes, you teleported us both safely and in one piece, and I would assume to your intended location."

"I did, and it was."

"Then you're definitely at mage-one status. Maybe even higher."

"I am amazing, aren't I?" I said, huffing and mock polishing my nails.

"Hmm, don't forget what I said about overconfidence in mages."

I scrunched my nose at him. "Come on, let me run at least one little victory lap here. I worked very hard for it."

"Okay, this once. Be prepared to work a lot harder from this point on though."

"Wonderful," I muttered.

He chuckled. "I should head home. I have a lot to prep for tomorrow's lecture." He gave me a soft kiss that left my lips warm and tingling, then smiled as he traced my jaw with his fingers. "Would you like to come over and help out, lovely assistant?"

I grinned wide. "Tempting as that is, I'm sure you wouldn't get much done."

"Oh, I intend to do quite a bit and finish the job thoroughly."

"I'll bet," I muttered, shoving his shoulder playfully. "No, I'll finish my salad and head back my own room, and let you do your academic work. Alone."

He made another disgruntled noise. "Not as much fun alone."

"Nevertheless. Now go, teacher. Before I have to send you to detention for bad behavior."

"Spoiled sport."

Marc gave me another kiss, then tossed several bills onto the table to pay the tab, even though I said tonight's dinner was on me. He said a man had his pride, as antiquated as that might be.

"Call you later," he said.

"You'd better," I returned. "You welch on it this time, bucko, and you'll pay the price."

He lifted a hand to me as he walked out the door.

I was about to finish my meal when I noticed that he had left his car keys on the table. Grabbing them, I dashed out the door after him.

Marc was already across the quiet street and to his car parked along the curb when he patted his pockets, suddenly realizing his error. He then caught sight of me as I raised his keys in the air, then checked both directions for traffic and dashed across after him.

It was the look of horror in Marc's green eyes that made me hear the blaring of the diesel truck to my left.

Right before I felt the painful body-slam and all went black.

CRYSTAL MOON

CHAPTER 11

"Jillian, love, please come back to me. Please wake up."

It was Marc's desperate voice pulling me from the quagmire of my coma.

No, not coma—my death-sleep curse. Sorcerers and mages couldn't go into a comatose state.

But how did I know this?

"Jillian, please. Don't leave me."

I knew, because I was told this *after* I already woke from it weeks ago. Which meant this whole thing wasn't real, just some twisted nightmare replaying horrifying scenes from my past.

"Jillian, love. Stay with me!"

Don't worry, I wanted to reassure the sad, desperate voice. *This is just a dream. You, me, we're not even here, not really.*

"Jillian, please!"

Even so, I had to wake up. I didn't want to be in this dream anymore, didn't want to be suffocated again by the black nothingness that pulled me under once before. I couldn't bear to hear that voice pleading with me not to leave him.

I would not leave him. I had to wake up.

I had to wake up now.

Slowly I forced my mind to surface back to reality and end this horrible memory dream. When my brain began to dim the lines of consciousness, a thousand painful sensations that were very real and physical nearly overwhelmed and sucked me down under again.

"Jillian, you can't leave me. We just found each other. Please."

I cracked my eyes open to the blurry sight of Marc hovering over me with a drawn, desperate expression. He was mussed, frantic, looking like he hadn't slept in days.

"Jillian! Oh, thank God!" he rushed out, kissing my forehead that rang out with agonizing pain. "Max, she's awake!"

God, this seemed like déjà vu.

Was I still dreaming then? Was I reliving the time I woke from my coma almost three months ago?

Only now I was confusing the players from that awful scene. Even Max Valerian, donning a doctor's white lab coat with stethoscope hung around his neck, came up beside the hospital bed and started to go through a cursory exam.

I tried to speak, but a muffled sound made me realize there was a thick tube taped to my mouth and lodged down inside my throat, pumping oxygen at regular intervals. Valerian checked the hallway, then snapped his fingers, and the tube disappeared, allowing me to gratefully breath on my own.

"W-where..?" I rasped.

Marc kissed my scratched cheek, answering quietly, "Fort Collins Medical Center. A truck ran you down last night when you were crossing the street to bring me my car keys. It was a hit-and-run, the bastard didn't even stop. Do you remember? It took all of Max's expertise to keep you alive through the night and heal you to this point."

I did remember. It all happened in a split second—me crossing the empty street, the truck that wasn't there before suddenly appearing out of nowhere, slamming pain, flying weightless in the air.

Utter darkness.

I shifted my eyes to the master mage beside my bed. "Thanks."

Valerian gave me a slight smile and nod. "Let's not test the limits of my knowledge and healing abilities again for a while, shall we, Jillian dear?"

Marc exchanged a look with the mage, whispering through gritted teeth, "There was no question this time, Max. I saw that truck suddenly appear. I felt the surge of magic, black mage magic. Then it was just gone. She was definitely and specifically targeted."

Max looked at me. I gave a stiff nod.

"Fine, I'll check into it," he said. "It may have been—"

I cleared my rough throat. "That wasn't the first time."

Both men shot me a wide look.

"My car accident three months ago," I reminded Marc.

Fury flashed across his face, and he nodded at Valerian. "She was hit by a car and left in a seven-week coma."

"Impossible," Valerian said.

"You're right. I have no doubt she was cast into a death-sleep curse, since they couldn't manage to kill her. Then someone brought her out of it, but I have no idea who. She didn't recognize the man."

"A truck," I corrected. "It was another truck, not a car. Just like the one that hit me." *Again.*

"Do something, Max, or I will," Marc stated low and deadly. "Some mage out there knows about her and knows where she is, and definitely wants her dead. I'm not giving that bastard another chance to finish the job!"

A nurse passing by looked into the room with slight suspicion at Marc's raised volume. Valerian pretended to check something inside the manila file folder he carried, and the nurse sent him a cheerless smile and walked away.

"We have to get her out of here now," Marc whispered. "She's not safe here."

"Wait another hour, then finish the healing spell," Valerian instructed. "I'll call up some images and try to discover who's behind this. You're right. Some mage knows who and what she is, and is trying to stop the prophecy by eliminating one of the keys. Why he hasn't been able to successfully do so…There must be a life protection spell around her and her two sisters. I'll check around to see if there's a renegade mage practicing dark magic again."

"And in the meantime?"

"Stay with her here until I can properly arrange for her formal discharge from this…human hospital."

The mage said the word with such distaste as he cringed at the surroundings that it almost made me laugh at his snobbery.

"That could take days. No telling who this mage is, or what he will pose as next to get to Jillian again."

That was a disturbing possibility. I myself had only recently mastered glamor spells, but I knew how convincing they could be.

Yeah, I didn't like the idea of staying here for any length of time now either. Especially since I could barely move a finger.

"I have to get her to my place where she can be thoroughly protected. I dare that mage to try and break through my barriers. Dark magic or not, he'll find himself in another world of hurt."

"Three hours should allow me enough time to alter records and memories around this place," Max said, checking his gold watch. "If I'm right and she's life protected, she'll be safe enough here until then. If we continued acting ignorant about this unknown dark mage, we might have a chance to drawn him out and bind him for the council to deal with."

Marc dragged a hand down his beard stubbled face and let go of a long breath. "Fine. Three hours, no more. Then I'm taking her myself, whether we find this assassin or not."

Valerian ignored his tirade, turning to me with a softer expression. "Get well quickly, my dear. I trust your safety in the hands of my very capable protégé. He'll make sure you stay in one piece to complete your destiny."

I twitched a smile and immediately groaned, even that bit of movement making me want to scream out with agony.

No, this definitely was no dream.

Valerian tucked the manila folder under his arm, then walked out and over to the nurse's station, already working his own personal magic with two female staff members who looked ready to expedite any of his requests.

Marc pressed a gentle hand to my head. "Where does it hurt?"

"Everywhere," I groaned. "I feel like I was hit by a truck."

He chuckled. "Don't worry, I'll take care of it. Then we'll find out who's trying to take your life, and put an end to theirs. In a much more painful way."

He cupped his palms and hovered them inches above my body. Immediately I began to feel the fingers of healing warmth flow into me.

"Max said to wait an hour," I groaned.

"He doesn't want to cause too much suspicion with the staff, but he's already taking care of that, so there's no need to wait. He'll have them convinced in no time that your injuries have always been minor. Close your eyes and relax."

"Easy for you to say."

He softly pressed a palm over them to coax them closed, then began to murmur a long, detailed incantation I wasn't yet familiar with in the language he said had been developed by a mysterious group of powerful mages called the "Ancient Ones". Only those of mage status could understand the language and invoke their magic. Thank goodness one of them was my boyfriend who didn't like to see me in pain. Or in the Intensive Care Unit.

A tingling sensation began at the core of my body that slowly caught and spread, tickling me with tiny electrical sparks that wrapped around and covered every muscle, every blood vessel and vein and ligament and fiber. Fractured bones gathered and snapped back together, welding themselves firmly into their rightful places. Internal injuries knitted back into place. Several deep gashes closed, the skin mending and melting to its familiar smoothness under human stitches that now only itched.

Mostly, the agonizing pain dimmed to a pinpoint, then fizzled out completely, and I sighed with deep, grateful relief.

"Thank you," I whispered.

Marc smiled and kissed my lips gently, keeping one hand pressed to the top of my head. "Rest now. We'll get you out of here soon."

"Don't go."

"Don't worry, I'm not going anywhere."

"You did last time."

He frowned. "Last time?"

I shook my head, closing my eyes. "Just don't go."

"I'm here, Jillian. Sleep now."

* * *

I woke to the sudden memory of where I was and what had happened. I snapped my eyes open and frantically look around the hospital room—a normal one, not Intensive Care.

I eased slightly, spotting Marc in the side chair below the window, his head lolled to the side and propped with his hand as he slept. He still wore the same street clothes he had on when I woke last time. Hopefully that meant that I hadn't been out too long.

A doctor wearing a white lab coat with a stethoscope hung around his neck walked into the room. When he lowered the iPad he was reading, I saw that it was Max Valerian again in disguise.

"Good morning, Ms. Azure" he said quietly, pretending to take my pulse and go through a cursory exam. "Feeling better now, I see."

"Thanks to my protector over there," I said.

"Sleeping on the job, too."

"You'd be exhausted too, trying to pull me from the grips of death and keep me from being murdered by some unknown enemy mage."

Valerian made a noise in his throat, and I wasn't sure if that was agreement or doubt. "How are you feeling otherwise?"

"Fine. I'm pretty much back to normal, in fact. You trained him well. Think you'll be able to spring me from this hospital soon?"

"That's the plan."

"And they won't try to keep me around in order to discover my miraculous, self-healing capabilities?"

He shook his head. "I've been altering records and rearranging several surgeons' and staff members' memories to make your injuries far less than what they were. It took some doing. You were in bad shape when they brought you in."

"Did you have to help them?" I asked.

He lifted a shoulder. "A bit. Their methods are so barbaric."

"They have the disadvantage of needing to heal people without the use magic."

Max snorted his derision at that uncouth prospect.

"Thanks again. Glad you're on my side."

"More than you know," he said.

"Have you found out who's trying to kill me yet?"

Max shook his head. "Whoever it is knows how to cover his tracks well. I'm not entirely sure how you were able to come out of your original death-sleep curse, in fact."

"I had a little help from a friend," I remarked.

He caught the odd timbre of my voice and tilted his head. "Yes, that's what Zander said. Care to elaborate?"

"Do me a favor," I said as the only form of explanation I could give him. "Don't stop working on your time-travel spell."

He fixed his blue stare with mine for a long moment, then simply gave me a nod.

"Get well, Jillian," he said. "Then get the hell out of here. Your sisters will need you. Very soon."

"Who are they? Can you tell me that much?"

Max shook his head. "But you will find them, and soon. That much is certain. Goodbye for now."

With that, he disappeared into a light red mist that immediately dissipated. My gasp startled Marc awake, and he shot to his feet.

"Jillian?"

"I'm fine," I assured as he dashed up to me. "Just thought I saw something."

"What?"

"Nothing. You should find out how soon the hospital will release me."

He raked a tired hand through his mussed hair and gave his head a hard shake to wake himself further. "I'm not leaving you here alone and unprotected, Jillian."

"I'll be fine for a few minutes."

"No."

"You're as stubborn as a mule, you know that?" I remarked.

"I do know that," he said walking up to my bedside. "How are you feeling?"

"Right as rain. Fit as a fiddle. I just want to get out of here."

He nodded. "I'll move things along to spring you. Don't go anywhere."

"Ha, ha."

I watched with amazement as Marc checked around, then cast a protection spell around my room before he left for the nurse's station. I actually saw the clear, iridescent shield vibrating around the place, something invisible to the human eye, and I must admit that it did give me an added sense of security against my unknown assailant.

After he left, I headed to the bathroom to check my reflection in the mirror. Not bad for someone who had been hit and nearly killed by a truck less than twenty-four hours ago.

With a wave of my hand, I freshened my appearance more. A snap of my fingers and I was dressed in street clothes. Now I just had to get out of there.

My cellphone now in my jeans pocket buzzed, and I saw that it was Helene. God, what was I going to tell her?

"Hey, lady," I said casually.

"Where the hell have you been?" she immediately blasted. "I've left three messages since last night!"

"Sorry, I let my battery run out and forgot to recharge. What's up?"

"Well, for one, I'm glad that you're still alive. Naomi Rogers said she saw something about you on the news last night, that you had been in an accident?"

I grimaced. "She must be mistaken. Anyhow, you have me now. What's going on?"

"There's been a huge glitch in the team lineup. Trenton in Archeology demands he and some of his cave dwellers get to come on the dig because of the parchment we found. He convinced the Board that it's more of an historical than geological site. That eliminates several of our people, including you."

"Me?" I shook my head, adding, "Do me a favor and email me anything about the changeup. I'll check around and see if I can get some added funding."

"And if you can't? The trip is in five days, Azure."

"I know, don't freak out. I'll think of something and get back to you."

She growled quietly. "Okay, fine. You've always been our miracle worker on these trips. Hope you can whip up some of your magic now."

"So do I," I muttered, then said my goodbyes and hung up.

When Marc returned twenty minutes later followed by a nurse with a wheelchair, I was pacing the room to get out of there. I had a lot to do, and I was running out of time. I needed to find the identity and location of these unknown sisters of mine, which I was theorizing as metaphorical rather than biological. I needed to help Marc find this unknown dark mage and stop him from targeting me, while still continuing to advance my own sorcerer skills. Now I had this other glitch with Helene to deal with too.

"About time," I grumbled, plopping down in the wheelchair to be discharged.

"See, I told you she's feeling better," Marc told the nurse dryly. "A nasty temper is always a good sign."

The nurse grunted his agreement, then wheeled me away with Marc in tow. It wasn't until we were halfway to Marc's house that I posed my next thought.

"Max keeps saying that I need to find my 'two sisters' before the time of the Red Moon Prophecy, so I think that's my first priority."

"Finding this dark mage is our first priority, Jillian," he said.

"Once I know who and where my sisters are, that might lead us to who's trying to stop the prophecy from happening. This mage might have targeted them as well. Or at least will be at some point."

"Possibly. Based on your eager expression, I take it you have a plan of action?" he remarked.

I nodded. "I need to talk with my parents, and force them to tell me the truth about my heritage and how I came to have mage blood inside of me to begin with."

* * *

"Well, I'm glad you're okay now, honey," my mother Ellen Azure said after I told her about the accident I had been in.

I sat in front of Marc's laptop computer at his house watching my parents on the screen. They were video-chatting me on my dad's cellphone as they sat in the coffeehouse they were in when I called.

"Yeah, it was just a small fender-bender," I told them, touching the pinking, healing scar on my forehead. "I wish Doug wouldn't have called you. I'm not even sure how he found out."

"He's your fiancé, dear," she said. "Of course, he would be concerned enough to call us."

"Ex-fiancé, like I said," I corrected. "And I'm not happy that he's still keeping tabs on me or the family. Anyhow, he greatly exaggerated the whole thing. I'm perfectly fine."

"Well, we're relieved to hear that," my mom said.

Marc was facing me and gestured for me to keep them talking. With a wave of hand, he instantly disappeared, startling me slightly.

"Hey, so how are you liking your new pottery classes, mom? Have you made any masterpieces yet?"

She chuckled, waving me off. "Nothing that will sell in any studio, unless I label it as modern art. Last week I made a ceramic plant holder that I'm pretty proud over though. The painting of it was the most difficult part. I didn't realize you had to be a design artist too, but I'm working on it."

"I'll expect a coffee mug soon."

"Purple on purple, of course."

I smiled. "You know me too well. Dad, what about you? Any new projects you're working on with your lodge buddies?"

"Just a bit of…Excuse me!"

I gasped at the sight of Marc behind my father carrying a couple of coffee cups, bumping into my parents. Both my mother and father jumped out of their seats, the cellphone dropping onto the table, the image now sideways. There was some slight scuffling and startled, gruff conversation. Then the video righted again as my mother came back on the line, looking flustered.

"Sorry, honey. Someone just tripped over your father and spilled his drinks all over us. We're going to have to get out of here to go change. I'll call you later, and we can catch up then."

"Sounds good." I frowned at Marc now standing in front of me again, holding two plastic bags, both with strands of white and silver hair. "Take care. Love you, bye."

I ended the chat and closed the laptop lid. "Did you have to do that?"

"I needed to grab some DNA samples to test for magic in their systems," Marc said. "I'll take them to the lab and have George Meyers run an analysis. He should be able to give me the results immediately."

"I saw you touch them both. Any magic that you can initially detect?"

He shook his head.

"In either of them?" I prodded.

"Neither one, I'm sorry. But it was very quick, since I didn't have a lot of time. George's test should confirm any mage anomalies, then we'll go from there."

* * *

I was greatly relieved when Marc finally returned three hours later with the DNA results.

"So?" I prodded, switching off the television and standing when he walked through the front door. "Any detectable magic in either one?"

"You might want to sit down again, Jillian," he said.

"Why? What did you find?"

Marc waited a beat before he finally said, "The couple who raised you, Richard and Ellen Azure, aren't your birthparents. Neither one. In fact, you have no genetic ties to either of them in any way."

He allowed that bit of news sink in a few moments.

I shook my head saying, "No. That's impossible."

"These tests don't lie," he insisted.

"No," I insisted. "They would've told me if I was adopted."

"Maybe you need to find out why they didn't."

I hugged myself and numbly gazed outside the living room window. The day was turning windy and cloudy with the threat of an approaching storm.

"Then it is possible that I do have two biological sisters out in the world somewhere," I remarked.

"Definitely possible."

I turned back to him. "Max must know something about them. He hints about them often enough. Maybe that's the next step we need to take."

Marc thought about, then nodded slowly. "All right, let's go see him then. I'm one of the only people who knows where he hides out."

He slipped one arm around me, his other hand, pulling out a stick of black obsidian crystal.

"My own conductor," he explained. "I'll need it to break through the barriers he places around his lair."

"Second star to the right then?" I remarked nervously, not sure if I really wanted to go to the one place Maximus Valeria felts safe enough to hide from the entire world.

"Trust me, this is no Neverland. Hang on tight, and don't let go."

CRYSTAL MOON

CHAPTER 12

Valerian's private domain wasn't anything I would have imagined for a master mage of his caliber, age and experience. Instead of a castle dungeon filled with damp, harled stone, iron sconces and chandeliers with dripping candles, this bright, airy sunroom was filled with exotic plants and flowers and modern furnishings. The villa itself, in fact, was set on a Mediterranean cliff overlooking a magnificent turquoise ocean spotted with sailboats and cruise ships.

Max was sitting comfortably on a green and white striped couch next to a natural looking fountain of cascading rocks. Only his eyes raised from the book he was reading when we suddenly appeared in front of him, and they weren't kindly met.

"What are you doing here, Zander? And you've brought your apprentice, I see. Nice to see you again, Jillian. I trust you're feeling better from your accident?"

"Cut the crap, Max," Marc ground out. "I'm sure you fully expected us."

Valerian closed his book and stood. "Not quite this soon. You could have at least allowed me to finish two more chapters before you intruded into my home and disrupted my quite time. I get so little of it these days."

"Why didn't you tell me about Jillian? You said she was the third key. You knew who she was from the very first, didn't you?"

"Of course. I've known from the first time I touched her."

"Then you know who her real mage father is."

"And mother," Valerian confirmed, then shifted his blue eyes to mine. "I'm sorry for not providing this information to you, Jillian, but you weren't ready to receive it yet. Nor would you have come so far in your lessons. In fact, I'm even considering taking you on as my own apprentice to further your education."

"No!" Marc and I shouted together.

"I'll teach her everything she needs to know," Marc vehemently insisted, slipping his hand protectively behind my back. "I've made her that vow."

"Which I can break at any time of my choosing," Valerian added. "She hasn't been officially registered, as you well know."

"I thought that was for my protection," I said.

Marc narrowed his eyes at the master mage. "No. That's was for *his* protection, so that he could change things up as he decides best without interference from the council. I should have guessed it. You are a manipulative bastard."

Valerian didn't react, but clasped one hand over the other in front of him. "Why are you here, Marcus?"

"Give me the names of her birthparents," he said. "Something tells me that it will explain a hell of a lot."

Valerian turned to me. "Are you ready to learn of your true heritage and ultimate destiny, dear one?"

He and I exchanged an entire conversation in that next look. It made me eager to find out more. And it terrified me to my very bones.

"Very well," he said, understanding my unspoken answer. "Follow me to my workroom."

Marc and I trailed behind him through the vast, modern house, room after spacious, tastefully decorated room. The only thing not of this current decade were the many sculptures and framed paintings, every piece an original from every century and style. Outwardly it appeared as if he was a collector of ancient and fine art, but chances were each had been given to him by the artist personally at the time of its creation.

I also noted that we passed no maids or cooks or servants of any kind. Then again, anything he wanted or needed could be conjured with the flick of wrist or recitation of a spell. Maybe even the house itself had been whipped up from magic.

"Will you be staying for dinner?" Valerian asked casually as we headed down a long hallway.

"No. We're gone just as soon as I find out who Jillian's real parents are."

"Suit yourselves," he said. "Here we are then."

With the flick of his hand, the double doors at the end of the long hallway opened, and we followed him inside its depths.

This room looked more like the kind of a laboratory a master mage would use, or rather Baron von Frankenstein with its long tables of bubbling glass bottles of every shape and size, along with shelves of colorful crystals and bizarre looking relics with another shelf filled with old books and dusty, tattered grimoires. All he needed was a barrel sized caldron and squawking black raven perched beside it to complete the picture straight from a Grimm's fairytale.

"Was this where he trained you?" I whispered to Marc.

He kept his voice quiet, never taking his narrowed eyes off his mentor. "Yes. Be careful, and don't touch anything."

Valerian moved to the end of the worktable. Then with a flick of the wrist, it was cleaned of paraphernalia, and a crystal ball set on a black, ornate stand appeared. He closed his eyes and pressed his palms to the glass, and colorful lights began to flicker and swirl inside. Two minutes, and he opened his eyes and stepped back.

"Come and see, Jillian Azure," he said.

"What is it?" I asked warily.

"Max has conjured a replay of your past," Marc explained.

"Your beginning, actually," he added with a wry smile. "See who you come from."

My heart beat like a drum against my chest. Did I really want to know my birth heritage? The couple who raised me were good and loving people, albeit human. Would it be disloyal to them to seek out my true roots?

Then again, they lied about my own birth and relation to them, so the lack of loyalty cut both ways.

Right now wasn't the time to deal with this, however. I needed to swallow any injury or pride and fear and finally learn the full truth of who and what I was.

Cautiously I moved towards the sparkling glass ball, then looked down into the confusing, flickering lights.

"What am I supposed see?" I asked.

Marc stepped my behind me and slipped his hands around my waist, then spoke quietly into my ear, "Place your fingertips onto the glass. It needs to know whose history to bring up."

Taking strength and comfort from his protective hold, I did as instructed. The swirling lights slowed and cleared, melting away into the foggy images of a dark haired man and a woman with long black hair, both very beautiful people. His arm was around her shoulder and she was nervously pressed against him as together they walked down some dark corridor.

"Who are they?" I asked.

"Your birthparents, I suspect," Marc said.

I look at them with new interest, studied their features and mannerisms. I couldn't see myself in either of these two people, and it made me wonder if Max had gotten this wrong.

"Why is there no sound?" I asked.

"There never is. We don't know why. But you can generally figure out what's happening anyhow."

I watched. There was a definite closeness shared between them, even if not yet actual love and devotion. That comforted me somewhat. I didn't know them, might never know them in fact, but it was nice that they seemed to care for each other before conceiving me, particularly knowing mages' prevalence with casual hookups.

I gasped as an enormous, shining warrior with wings and armor rounded a dark corner behind them, brandishing a brilliant sword. He looked like he was made from pure light, but the glazed red of his eyes told me he meant to kill them.

"Fey," Marc explained, then nodded when I turned around to him with drawn brows. "There are a lot of different supernatural beings in this world that you don't yet know about."

"Wonderful," I muttered, turning back to the silent movie.

The warrior fey drew closer, his sword raised higher. I wanted to scream at the unsuspecting couple to watch out, to run. Of course, this was just a movie, a rerun, the event already taken place in the past.

I saw the man covertly draw a chisel and hand it to the woman, then drew a hunting knife attached to his belt. He knew then.

As one, they both turned and faced the shining monster. There was a vicious struggle between the man and fey, until the man lost the advantage, now flat on his back. The fey raised his broadsword to plunge down for that final death blow, but the woman jumped onto its back and plunged her chisel into its neck.

The fey went rigid, then collapsed into a heap. Its shining lights winked out, and the remains instantly flamed up and dissolved into a heap of ash.

The man looked at the woman with a mixture of worry, relief and awe. I smiled as he took her hand and kissed it.

"He loved her," I commented, recognizing this look very well. I saw it in Marc's face, and in my own.

"He did," Valerian confirmed. "Until she betrayed him."

"Betrayed him? How? Why?"

"Watch," he instructed.

I turned back to the crystal. The scene dimmed out and a new one appeared. They were now at the gates of an airport, holding each other tightly. There was a sign above them that read they were in Dublin, Ireland.

They kissed desperately, then broke apart, and the man watched as she left to get into the flight boarding line. When he turned and walked away towards another gate, she ducked around a corner, then disappeared.

"Whoa! Where did she go?" I gasped.

The answer came in the next image. The woman suddenly appeared in the middle of a quaint, rustic cottage that was a cross between something you would see on Cape Cod and in the Enchanted Forest. A middle age woman with blond, curly hair was there as well and looked greatly relieved to see her.

They talked. The woman pulled something from her pocket then opened her palm to reveal a large garnet stone.

Then the image died out completely.

"That's all I get?" I asked Valerian.

It was interesting, fascinating even, but not very helpful. I still didn't know who these people were, or the reason they split up. And nothing at all about me specifically.

"These recalls are never specific," Marc explained, his jaw muscles working hard. "You only get bits and pieces. Usually the most significant."

"But that didn't tell me anything. Who were they? And why did she leave him?" I turned to Valerian, adding, "And who was that other woman, the one at the cottage? She seems oddly familiar."

Marc glared Valerian who lifted his chin. "She would be. You would have met her at the charity dinner three weeks ago if I hadn't snagged her attention first. Her name is Rhiona Kennish, and she's the aunt of Brenna and Rosalyn Callaghan. Apparently yours, as well."

"Mine?"

Marc pulled his glare from Valerian and looked at me. "Jillian, Brenna Callaghan is your birthmother."

* * *

Marc wanted to teleport us that very minute to Santa Barbara, California where the Callaghan clan lived, but I didn't want to impulsively confront my alleged family until I thought things through first. In the end, he agreed to take us back to Fort Collins and grudgingly drove me to my hotel.

"I still don't like you being here alone, Jillian. It's too dangerous, even with my protection spell."

I checked around my room, smiling to see the clear, iridescent shield in place. I would have to order room service, but staying inside was part of the agreement for sleeping here tonight.

"I need to think about what all this means," I told him again. "For that I need solitude, at least for tonight."

He grunted, then kissed me, grazing my cheek with the back of his fingers. "I don't like it, but I guess I understand. It'll give me a chance to arrange for my classes to be covered tomorrow."

"No, don't. I can stay here until you're done for the day. We'll visit the Callaghans afterwards."

He shook his head. "It's final exams. I just need one of the other professors to pass out and monitor the testing. It's more of a babysitting job anyhow."

The end of the spring semester, and the beginning of summer break. It was the reason for Helene's trip timing.

Part of me was glad that Marc was skipping his final class. He refused to let me visit the Callaghans without him, and I was anxious to talk with them all face to face as soon as possible.

It was a restless, sleepless night, making me regret not having Marc spend it beside me. I didn't seem to breathe easier until he showed up at my door the next morning.

"Ready to meet your family?" he asked.

Last night I contacted Rosalyn Callaghan and mentioned that I would "be in her neighborhood" and would like to get together. She readily agreed, but hesitated when I asked that her aunt and mother join us, that there was something they both would find of great interest.

"Mom rarely goes out these days," Rosalyn explained. "And I'm never sure about Aunt Rhiona. She's sort of a free spirit who comes and goes."

Free spirit indeed, I mused. Dropping another mental bomb on me, Marc told me that my newly discovered aunt, Rhiona Kennish, was also a sorceress of the twelfth power, something he verified when they first met at the charity dinner. So I had sorcerer as well as mage blood. No wonder I was a mystery to everyone.

Did Rosalyn, who was also my apparent sister, know our mother was a sorceress? Was she a sorceress, or mage, herself?

I had so many questions now for all of them.

"Just tell her that I have all the active luminaries she's been trying to find," I said at Marc's coaxing.

This was a reference she and my mother as powerful sorceresses would understand. And that now we knew what they were as well. All cards were on the table.

"Sure, okay then. See you tomorrow at the hotel beach café," Rosalyn said.

"What if we're wrong?" I asked Marc after I had clicked off.

"We're not," he said. "I felt Rhiona's magic the moment I shook her hand at the charity dinner. I'm sure she felt mine as well. In truth, that's the only reason she went me that night, to discover who I was and why I was there."

"Why didn't you tell me?"

"Because the woman and I only verbally circled each other, neither one giving over, so it came to nothing. This was even before I knew about your own magic."

Yes, I had a truckload of questions for my birthmother, my aunt and my sister when we met again.

"Let's go," I said, straightening my summer dress. "I don't want to be late for our lunch."

I was too nervous to trust my own directional magic, especially for that distance, so Marc slipped his hand around my waist and teleported us to the Santa Barbara Hotel in California.

It was agreed that until we discovered what Rosalyn herself knew of our supernatural heritage, we would be careful with what we shared. If she didn't know, Marc would take Rhiona Kennish aside and find out why.

It was a warm, sunny day when we arrived at the California coastal town. Marc took my hand and led me around the grounds of the Spanish styled hotel to the outside beach café. Rosalyn was the first to spot us and wave us over from a corner table.

My heart leapt at the sight of her, this time knowing she was my birth sister. Rosalyn hugged me lightly, and it was everything I could do not to pull her into a tight embrace. I had always wanted a sister, but I still needed to tread lightly. I didn't know if she had any inkling of what we were, of what she herself might become.

It was Rhiona's turn to greet me.

"It's nice to finally meet you, Jillian," she said. "Rosalyn's told me many good things about you."

"I have," Rosalyn assured.

The woman pressed both of her plushy hands over mine, and her eyes instantly widened.

"Mage, then?" she asked Marc with disbelief. "Are you certain of this?"

"Impossible, but true," he confirmed. "That's why we're here. To find out how this came about. Is Rosalyn..?"

Rhiona waved him off. "She's fully in the know, not to worry." Panic flashed across her expression then. "Who else knows of the girls?"

"Just my own mentor, Max Valerian," Marc said. "He claims Jillian is one of the three keys to the prophecy."

"She is, as is Rosalyn. Valerian, huh?" She grunted. "I suppose I shouldn't be surprised. How are you connected with him?"

"He was my master-mentor."

"Really? He would have been a good one. A dangerous one, too."

Marc arched a brow, giving her that. "There's someone else who knows of Jillian, maybe all the three keys to the prophecy. Her life has been threatened more than once."

Rhiona's straightened then. "That can't be good."

"It's not. Max and I suspect a dark mage who's trying to stop the Red Moon Prophecy from taking place. If he is, then Rosalyn and their third sister aren't safe either."

"Pleiades and all the stars," Rhiona cursed. "You could be right. We'll need to talk this out, figure our next move."

I could see the waitress anxiously hovering on the sidelines waiting for our order. We were also drawing very curious stares from the other patrons with us just standing here.

"Maybe we should sit and have some lunch first," I suggested. "I try not to make life altering and death defying decisions on an empty stomach."

"Yes, yes," the woman said, flapping her hand. "Good idea, child."

Orders were placed, but all of us were more eager to talk after the waitress left.

"So you officially claimed your mage heritage then," Rhiona said.

I described the disastrous scene in Marc's classroom lab and his testing my newly discovered magical abilities afterwards.

"He's been teaching me the craft. I'm still very new at it."

"Don't let her fool you," Marc added. "She's already far surpassed any three-year mage. She's quite talented."

Rhiona took my hand and squeezed, her head lowered and eyes closed in concentration. Fifteen seconds later she opened them again, releasing my hand.

"Amazing," she said to Marc. "You can't have her certified. No one else must know of her, not even the mage council itself."

"They don't, not yet." He leaned forward, lowering his voice even more. "Rhiona, you must give me the name of Jillian's and Rosalyn's birthfather. He must be approached with the knowledge of their miraculous birth."

Rosalyn snorted. "He knows, don't worry."

I looked at her tightening expression. So she knew our birthfather, or of him at least.

Obviously he didn't want us—typical philandering mage. Making babies, then making tracks.

"Did you know about me when we first met?" I asked her.

She nodded, smiled. "That's why we went to Colorado, to find you. Aunt Rhiona had cast a memory-loss spell on herself after she arranged for all of our adoptions in order to protect our identities. The spell was time-lapsed and was set to dissolve on our twenty-fifth birthdays. And it did, one by one. You were the last of us."

"Once I remembered who your adoptive parents were," Rhiona added, "it was just a manner of some detective work. Fortunately, Rosalyn is engaged to an actual police detective who found you immediately."

"Why didn't you tell me who you were to begin with?" I asked Rosalyn.

"And say what? That you're my long, lost triplet sister who was separated from us at birth because we're some mystical saviors of the future world?"

I chuckled nervously. "Yeah, that wouldn't have gone over well, I suppose. At the time, anyhow."

With all barriers down now, the conversation progressed quickly as we ate lunch. By the end of it, I knew what I really wanted most of all. And now I knew I was ready for it.

"I want to meet our mother, Brenna Callaghan," I said. "I want to know the whole story, everything."

Rosalyn grasped my hand across the table and nodded. "She wants very much to meet you too, Jillian. She would have been here today herself, but didn't want to force the issue. She wanted it to be your choice."

"Then let's go see her," I said. "As soon as possible."

"She'd really like that."

Rhiona watched us both, then grimaced saying, "One more thing you both need to know. It's probably something your mother should have mentioned a long time ago."

"What is it?" Rosalyn said.

"Brenna isn't half sorceress," Rhiona said quietly. "She's half mage. Her mother, your grandmother, was born full mage, not sorcerer. Our mother never knew how, although she did have an affair about that time with a powerful master mage by the name of Fredric Thornston. He was working on some genetic spells during that time that may have had…side effects."

"I've heard of Thornston," Marc said, frowning. "Didn't he instigate the Brazilian mage war fifty years ago?"

Rhiona nodded. "Was killed then too. Poor Mary showed real promise to her mage genetics too. I often wondered how far she might have advanced if she had lived."

"So that explains why Rosalyn and I are mages then," I said.

Rhiona and Rosalyn glanced at each other again, but it was our aunt that answered that question.

"No, dear. Brenna Callaghan is a werewolf, and the Alpha of her wolf pack."

"And so am I," Rosalyn added.

* * *

If it hadn't been for Marc's confirmation that such a supernatural species existed, I would have turned tail and run away from these crazy people.

He and I rode in the backseat of Rhiona's sedan as she drove up the arid, forested mountainside toward their home for me to meet my birthmother for the first time. I supposed one of us, with the exception of Rosalyn, could have just teleported us there, but I was glad for the extra time to process all that I had just learned.

First, I was only a quarter mage, which meant that my birthfather was only human. It also mean that the magic in my blood by all rights should have been too diluted for me to do much of anything. Why I was such a phenomenon was another question I hoped Brenna Callaghan could answer.

Secondly, Rosalyn claimed she was a fully shifting werewolf. A powerful one at that, she was discovering with every new day that passed. Again, this was another puzzle, since her werewolf genetics were also cut by a quarter. In that case, I could have become a werewolf too, which would've been very inconvenient since I was deathly allergic to all canine dander.

Thirdly, Brenna Callaghan gave birth to three daughters who she had separated and given away to be adopted by those who were sworn to secrecy about us. And still no one would tell me why.

"Do you know who our third sister is?" I asked right before we left the café.

Neither woman would answer me though. When I brought the subject up again later while we were driving, Rosalyn said that it wasn't for her to say, not until I spoke with our mother Brenna. So I rode up the mountain towards their home in relative silence, a million questions jockeying for priority to be asked when I finally met this mysterious wolf-mage woman.

We drove over a river bridge, and the road ended a few hundred yards away into a clearing that boasted of an expansive log cabin styled, three story mansion. Several children were playing and chasing each other in the front yard, which was beautifully landscaped. The road itself forked in two directions, both continuing on either side of the enormous estate.

We parked directly in front of the wide steps leading up to a covered porch and double doors that lead inside. When we all stepped out, the children playing halted their games and immediately ran up to Rhiona and Rosalyn, embracing them both. A few asked who we were, but the older woman shooed them away with maternal warnings to mind their manners and their own nosy business.

Marc stepped beside me, slipping his hand behind my back, then whispered in my ear, "Stay close. No quick movements. Wait until we're alone with Brenna before you ask anything."

I was going to ask him why, until three very large, intimidating males exited the front doors, barring our way. Instinctively I took a step behind Marc and kept my eyes on the men at all times.

Werewolves.

These men, all of them, were very lethal werewolves. Probably the toughest of the bunch, as well, sent to guard their alpha queen from intruders. Like me.

Rosalyn lifted her chin to them. An authoritative and regal move, I noticed.

"Brother," she stiffly greeted the largest one.

"Sister," he returned gruffly.

"We're here to see Mom." When he didn't move, she added, "She's expecting us. All of us."

The blond man shifted a narrowed stare my way, then back to Rosalyn. He gave a stiff nod, then stepped aside, gesturing for the other two to do the same. They obeyed.

"Don't worry," she turned back to tell me with a slight smile. "Their bark is worse than their bite. Most times."

"Comforting," I murmured, cautiously following her inside.

There were several more people milling about as we walked inside the large living area, all cautious and curious at our presence in their hidden sanctum. I would have run screaming away had Rosalyn not been with us. Every one of them looked like they wanted to tear my head off with one lethal claw swipe. I had no doubt they could do it, too.

"Where's Mom?" Rosalyn asked one of the women staring at me with wide hazel eyes.

The woman didn't pull her unblinking, ultra-focused stare from me when she answered, "In the office."

"This way," Rosalyn instructed us.

We continued to follow her and Rhiona down two long hallways until coming to a thick set of double doors. When we walked inside, I saw that it was a very modern, but elegant library or study, one wall covered floor-to-ceiling with shelves of books. The opposite side was a huge bay window with two overstuffed chairs. There was a large antique desk in the corner, and two couches facing each other in front of the fireplace with blaze flickering in warm welcome. That's where the young black haired woman stood, the one I vividly remembered from the scene replaying in Max's crystal ball.

"You're Brenna Callaghan?" I asked in slight disbelief, because this woman looked no older than me, or Marc, or even Rosalyn herself.

This was her mother? Our *mother*?

She brightened, silver eyes glistening with unshed tears as she walked over and stood in front of me. She started to raise a hand to my face, then quickly lowered it.

"I am. It's so nice to finally meet you, Jillian. I've waited…well, all of your life."

I blinked hard, frowned. "You're, uh, not what I expected."

"Oh?"

"For one, you're so…young," I blurted, then regretted my impulsive tongue.

"We werewolves have longevity," Rosalyn leaned in and spoke with amusement. "We'll stay young for centuries. Cool, huh?"

I gaped a moment, then frowned. "Does that mean I..?"

I turned to Marc who shook his head, reminding me, "Mages live the same lifespan as human beings."

Well, that was disappointing. I happened to be the lucky sister with the mage dominant genetics and shorter lifespan. I suppose I was no worse off than when I did believe I was fully human, but still.

"I have questions," I said finally.

Brenna nodded and turned to Rosalyn and Rhiona. "Can you please give us a few minutes alone? Tell the others we shouldn't be disturbed."

"Will do," Rosalyn said.

Marc sent me a look of encouragement, then left with the other two women, closing the door behind them. Now that I was at last alone with my birthmother, I had no idea where to go to from there, every question I had emptying from my head.

"Would you like to sit down, Jillian?"

She gestured to the couches by the warming fire, and I followed and sat across from her.

"I can't get over how beautiful you grew up to be," Brenna said, smiling. "You favor my father and brother, I think."

"Oh. I wondered," I said. "Valerian pulled up an image of you and your...my birthfather, and I didn't look like either one of you."

"Rosalyn favors him," she remarked. "Amelia takes after me."

"Amelia? You know who our third sister is then?"

"They didn't tell you?" Brenna frowned at the shake of my head. "I suppose they thought it was my story to tell. And it is. Which you deserve to hear, if you'd like."

"I do. Please."

Brenna Callaghan settled in for a lengthy, detailed story, so I did likewise. All the stops were gone now, and I was about to learn the truth of my history, my present, and perhaps even my future. What I didn't expect was the thing she told me next.

"I was the daughter of Quinn Callaghan, the High Alpha of our wolf pack based in Dublin, Ireland," she began. "Davin was the true blood son of Samuel Laith, the sire who claimed all of the United Kingdom."

"Wait, my birthfather is a werewolf too?" I asked.

Which meant I myself was three-quarters as well.

How did I not turn into one myself then? How did my mage DNA become dominant over that?

"No, Jillian," she said. "Your father, Davin Laith, was, is, a true blood vampire. As is our third daughter and your sister, Amelia."

CRYSTAL MOON

CHAPTER 13

I squirmed in my cramped airline seat next to the window. It was late, and everyone in coach who wasn't already asleep was switching off their overhead lights and settling to sleep through the long hours between the Atlanta airport to London-Heathrow. Even Marc with folded arms across his chest was adjusting himself to sleep off the endless flight hours.

"We could have just zapped ourselves there," I grumbled.

Marc kept his eyes closed when answering, "Too many people knew we were going to Ireland already. We had to do things the old fashioned way to avoid suspicion."

"Too late for that. The mage trying to kill me must already—"

I silenced when the woman behind me made a small choked sound. I couldn't be sure if it was just an unconscious reflex, or if she had really overheard what I said.

"I mean…"

"I know what you mean," Marc mumbled. "We still needed to get there the regular way, even if he knows about you. There are always others to worry about, like Helene and the team. Stop using your new abilities as a lazier way to live, Jillian. You have to learn to be inconspicuous if you don't want to accidentally give yourself away."

I made a disgruntled noise. He was right, of course, but I didn't exactly like it.

I fingered the business card in my hand given to me by Brenna Callaghan with the name of Davin Laith along with his personal cellphone number. Yesterday after returning to Fort Collins I gathered the nerve to call him. Now we were heading across the Atlantic Ocean three days earlier than planned to meet him and my other sister for the first time at their country estate home outside of Cambridge.

My family, the vampires. Full, blood-drinking vampires.

A shudder shivered through me at the thought.

"What's wrong?" Marc muttered, cracking open one eye.

"Did you know my dad was a…you know?"

I checked my words and the people behind us. They all looked asleep now. Still, I shouldn't assume anything at this point.

"No, or I would've told you," he said.

"Really?"

"Yes."

"Rosalyn says that I smell very human," I whispered.

"Genetically speaking you are human like any other sorcerer and mage."

"Oh." That was something then, I supposed. "Hey, that won't ignite my father's or sister's bloodlust, will it?"

"Jillian," he grumbled irritably.

"It's a possibility. If I smell human, I might taste it."

Marc chuckled darkly. "You do. I can personally vouch for that. Very tasty, too."

"Ha, ha."

"Go to sleep, please."

"Fine."

I gazed out through the porthole, but only saw blackness beyond the lighted wing. To think that I was actually half-vampire and only a quarter mage. Yet, it was the magical side of my genetics that surfaced and became pronounced. How was that even possible?

"Do you feel any differently about me?" I asked Marc, touching his thigh. "Now that you know that I'm not a full mage."

"No, Jillian. Besides all of us are technically only half mage, including me."

"Yes, but I'm only a quarter, and the other parts are…other things."

"Still no. Now please get some sleep. It's a long way to England, and I'll doubt you'll get much after we land."

Five minutes later, I was going to ask Marc another question, but heard his deep, heavy breathing to indicate he was asleep. I was too keyed up to drift off into any semblance of it myself, still trying to sort out all that I had learned.

Once again, I replayed the conversation I had with Brenna in front of the stone fireplace less than two days ago, the story she shared of her brief, but intense encounter with Davin Laith.

"I was the daughter of Quinn Callaghan, the High Alpha of our wolf pack based in Dublin, Ireland," she began. "Davin was the true blood son of Samuel Laith, the sire who claimed all of the United Kingdom."

"Wait, my father was a werewolf, too?" I asked.

"No, Jillian. Your father, Davin Laith, was…is…a true blood vampire. As is our third daughter and your sister, Amelia. She lives with him now on his estate in Cambridge."

Brenna said it so matter-of-factly, as if she were telling me my birthfather was a plumber or electrician. She apparently didn't know that I didn't know such creatures even existed. I was still wrapping my mind around the idea of real, howl-at-the-full-moon werewolves.

I nearly fell off the couch, but thankfully steadied myself in time.

"When you say vampire…"

"Oh dear, you didn't know, did you? I'm so sorry for putting it so bluntly." She twitched a smile at my gaping expression, adding, "Don't worry. He's not the ghoulish fiends of folklore. Most times you would never know a modern vampire apart from any other human person, with a few exceptions to their…lifestyle."

"And dietary restrictions."

"That, too."

Brenna handed me a photo of the vampire in question printed off an internet article. I had seen him before from Max's crystal recall, and she was right. Davin Laith was an aristocratically handsome man with dark hair and sculpted, olive toned features, but gave no indications that he was one of the walking-dead.

It did make me curious about the realities of their species, but asking at that moment wasn't the best time. Brenna had a story to share, and I had already sidetracked her enough from it.

"Max pulled up a recall image of you both," I said, handing the photo back to her. "You were together inside some dark cavern or hallway."

I saw the nod and soft smile as she gazed down at the photo in her hand, noticed her fingertips lightly touching the image.

She loved him then. Maybe she still did to some extent. It was strangely reassuring to know that I was something more than the unwanted byproduct of a careless fling.

"Yes, we were inside the ruins of the Ancient Ones near Spanish Point in Ireland, hunting for the knowledge stone together," she said, tears glistening her silver eyes. She blinked them away and offered me a trembling smile adding, "I know that it sounds cliché, but even though it happened nearly three decades ago, it still seems as if it were only yesterday."

Brenna then told me the entire story of her four days spent with the one man in her life she truly and passionately loved. I tried not to interrupt her, but every other minute there would be a new twist or bizarre information that stunned me and needed further explanation.

"Wait, so *you* essentially became the legendary firestone then," I remarked with amazement.

She stood and walked up to the crackling fireplace, opened a small crystal bowl and pulled something from it. Sitting down next to me, Brenna then opened her palm to reveal a large, smooth garnet.

"This is it? The firestone?" I asked.

Brenna handed it to me. "As you can feel, there is no magic inside of it now. All of the information contained within it transferred into me when I took hold of it inside the sea cave that day. It very nearly killed me in the process, too. It was Davin who pulled me back from the edge of near insanity. He saved me. Again."

"Whoa, so you know everything about everything now. That's…daunting."

"No, I'm not omniscient by any means," Brenna explained. "That was always the assumption by those who studied the ancient texts, but it wasn't the reality. I was given the foreknowledge of things regarding only one very specific event—the Red Moon Prophecy. And our family's part in it."

"Yes, I've been thoroughly apprised about that annoying prediction myself," I grumbled. "I'd love to know who to thank for that bit of honor bestowed on us, then send him a live snake sandwich."

Brenna clutched my fingers and gave them a gentle squeeze. "I imagine all of this has been an enormous disruption of your life, Jillian, and for that I'm truly sorry."

"Not your fault. Anyhow, you know what's going to happen to all of us then."

She shook her head. "Not specifically, and not the outcome. Only the potential for the outcome should you three succeed, and more importantly, what will happen if you don't."

"Great, no pressure at all then. What is it that we're all supposed to do anyhow? No one has ever said."

"That much isn't clear, even to me. I'm sorry. I wish I could give you more, help you and Rosalyn and even Amelia to know what to expect, how to prepare. I feel incredibly helpless in all of this."

I processed all of this for a moment, fitting a few other pieces together—such as this unknown mage stalking and trying to kill me.

"I saw another image of you and Davin," I said. "You separated at the Dublin airport. You didn't get on the plane you were heading for though, but popped into some cottage. Your Aunt Rhiona's?"

"Yes," she confirmed. "She and I immediately left for the United States after that. Washington State, to be exact. The Bryant wolfpack that claims the territory hid and protected us until you three girls were born. It was the one place I knew Davin wouldn't be able to look for me. Vampires and shapeshifters weren't on easy diplomatic terms at that time."

"You didn't want him to know about us, because you didn't want to endanger him," I remarked.

Brenna looked at me with a tearful, grateful glow, clasping my hand in hers. "You know, you're the first person who has understood that."

It made sense. Like the dark mage trying to kill me now, there would have been others who would have tried to either kidnap or kill one or all of us to manipulate the prophecy for their own purposes.

"If Davin knew, those wanting us would torture the information from him," I guessed.

She swallowed hard and nodded. "I knew Davin like I know my own soul. Even if I disappeared, he would question why and would never stop searching for me, putting him and all of you at risk."

"So you had to make him believe that you betrayed him," I added for her.

Only the gem he assumed Brenna stole for her own greedy purposes was nothing more than a relatively worthless piece of costume jewelry.

"Your identities and locations needed to remain secret until you three came into our full individual powers after your twenty-fifth birthday," she continued. "So Rhiona used her own magic to locate three adoptive families, then cast a memory-loss spell on both her and I so that we could never divulge this vital information."

"When Rhiona's spell dissolved last fall," Brenna continued, "Davin's ambassador mage, Max Valerian, was able to recall the image of my giving birth to Amelia and Aunt Rhiona handing her to her adoptive parents in Everett, Washington. Davin then approached her with this information, with a desire to know her. But he himself only knew half the real story, so like him, Amelia wishes to have nothing to do with me. Not that I blame either of them."

Then later the spell dissolved further to reveal that Brenna hadn't given birth to just one daughter, but two. Davin wanted to gain the love and relationship of his second daughter as well, but Brenna had approached Rosalyn first.

"It was such a mess," Brenna groaned with shaking head. "I didn't mean for this to drive a wedge between Amelia and Rosalyn. I've tried convincing Rosalyn to make amends with her sister, that I didn't care what Amelia thought of me, if they could only have a good relationship themselves. But Rosalyn is just as stubborn as her father and won't ever give an inch for reconciliation."

Then there were three. When all threads of the memory-loss spell disintegrated a few months ago, both Rhiona and now Max was able to see my own birth scene and the adoptive handoff. I privately vowed to have a nice little chat with the manipulative old mage next time I saw him. And he wasn't going to like it one bit.

"Okay, so everyone is finally in the know now," I said. "Why don't you just contact Davin yourself and tell him the whole truth?"

Brenna stood up and paced in front of the fireplace. "No, I can't. It's too late. Too much time has passed. Too much has happened. He could never forgive me for my deception or from keeping you girls from him. He's said as much through Amelia."

"Well, maybe Amelia can help convince him," I reasoned. "All of us sisters can."

Suddenly, brokering a real truce between them became very important. Images of all of us together as a complete family made my heart race with a deep seated longing I never felt before.

Brenna halted, shook her head. "Amelia won't even speak to me. She hates me for what I did to her father, to all of you. No, it will never happen."

"Okay, then I can—"

"No! Jillian, I won't have you put yourself in the middle of this," she said, gripping my hands. "Promise me that you won't say anything about what I did to either of them when you meet. It's more important that you girls make peace, and Rosalyn and Amelia are already at war with each other over this."

"Well, that's just plain childish. If we all just…" I grumbled at Brenna's wide, pleading stare, saying, "Fine, I promise I won't tell

Davin or Amelia what really happened. But you should. He has a right to know the truth and make up his own mind."

She eased and drew me into a desperate embrace. "Talk to your father. As soon as possible."

So here I was, halfway across the Atlantic to meet my birthfather and my unknown triplet sister for the very first time, both who just happened to be full, fang-biting, blood-sucking vampires. I hoped they didn't prefer mage blood.

Mages.

Fey

Werewolves.

Now vampires.

How many more mythical creatures existed in this new, strange world of mine?

I shifted uncomfortably in my cramped seat, tugging the thin blanket up over my shoulders. I forced my eyes shut for only a minute before they popped open again to look up at the digital map showing our progression across the ocean. It was barely a blip away from the coast of the United States.

God, this was going to be a very long, grueling flight.

* * *

"Did you get any sleep at all?" Marc chided when we disembarked the plane and walked down crowded hallways through the busy London-Heathrow Airport.

"I dozed here and there," I said, my feet literally dragging, my brain sluggish with the lack of said needed slumber.

"We could check into a hotel and meet the Laith's tomorrow instead," he posed. "I'm sure they would understand."

I tiredly waved him off. "No, the sooner, the better that we meet and get this over with. Davin said not to worry about transportation, that he'll arrange something for us when we arrive."

"Fine. I'll get our bags if you want to go splash some water on your face. You looked like death warmed over."

"Ever the flatterer," I grumbled snidely. "Actually, I will hit the ladies room."

Because he was probably right, and I didn't want to give my birthfather and sister too awful an impression when I first met them.

Marc kissed me. "Don't take too long. And don't wander off."

"Yes, daddy."

He arched a brow at me for the crack, then headed for the luggage carousel, and I headed for the nearest ladies' room. By my dreadfully worn appearance, I was glad I did as well. I refreshed myself as best as possible, then headed out and met Marc who now had all of our suitcases.

"You're sure you don't want to postpone meeting your family until tomorrow," Marc said as we pressed through the crowds towards the exit.

"It's too late either way," I mentioned, seeing the limousine parked by the curb as soon as we walked outside, a sign with our names carried by the waiting driver. "Wow. When Davin said he was going to arrange ground transportation, I thought he meant a cab."

Marc twisted a grin. "He didn't tell you that he's a billionaire?"

My eyes went wide and shot to him. "No, he didn't. You knew?"

He lifted a shoulder. "Haven't you ever heard of Laith International Holdings?"

"Yes, but…Wait, are you telling me that he's *that* Laith? Holy frigging smokes!"

We drove another half hour through the city and suburban areas until we reached the city of Cambridge. Then we were driven another fifteen minutes outside the town and through the rural countryside, finally taking an even more remote road into the grassy, rolling hills straight from a Jane Austen book until we reached the locked gates of the wall surrounding the enormous estate.

A quick check with the person manning the gate, and we were through heading up to the estate that looked similar to the classic ones reserved for movies of the eighteenth-century era. I had been extremely impressed with my well-to-do birthmother's mountain manor, but this far exceeded anything I could imagine for anyone holding less than a duke's status.

"Maybe I should have waited until tomorrow, so I could be more formally dressed," I remarked.

"I doubt your family will care what you look like, Jillian," Marc generously said, giving my hand a light squeeze with his own. "They'll just be glad to finally meet you."

"I hope so. I'm not so sure now."

It was too late to change my mind and turn back now though.

The lowering sun was setting off rays of dark orange below a cobalt darkening sky. The late hour reminded me that for these nocturnal people, it would begin a new day.

Marc had filled me in on some of the truths and myths about vampiric beings. One of them was that direct sunlight was lethal to them and acted as a poison to their ultra-sensitive skin. So it was much easier for them to move around at night to avoid the deadly U.V. rays.

We were let out by the front walkway steps, and I gripped Marc's had for support as I nervously ascended the wide cement steps. The right front door was opened for us before we could knock, and the servant opening it stepped aside as we walked into the large foyer.

Immediately a young couple descended the grand staircase. The tall blond man was unearthly attractive with the kind of surreal beauty you imagined of an aristocratic vampire. The black haired woman beside him was his perfect match, and looked startlingly similar to Brenna Callaghan.

She eagerly came up to take my hands in hers. "Jillian?"

"Amelia?" I ventured.

"Yes. It's so great to finally meet you! This is my husband, Ethan Valter," she introduced.

Introduction were made all around. Amelia then escorted us into a more comfortable sitting room where coffee and tea and pastries were served. I was relieved that, aside from their striking beauty, they appeared every bit as human as Marc and I. Nothing like the frightening images I had of them with gray, corpselike skin and gnarly, crooked fangs and blood-red eyes.

"Dad will be here shortly," she said, sitting across from us on the second couch. "He had to wind up a business phone call."

"That's fine. It gives us a chance to talk," I said, grabbing a scone and some coffee.

As I nervously sipped and nibbled, I realized with a start that neither Amelia or Ethan partook of the refreshments themselves, giving me a hard reminder of what they were. Covertly I tried to see if they had fangs, but their smiles looked just as normal as everyone else's. A bit disappointing, actually.

Amelia kept staring at me in wonder, and I must confess that I found myself doing the same to her. It wasn't every day that one met their lost triplet sister.

"I understand that you're a nurse and Ethan's a doctor," I politely began.

Sharing one's career was generally a good ice breaker.

"We are," Amelia said, brightening at the subject. "We actually met when working together in the emergency room at Everett Memorial Hospital in Washington State last fall. I didn't know he was in reality a spy for my father."

They chuckled at the reference, then both shared their story back and forth at different parts. I found that I liked them both very much. Even if they were blood-drinking vampires.

"You didn't have any clue that you were adopted either then," I remarked to Amelia.

She shook her head, squeezing her husband's clasped hand in her lap. "That was the main condition of my adoption, my mother told me. Our birthmother lied that our father Davin was an extremely dangerous man, and that it would endanger my life if he ever knew about me."

I wanted to tell her that in a manner of speaking that was true, but by the rigid tone of her voice, I could feel the stubborn animosity.

No, she definitely wasn't yet ready to hear our mother's side of the story just yet.

"What about your parents?" Amelia asked me. "Did you know you were adopted?"

"Nope," I said. "I didn't even question the fact, since I have the same coloring as several people in my family. They still don't know that I know. I plan to ask them about it when I get back from this trip."

"Brothers or sisters?"

"No, an only child," I said.

"You hold them no ill will for keeping this information from you then?" she asked.

"None," I said. "I'm sure they had their reasons. People aren't perfect, I've come to learn. They make mistakes. So I never make any judgements without hearing all sides of a story first."

Amelia's back went up at that. I didn't mean to cast aspersions at her, saying she was being stubborn and unreasonable for not talking with our birthmother and hearing what she had to say, even though it was true.

"I'm sorry, I didn't mean   "

"Davin should be done. Oh, here he is now. Great timing." Everyone stood as the man I remembered from Brenna's printed photo entered the room. "Dad, this is Jillian Azure, and her friend Marc Zander."

My heart leapt when the man walked up to me and pressed my hand between his and he smiled wide. "So very nice to meet you, my dear one. I couldn't believe it when Max told me of your existence."

"A good surprise, I hope."

"A very good surprise," he assured. "Sit down, please, we have so much to talk about. I want to know all there is of your life. Max tells me that your mage blood surfaced as dominant of the three, and now he's working with you to increase your abilities."

"Marc here is actually my teacher in the arcane arts," I said, lacing my fingers through his. "He was apprenticed himself by Max Valerian."

"Is that right?" Davin remarked, shifting his focus to him.

Marc gave a nod. "She's shows great promise, sir. Even Master Valerian is impressed."

"That's very good to hear," Davin said, then patted Amelia's shoulder. "We might have a possible future mage consultant for the coven someday then? What is that you do again, Jillian? A professor of science?"

"Geology, to be more specific. That's another reason we're over here in the British Isles now. We have a geological and archeological team gathered to find and extract some rare geodes near Spanish Point, Ireland."

Davin straightened at the reference. "Spanish Point?"

So his own mage ambassador didn't inform him of the coincidental information. What else was Magic Max keeping on the downlow? And why?

I nodded. "We're first meeting a man by the name of Mike O'Halloran in Dublin. His late father was a history professor at the university there and the person who discovered them."

Davin frowned. "O'Halloran? Was the professor's name Sean O'Halloran, by any chance?"

"Yes, actually. Why? Did you know him?"

His expression gave nothing away. "By reputation. In any case, if Professor O'Halloran gave you this lead, then it will definitely be worth your while to follow it."

"That's good to know then. I'll pass that information onto the lead of this dig."

Davin then looked to Amelia, adding, "You should go with them on this trip, Amelia dear. You as well, Ethan."

"Whyever for?" she remarked.

"For one, you both have been working so hard these days, you never take time for yourselves. Think of it as a short holiday together. I'm also certain Jillian and her team could use the extra pairs of hands. Having medical professionals to attend to any injuries would be an asset, I would believe. I would fund the entire expedition, of course."

"That's not necessary, thank you," I interjected. "The dig has been fully funded."

By the mother of his three daughters, in fact, I was tempted to add. But I promised Brenna to keep my trap shut from blurting the truth of their original encounter, so I would at least try to refrain from bringing her up.

Of course, if Amelia came on the dig with us, and just by coincidence ran into Rosalyn who would also be joining us…

The thought of getting my two bullheaded sisters in the same place, with me acting as referee to call a truce between our warring families, was too good to pass up.

Yes, this dig was working out so much better than I first expected.

"Actually, we could really use the medical expertise," I said. "You can't imagine the number of injuries and illnesses that happen during one of these expeditions."

"That settles it then," Davin said, brightening. "Amelia, you and Ethan will leave with Jillian when she goes. Please make use of the company jet as well. You will need to take some time to gather needed equipment too. Ethan, please make a list and see to that immediately."

Amelia sent him a withering stare. "Are you trying to get rid of me, Dad?"

"For a while, perhaps," he said, smiling. "If I'm ever to have any grandchildren, I'll have to give them a sporting chance. Ethan, I'll expect you take this opportunity away from your jobs to thoroughly do your part?"

"Dad! Please."

* * *

"So you knew the whole time?" I remarked with amazement.

"That you were tricking Amelia into coming with you in order to force her to talk and make peace with her sister?" Davin laughed lightly, adding, "You don't get to be the CEO of an international holdings corporation without knowing what's going on all around you. And I applaud your efforts, Jillian. I hope it works. I don't like to see you three girls at odds with each other."

The night before we left, Davin asked me to join him outside for a stroll in their night blooming garden. It was fragrant and breathtaking walking amongst the fragrant jasmine, clematis and cereus with the half moon beaming down silver streaks onto the path.

There was a long moment of silence before he asked quietly, "How is Brenna? Did you find her…well?"

"Yes, she's good, happy. Wait, you knew I went to see Brenna Callaghan too?"

He nudged a shoulder, his hands clasped behind his back as we walked along the dark brick and stone footpaths. "I assumed Rosalyn herself gave you my contact information, so it didn't take a genius to know you would be curious to talk with your birthmother whom she's close to."

I frowned up at him. "But Amelia didn't want to."

"Amelia is very headstrong and won't consider the possibility that Brenna had her reasons for stealing the firestone and escaping to the U.S. After all, she believed my coven was responsible for her family's massacre. She had no reason to trust me with the lives of our daughters. I understand that now."

"You do?"

"My dear, I'm pushing close to two centuries of age. Hopefully I've gained some insight and wisdom in that length of time."

I clenched my jaws to keep from spilling the true story, at least the truth from Brenna's perspective.

God, this was unbearable!

If only they would just get together and confess everything to each other. Then they could mend…

"Davin, why don't you come along with us on the dig?" I asked, my heart racing at the possibilities of my next scheme. "Rosalyn will be there. It will give you a chance to meet her face-to-face."

CRYSTAL MOON

CHAPTER 14

I stood along the sidewalk, gazing into the window of the antique store filled with hand-carved chairs, painted ceramic bowls and a set of multicolored glass vases. I shoved my hands into my coat pockets, my body tightly braced against the icy wind that had picked up.

The overcast clouds had darkened the late afternoon street in Dublin even more, threatening a thunderstorm. Good weather for vampires to be out and about in. Not so much for me.

Marc came up behind me and slid his arms around my waist to draw me against him, his body heat warming me deliciously. I raised my eyes to his sympathetic expression reflected in the shop's window.

"I'm sorry your father chose not to come with us, Jillian," he said, resting his chin on my shoulder. "I know you're disappointed, but he's the sire of his coven. Most never venture far from their home base for security reasons."

"It had nothing to do with security," I remarked glumly.

"What then?" When I didn't answer, he turned me around to fix his green stare with mine. "Jillian, why did you really want him to join us?"

"No reason."

"Bull crap. Spill it."

"What time is it? Do you think Amy and Ethan will be much longer in the store? I'd really like to go to the *Temple Bar* for something to drink. It's just down this next street."

"Jill. What's up?" he stubbornly persisted.

My cheeks flushed. Marc's expression immediately changed when figuring it out.

"It wouldn't have happened, Jillian. Even if Davin did come with us, Brenna is still in California, a half-world away."

"Which you or I could remedy on a moment's notice," I added.

He heaved a growled breath, drawing me against me. "Didn't know I fell in love with such a romantic idiot."

"Say that to me again, and you'll find yourself turned into a warthog."

"Jillian, love, you're just going to have to accept that your birthparents for whatever reason chooses not to be together of their own freewill. It's not for you to force them together in hopes they'll rekindle something they shared for one long, intense weekend some twenty-seven years ago."

I looked up to him. "But what if it is? What if I can be the one to finally get them together and talk and—"

Marc pressed two fingers gently on my lips. "If they had wanted to communicate with each other, they would have done so already. Brenna herself gave you Davin's personal number, which meant she had it in her possession and chose not to use it. Not to mention that she could have texted or emailed him."

"But if she was just too—"

"No, Jillian," he cut me off. "It's their lives. You have to respect their wishes and their silence to each other." Amelia and Ethan then exited the shop door. "Here they are. You said something about grabbing a drink before heading back the hotel?"

The reminder startled me, and I grabbed my cellphone, instantly easing at the time. We still had twenty minutes.

"Yes, I was reading about this famous Irish pub down the street called the *Temple Bar*," I remarked to everyone. "We should go try it, get some photos of all of us like proper tourists."

"Yeah, I've heard of it. Sounds great," Amelia said, Ethan readily agreeing.

"We'd better scoot then," I added. "I hear it fills up fast this time of day."

Marc narrowed his eyes at me, lifting his chin. "Jill?"

"What?" I remarked with too wide eyes.

He dryly sniffed and slid his arm around my shoulders as we followed Amelia and Ethan to the pub at the end of the busy street.

The Temple Bar itself was set in an historical brick building on the corner in downtown Dublin. It was crowded when we walked inside and grabbed a table. I checked my cellphone again, ignoring Marc's scrutiny after he ordered us all a round of the house whiskey.

"I miss this," Amelia remarked, smelling and gazing at the amber liquid in her hands that was more of a prop to her and Ethan. "The different flavors."

"I never thought of that," I said, sipping my own. "Yes, I don't think I'd like that part of…your new lifestyle."

"It's not so bad really," she remarked. "Tradeoffs. I have a lot of advantages now."

Like living for several centuries instead of only one like me. Yes, a very good tradeoff.

Ethan kissed the side of Amelia's head and whispered something to her in a decibel too low for us or any human to catch. She twitched a sad smile, then turned to face him and shook her head, giving him a kiss.

"So how did you find out about your own…predilections?" she then asked me.

"A long story that began when I visited my friend Helene at the university and running into this creep here," I said, nudging Marc playfully.

I told her the story of the disaster I caused in his classroom lab after accidently retargeting his laser towards the ceiling and setting off fire alarms and sprinklers. We all laughed hard as I recalled and acted out portions of the incident, Marc filling in a couple of gaps.

"So I said, 'Are you crazy, you freak. I'm nobody's slave.' And he said, 'Not a master as in…'"

"You didn't tell me that *she* was going to be here," snarled from behind us.

Marc turned around and muffled a curse.

I squeezed my eyes shut for two seconds, before I forced a toothy smile and stood up to greet Rosalyn and Brian who just arrived. "I'm so glad you found us! Sit down, please."

"No thanks," she spat, glaring daggers at Amelia who jumped up and looked ready to storm away as well. "It's a bit too crowded and foul smelling in here for my taste."

"Probably just as well," Amelia snarked back, her eyes beginning to glow. "I don't think they allow dogs inside the place for health code reasons."

Rosalyn's own eyes glowed the color of our whisky, her canine's beginning to lengthen. "Yeah, bloodsucker? You want to start comparing—?"

"Whoa! Both of you take it down several degrees," I said, standing between them, just in case it exploded into physical violence. "We're all here in the same, very public place, so let's just cool it down and play nice. Okay?"

Reluctantly Amelia's eyes dimmed and she sat back down, but kept her glare focused on Rosalyn who remained standing. "Is that why you wanted us to come here, Jillian? You set this up?"

"You tricked me?" Rosalyn accused with outrage. "And here I thought you were the good sister. Should've known better. Come on, Brian. We're outta here. Jillian, I'll see you at the dig."

"Wait, she's coming with us to Spanish Point?"

"Of course, Sherlock," Rosalyn stated to Amelia. "My family and I are financing the whole thing, so I'm coming…Wait, you know about the dig?"

"Of course, I do. We're coming with Jillian as medical consultants."

"Yeah, over my furry dead carcass, corpse."

"That can be easily arranged, mutt."

Okay, so it probably wasn't the brightest plan I had. Still, if it had worked, it would have been worth all the grief I was getting now.

Well, the best defense is a stronger offense. It helped me once before.

I eyed them both fiercely. "Stop it, both of you! Let's all just sit down. We're making a scene, and none of us wants to draw undo attention, do we?"

A few people looked in our direction, but loud, hot and perhaps even mildly physical confrontations at an Irish bar wasn't extraordinary enough to warrant more than a cursory glance from spectators. Thank goodness for small favors.

I pulled a chair out for Rosalyn, and she reluctantly lowered herself into it at the same time Amelia did her own. Both of their husbands eased their own protective, aggressive stances and sat down as well, but the mood at the table was still a sizzling powder keg that could explode at any moment. It was now or never to come with everything.

"Okay, so I sort of tricked you both into meeting here tonight," I admitted. "And coming on the dig itself. So yes, that's on me. Sorry."

"Not forgiven," Rosalyn grumbled.

"Sorry again. Look, I know you both have your reasons to be upset with each other. No, Rosalyn, I don't want to hear it again. You either, Amy. But it's long past time both of you laid down the gauntlet and made peace."

"Not happening," Rosalyn stated.

"Ditto," Amy ground out.

"Okay, a temporary truce then," I added. "At least until we're all finished with this project. After that, then you two can both go back to hating each other claw and fang. Agreed? It's what our parents really want."

Both sisters gaped at me.

"Dad knew about Rosalyn coming?" Amelia remarked.

"Brenna told you to do this?" Rosalyn accused at the same time.

"Yes, to both of you," I said. "More importantly, they both believe this project at Spanish Point might have something to do with the Red Moon Prophecy that all three of us are a part of. And it's going to take all three of us together to find out what that is."

"No way," Amelia snorted. "I'm beginning to doubt all that prophecy hooey that Valerian spouts off about in the first place. I've never trusted that manipulative mage."

Rosalyn arched a brow in silent agreement.

I couldn't say that their suspicious of the man were unfounded, but I didn't want to give them another reason to leave when we were so close to the opportunity to join together as a family.

Maybe Marc was right, and I was just fooling myself into romantically believing it could ever happen. Still, I had to try.

I pulled out my cellphone to show her the snapshot of the parchment text. "This came from inside one of the geodes found by the late Professor O'Halloran. Helene and I are set to meet with his son tomorrow, and I'd like for both of you to join us."

"Why?" Amelia asked.

"No good reason. Still, all three of us are here now, and I believe that it has something to do with the prophecy itself and our part in it. We're meeting in the early evening so that it won't be a problem for you, Amy, no matter the weather forecast."

"Fine, I'll be there," she stated after a long, tense pause.

"Well, if she's going, I'm going," Rosalyn added, then stood. "But I don't have to stay here now. Text me the when and where, and I'll see you tomorrow."

She stood and walked out with her husband. Amelia made her own exit excuses, furious at me for tricking her into meeting with her werewolf sister. It had been a dirty trick, but it had been for a good cause.

Of course, that's the line of reasoning Max Valerian disturbingly used too.

Alone now with Marc in the busy pub, he downed his whiskey in one gulp, then arched a brow at me.

"Well, that went well," he said. "Nice going, Churchill."

I kicked his shin hard for the crack, then downed my own shot of whiskey and waved the waitress for another.

* * *

The next night, I introduced Helene to Amelia as an extended family member who offered her and her husband's medical expertise for the team. Helene saw the wisdom in having medical professionals on hand knowing the many injuries that occurred during these trips, and was enthusiastically onboard when they both insisted their services be strictly voluntary and pro bono.

After Rosalyn joined us in the hotel lobby, we drove to Mike O'Halloran's rustic country house outside of Dublin. The man was burly, pockmarked and semi-bald, dressed in khaki work clothes. Unmarried and alone, he seemed a bit awkward hosting a gaggle of four women as he invited us all inside.

"Thank you for meeting us, Mr. O'Halloran," Helene said, sitting on the worn couch across from him. "We're all ready to start work at Spanish Point. We just need the exact location that you promised to give us."

"Mike, please," he offered, pouring tea for each of us. "I have something else besides the grid map as well. I'm sorry not to just send it to you, but my father had left written instructions that I hand it all to you in person, not to trust any delivery services, you understand."

Helene waved him off. "I do, no worries at all. We're glad to stop by and thank you personally, in fact."

"I'm glad then," O'Halloran said. "Frankly, I'll be glad to be rid of the last things my father left behind. Cake? I have a bit of angel food in the kitchen."

"Thank you, no," I answered. "Whatever your father left for us will be more than enough, then we won't trouble you further."

"No trouble a'tall. I'll go and get them then," he said, then shuffled away and up the thin staircase. "Excuse me a bit, ladies."

We all sat and silently drank our tea as if this was any other social call. I waited until O'Halloran was out of sight and earshot before I turned to Helene sitting next to me.

"What else do you think he has for us?" I whispered Helene next to me.

"More geodes, I hope," she said quietly. "And with any luck…"

Her expression froze. In fact, so did her entire body.

"With any luck, what? Helene?" I waved a hand in front of her face to see that she was stiff and unblinking, then gave her arm a shake. "Helene!"

"Don't worry," O'Halloran said as he trudged down the stairs. "She's just having a bit of a nap right now."

"A nap? What's wrong..?" My stomach dropped with disbelief, and I shot to my feet. "Oh God, you're a sorcerer!"

He straightened with mock indignation. "Master mage, I'll thank you very much."

Rosalyn and Amelia both jumped up and moved protectively beside me. O'Halloran rolled his rheumy eyes, then swiped a hand across his face that melted and reformed to that of Max Valerian himself, now slimmed and dressed in his usual expensive business suit.

"Max?" Amelia shot out while Rosalyn cursed.

"Why the smoke and mirrors?" I accused. "Where's the real Mike O'Halloran? What did you do to him?"

"I am the real Michael O'Halloran," he said with slight irritation. "As well as his father Sean O'Halloran twenty-seven years ago."

"Who?" Rosalyn asked.

"He was the professor who directed Davin to the cavern at Spanish Point where they found the firestone," Amelia answered.

"A simple glamor spell," Max explained with an absent gesture. "Jillian, I'm disappointed you didn't catch on from the first."

So was I. Having mastered the ability myself two weeks ago, I now saw many of the signs that would have told me as much. I inwardly kicked myself for not paying attention.

"So you knew the firestone was in the ruins all along?" I remarked.

Max nudged a shoulder. "An educated assumption, after studying the ancient texts."

"Why didn't you just give Davin that information as yourself to begin with?" Amelia asked.

I narrowed my eyes at the mage. "Because he needed Brenna and Davin to get together. They had to find the stone together, right?"

Brenna had explained their meeting in detail, including one moment when he met the alleged professor in the pub to discuss the location of the ancient ruins. She had been spying on Davin, still believing him and his coven to be responsible for her pack's massacre, still bent on seeking revenge.

Until he rescued her from certain death when he followed her and her attacker out of the same pub that night. That was beginning of their truce, and of their partnership, and their love affair.

"Very good, Jillian."

"But why?" Amelia said.

"Because alone, neither could have made it through the barriers and attacks to reach and claim it," he explained.

"And once they did, you planned to take it from them," she figured out. "I was wrong about her then."

"You greedy bastard!" Rosalyn viciously yelled. "You accused *my* mother of stealing the firestone for her own purposes!"

"Worse, you let *my* father believe she betrayed him for it," Amelia added. "You're the real greedy manipulator in all of this, aren't you, Valerian? I knew it."

Max shifted his bored stare to her. "You don't know anything yet, child. But you're about to. It's time all three of you learned the full truth of what happened, so that we can finally get down to real business."

"Learn what?" Rosalyn demanded.

"Wait, how can we trust anything you say?" Amelia shot back.

"You can't," he answered coolly. "But I'll tell you nonetheless and allow you to draw your own conclusions. This world is depending upon it."

"The world? What kind of B.S. is that?" Rosalyn spat.

"We're listening," I said for all of us.

"To begin with," Max said. "Until Rhiona Kennish's memory-loss spell began to disintegrate on your twenty-fifth birthday, I didn't know a single one of you existed. Which was its purpose, of course, the sneaky little sorceress. I interpreted the keys to the Red Moon Prophecy to being only your parents. Now I see the poetic perfection in its true meaning. Three young women fully claiming one-third of each supernatural legacy—vampire, werewolf and mage."

I frowned at Amelia and Rosalyn, then shook my head at Max. "Your math doesn't add up. Our mother is half-wolf and half-mage, but our father is full vampire."

"Unless…" Amelia said, scrutinizing him. "Oh, God. Really?"

He arched a brow at her, cracking a slight smile. "You always were the quick minded one, my dear granddaughter."

"Granddaughter?" Rosalyn remarked.

"Of course," Amelia ground out, narrowing her eyes at Max. "You had an affair with Davin's mother while she was married to Samuel Laith. You're his real father."

He shrugged, then looked to me for understanding. "You know a mage's life is a lonely, solitary one. We find our comfort where we may."

"He means that mages like to have hookups at the drop of a hat," I said. "No permanent commitments needed then."

He shrugged in a "what can I say" unspoken comment.

So we were all equally one-third mage, werewolf and vampire. Each of us fully taking on the one side that called to us through love and destiny, and perhaps even the prophecy itself.

"I take it Davin doesn't know about his true heritage then," I said to Amelia.

She shook her head. "Not a clue. So why the secrecy all this time, Max? At least to him."

"I suspect the same reason Rhiona Kennish kept your existence secret—to hide and protect him from the upcoming dark mage foretold in the prophecy by the Ancient Ones, the one labeled as Mars. He is my son after all, and I do care for his wellbeing."

Mars, the Greek god of war. The one who would bring ultimate destruction to this unsuspecting and unequipped world.

"What do you know of this dark mage then?" I asked.

"Unfortunately as much, or as little, as you," he said. "I cast a locator spell for the text describing this dark mage hidden by the Ancient Ones, but was able to find only the one geode where they hid a portion of it.

"My suspicion is that they hid the other fragments to safeguard the secret in other geodes around the same area. All three of you must go to Spanish Point and find them. When the text is complete, you will know where to locate this dark mage and how to defeat him."

"Defeat him at what?" I asked.

Max turned to me, answering, "According to my readings, I believe this mage discovered the ability to open a portal that leads to the Dark Dimension, one only he knows about."

"No," I breathed heavily with dread.

Which meant he would have the ability unleash an army of demons bent on the destruction of this world. And only we three would have the ability to stop him.

If we could find this ancient text first in time.

"According to my calculations, you have less than two weeks to accomplish this," Max concluded. "That's when the next full blood moon will rise.

* * *

It was late afternoon the next day when I finished my prep for tomorrow's grueling dig and left my hotel room to walk along the beach at Spanish Point. The clouds were gathering, throwing magnificent colors in the sky and across the glittering ocean waves, the breeze light and cold even at this time of year.

My shoes sunk into the damp sand as I strolled, looking at the nearby craggy cliffs as a few rogue waves crashed and flowed up to my feet, never quite reaching. The solitude was nice and sorely needed. So much had crashed down on me the past few months, most of which I was still having a difficult time processing.

Had it only been three months since I first woke up in that hospital bed and my world turned on its axis?

It made me think of Doug, and I once again felt guilty at the cruel trick Fate had played on him.

He had faithfully stayed by my side while I was in my death-sleep, night after night, week after week. The poor man must have come to some sad resignation of his inevitable loss to have my cellphone shutoff, ready to bury the woman he loved and planned a future with. Then I miraculously wake and don't even recognize him, only to leave him the day after I returned to our home.

God, I was such a slime for running away like that.

Of course, if I hadn't, I never would have met Marc, again, and discovered my magic, or my birthparents and sisters. It was frustrating to reconcile the guilt and gratefulness of my actions.

I felt the sparking sizzle in the air two seconds before Marc appeared at my side to take my hand. I turned a sad smile to him, and he leaned down to kiss me, tracing my jaw lightly with his fingers.

"What's wrong?"

I lifted a shoulder, while still meandering across the beach, now with him beside me. "Guilt. Worry. Confusion. You know, the usual."

"The worry and confusion, I get. Why do you feel guilty though?" he asked.

It would be insensitive for me to tell him, although I knew he would graciously take it in stride and be understanding, even encouraging and supportive.

I shook my head, and he accepted my silence.

"Ready to get your hands dirty tomorrow?" he asked to change the subject to something more upbeat.

"Yep. Looking forward to it. You?"

"Always," he said, looking out at the restless ocean. "We could have done this faster, if we had just come on our own though. It could have remained secret then too."

"And alert this unknown mage as to what we're doing," I added, shaking my head. "No, this is the perfect camouflage."

"Don't you think this mage already knows? That's the reason he tried to kill you twice."

"Maybe. But if there's even a slight chance that he doesn't know what we're really doing here, it's worth the ruse of working with a college geology team."

He obviously disagreed with me, but didn't argue. That was good. I wasn't in the mood to fight, and didn't have the strength or the logic to battle his better reasoning.

"What if we fail, Marc?"

That was the biggest burden on my shoulders now.

Billions of people and future generations were depending on us to succeed, and they didn't have an inkling that their lives and future depended upon three women doing what they had been created to do. We were going to battle with an unseen enemy, and we couldn't fail. We couldn't. Even if no one but us knew about it.

Marc halted and turned me to face him straight on, my insides melting with the intensity of his green stare, the wind whipping his black, wavy hair to one side.

"You won't, Jillian," he said simply, confidently. "I've doubted so much in my life, but there is one thing I have full confidence in. You are the most incredible, amazing, talented woman I have ever had the privilege to know, Jillian Azure, and you will succeed at anything you choose to do."

"But I don't think—"

"No, let me finish," he cut in. "Jillian, I love you. I don't know what I did to deserve you loving me back, but I thank all the powers that be that you do, and I'll do my level best to live up to that honor every day, to make you happy that you've chosen to be with me, now and in the future.

"Still, it's a future not set. Not until you and your sisters do what it is you were made to do, so that you and I and the rest of this world can live and love as we choose."

He kissed me and held me, adding, "You will succeed, Jillian Azure. I'm completely confident in that. That's what I intend to tell our children as they grow up and long after that. That you fought for us, all of us in this world. And you succeeded."

Marc flicked his hand, and suddenly we were back in my hotel room, clawing, tearing off every barrier between us until we were skin-to-skin.

Desperation forced our joining, our claiming, repeated again and again to alleviate any doubt and worry I had in our future together. When he poured himself inside me, he was offering all of himself, every last ounce of strength that he could give me. It was a declaration in itself, that he would never be apart from me, ever.

It was what I needed to get me through the sleepless night and for the true battle to come. As I clung to him when dawn broke through the curtains, I was ready to face this day and all that it brought

Including the monster I was determined to find and destroy.

Crystal Moon

Chapter 15

The first day was expectedly uneventful, everyone mainly introducing each other of the thirty-person team, organizing tasks, setting up equipment and grid targets.

Ethan and Amelia set up a medical tent where they would treat the sick and injured, which happened frequently on these projects. Mostly it was the perfect place for them to remain out of the deadly ultraviolet rays during the sunnier days.

The next day everyone got down to business and eagerly picked up their shovel, pick or other equipment that would hack the rocks along our first grid section. Memories of previous projects returned in small fragments as I myself dug and picked away. I remembered the enthusiastic first two days of a dig that slowly diminished as the long, tedious, and physically taxing days went by and the novelty wore off.

"How long before you think we should explore on our own?" Rosalyn asked me quietly.

It was the end of the grueling workday, and we were sitting on the forested rise above the worksite. She and Brian were already proving to be huge assets with this physical labor, neither afraid to get down and dirty, and both having the incredible strength and endurance of their werewolf species. Not exactly the most romantic place for a honeymoon, but they didn't seem to mind.

"Another few days, at least," I said, pulling off my soiled work gloves and sitting back. "By then, the initial excitement of the trip will dim down. Then there won't be as many people hanging around afterhours observing what we do."

"I really want to see if we can find that secret cavern mom told us about where she and Davin Laith found the firestone," she said, surveying over the rolling, green landscape. "I still think we might find something there."

"Max doesn't think so."

Rosalyn snorted. "Yeah, I don't trust that mage as far as I can throw him."

I took a long pull from my water bottle, then capped it again. "You're not wrong to be cautious of the man, but I don't think he'd steer us wrong. Not in this. He wants us to find the text pieces as much as anyone."

"Yeah, well, I'm still having a hard time believing it. The things Aunt Rhiona told me about him…" She shook her head.

"At least he's on our side," I said, not disagreeing with her.

Rosalyn shrugged.

"Mom says hi, but the way," she added. "She hopes you'll take some time and come visit Callaghan Lodge again. You're always welcome, you know."

I nodded, smiling. "Thanks, I appreciate that. There's still so much I want to ask her."

"You should give her a call," Rosalyn suggested.

I wiped my dirty, sweaty forehead with the back of my arm, saying, "I will. There's still too much to worry about with this hunt for the geodes first."

The sun had set, and I gazed down the hillside to the distant worksite below. Parked vehicles were leaving. The few remaining workers were winding up their own tasks. That included Ethan and Amelia as they headed back and forth from their own car.

"Still say you shouldn't have invited the bloodsuckers," Rosalyn muttered, following my gaze below. "We could've done this without them."

"Maybe, but it'll be nice having medical professionals on immediate hand. You don't realize how many injuries happen on these trips."

"Hmm."

"You really should get over your animosity towards Amelia," I told her. "Like it or not, she is our sister, and we're going to need her if there's any truth to this prophecy battle coming up."

Rosalyn grunted again. "I guess. It would be easier if she just accepted our mother as easy as you did."

"*I* didn't have any preconceived ideas regarding our birthparents' history," I reminded her with arched brow. "Be patient with her. She only recently heard the truth about Brenna, and not even the entire story in full yet."

"She had plenty of opportunity to find out before this," Rosalyn said.

"Maybe, but she wasn't ready to hear it. I think she is now, or will be very soon. It isn't easy to learn that your own birthmother gave you up to perfect strangers. I know. I'm still having a hard time wrapping my head about my new…heritage."

There was a long pause.

"Do you harbor any animosity towards our mother for giving us all up?" Rosalyn asked.

I shook my head. "No. Not much, anyhow. Brenna Callaghan did an incredibly brave and heartbreaking thing by doing what she thought best to keep us all alive. I'm just thankful that I have a chance to get to know her now. Davin Laith, too."

"Hmm. I wish others thought that way," she remarked, narrowing her eyes at the small, distant figure of Amelia as she exited the medical tent with a bundle in her arms.

"She will," I said. "In time."

"You didn't need it."

"I didn't have either one of my birthparents' families trying to coax me to their side," I reminded.

Rosalyn cracked a grin. "No. Just our evil grandfather determined to pass on his own dangerous legacy."

I suppose she was right. It was the first time I had considered that aspect.

I was going to take another drink of water. Instead, I pulled out a small flask of Irish whiskey I had purchased at the Dublin bar from my shirt pocket and offered it to her.

"Here's to family?"

She grinned and held it up. "No matter what species they may be. Cheers."

We both drank and laughed, sharing things about our head-bending, ridiculous familial situation, and the times we both discovered what we were.

My cellphone buzzed. The caller I.D. showed that it was Doug, and my stomach guiltily gripped. I didn't blame him for trying to reconnect, trying anything to repair our damaged relationship, but he needed to accept the fact that whatever we once had was now over. And probably shouldn't have started to begin with.

I answered it. "Doug."

"Jillian. You answered. I…wasn't sure if you would."

Rosalyn must have sensed the sensitivity of the conversation by my expression and gestured that she planned to button down the worksite for the night with the others. I lifted a hand in goodbye to her, mouthing my apologies. She shrugged, waved—no big deal.

"Sure, I answered," I said, forcing a calmer, more casual tone. "How are you?"

"I'm okay. God, it's great to hear your voice. I've missed you."

Another pause.

"Was there something you wanted?" I asked.

"Yes, actually," he said. "I was thinking about driving up to see you. Before you say anything, this isn't some cheap stunt to try and get you to come home with me. If…If you really feel that you need to stay up there in Fort Collins, then I won't try and convince you otherwise. I just wanted a chance to see you for a bit, talk. I hate the way we left things last time."

I bit my lip, gazing down at the worksite where Marc was talking to Helene about something.

"I hated the way we left things too," I admitted.

"Then you'll meet me?" he asked with new hope in his voice.

“Actually I can’t right now.”

“Why not?” he asked a little to roughly.

“You remember Helene’s dig in Ireland? I’m here now. In Ireland.”

“What? I thought that was a month away!”

“It was a month ago that I told you,” I reminded. “We’re all here now.”

“For how long?”

“I don’t know. A couple of weeks at least. It all depends on what we find, or if we find anything at all.”

“Then you’ll be back home,” he added.

“To Fort Collins, yes.”

“Right. Of course. Maybe I can drive up then.”

I frowned, swallowed hard. “Doug, it probably isn’t a good idea for us to meet at all. Not yet, at least. Not for a long while.”

There was another pause before he came back on the line.

“There’s someone else, isn’t there? It’s that guy I caught you with at your hotel, isn’t it?”

I pinched my eyelids shut, unable to deny his accusations. Even so, I would still feel the same nothingness for Doug if Marc and I hadn’t come together, so it was cruel to give him any false hope.

“Doug, I’m sorry, but I told you last time that it was over between us, and I haven’t changed my mind.”

“Where are you in Ireland? Tell me exactly where you are, Jillian.”

My brows hiked. “Why? Do you plan to hop and plane and come all the way here to Spanish Point to plead your case? Please understand that even if we saw each other again, I won’t change my mind. Whatever we might have had in the past is gone now, over. Accept this and finally move on with your life. You’re a good man who deserves have some happiness.”

“I have that with you, Jillian.”

"Had. Past tense. I care very much for you, Doug, but I'm not in love with you, at least not anymore, and I know that I won't be in the future either. Goodbye. And I do hope you find someone else who will make you happy."

I hung up before he could say anything else that would make me change my mind or feel even more guilty than I did already. I watched Marc with Helene in the distance, pointing out something on the grid map spread out on a folding camp table. He looked up and spotted me, smiled and lifted a hand. I nodded back, sighing heavily.

Yes, I had made the right decision. Marc was who I wanted, needed, who I was meant to be with. I couldn't draw breath on this earth, if he wasn't with me now.

Still, it didn't make things any easier to cruelly injure another man who obviously still harbored deep feelings for me and who had patiently, faithfully saw me through the worst time in my unconscious life.

Frowning at something he saw on my face, Marc spoke to Helene, then left her and hiked up the long, grassy ridge to where I sat.

"Hi, beautiful."

"Hi, yourself, Magic Man," I returned. "Give us a kiss then."

He sat down beside me, obliging me with a slow, thorough and mind-numbing kiss that only confirmed my choice. I still couldn't shake the guilt I felt over Doug, though. He was the innocent and most harmed party in this entire bizarre situation.

"What's wrong?" he asked through kissing the side of my mouth, then pulling back and fixing his stare with mine.

"Why would you think that?"

"Shall I list all the different nuances of your expressions that tell the entire world what you're thinking?"

I let go of a long breath. "I'm just tired. It's been a long day. And week." *And month and year and life.*

"It has, but there's something else. What's up?"

"It's nothing."

"You're lying, but okay," he said.

I sent him a narrowed stare. "You can be very annoying sometimes, you know that?"

"I do. But I'm also right." Marc glanced over his shoulder to the worksite below, then back to me. "Everyone's packing it in for the night. Let's head out ourselves. Helene mentioned something about a group of us going to the local pub for a drink."

I stood, brushing the grass, weeds and thistle heads off my pant legs. "You go. I just want to head back to the hotel and take a long, hot bath, then collapse into bed."

"Hmm. Think I like your idea better."

"Alone," I added pointedly.

He frowned. "Brushing me off?"

"For tonight only," I said as we plodded down the grassy rise together. "I really am tired."

Marc stopped and turned me to face him straight on. "What's really going on, Jillian?"

Flushing, I pressed my cheek against his chest, his arm instinctively coming around to hold me against him.

How could I say that I was incredibly conflicted between Doug and him? Yet, I wasn't. Not really. I knew who I couldn't live without. It still didn't make the decision easier though.

"Jill?"

I raised my face to him and kissed his chin scratchy with the shadow of an evening beard. "I'm good, really. Let's just go. Tomorrow will be better."

He sent me a look of doubt, but led us down to the worksite to collect our things and leave for the night.

Back at the hotel, Marc walked me to my room. I'm sure he wanted to be invited inside, but I needed this night alone to take a breath and process every strange thing in my life before I could face tomorrow and its own new calamities. He looked both disappointed and worried when I said my final goodnight, kissed him, then closed the door, but I planned to make it up to him tomorrow.

Grungy, filthy and exhausted, I let my muddy, dusty clothes and work boots lie where they dropped, then eased my aching body into the scalding, bath-salted water inch by inch, until I lay back in utter relief. I remained there until the water cooled and my muscles eased, then donned my bathrobe and padded back into the main room, startling to see Max sitting there in a side chair, perusing through a local newspaper.

"You took long enough," he stated irritably, not taking his eyes off the article he was reading. "I trust you're feeling better now?"

"What are you doing here?" I demanded, firmly tying the ends of my robe.

He folded the paper down on the table and stood. "Now is that any way for you to greet your aging grandfather?"

I snorted. "No, but well deserved punch in your interfering nose might get me turned into a slimy toad."

He tsked. "I would never disrespect you by turning you into a revolting amphibian, Jillian. You would be more of a turtledove. Or even a monarch butterfly."

"What do you want, Max?"

"You need to come with me to my private workroom," he said. "Now."

"Sorry, I'm tired of this day and your games. I just want to order some food to be delivered, eat it, then go to sleep, not necessarily in that order."

He snapped his fingers, and I was suddenly fully dressed in street clothes, my wet hair now dried and braided back. Which pissed me the hell off.

"No, I said!"

"Trust me, you'll want to see this. Now, let's be off."

Before I could protest again, we appeared in the laboratory I remembered from my previous visit to Max's hideaway manor in the Mediterranean. The place looked even creepier than the last time.

"Another gaze into your crystal ball?" I sniped.

Max shifted a withered stare at me. "Need another rerun of your tiresome, suburban human past?"

"No."

"This is something else."

Against all of my logic and self-preserving instincts, I was too intrigued now. The man had played and reeled me in like a fish on a line.

"Ten minutes," I said. "Then I'm going back."

"If you wish it," he said, guiding me across the room towards four large, uncut geodes.

I gaped at him. "You already had the missing geodes?"

Max picked up one. "No. Those are still hidden somewhere in Ireland. Which you had better find much sooner, rather than later. These hold else."

"What?"

He handed the rock to me, and my palms warmed around it. Reflexively I shook it, but heard nothing loose inside. The geode itself grew warmer, then hot. So hot that it started to glow.

Before I reflexively dropped it, Max gripped my wrist and began to murmur incoherent words in the mysterious language of the Ancient Ones. I try to pull apart from the geode and him, but we were all glued together.

Then the geode vibrated roughly, cracked in two.

And Max disappeared.

"Max?" I yelled, dropping the rock halves and whirling all around. "Okay, this isn't funny. Where are you? Max?"

Suddenly he blinked back to my side, a look of triumph on his face.

"Where the hell did you pop off to?" I demanded, my heart pounding like a jackhammer. "And what's with all the dramatics?"

Max picked up the two portions of the broken geode, revealing pink and burgundy crystals, his smile widening.

"You were the key," he said, placing it beside the others. "I thought as much that very first day we met."

"Yeah, I know. Me, Rosalyn and Amelia are the three keys foretold by the Ancient Ones and all that. I don't care about that. What about this geode?"

"No, Jillian," he said. "Not the prophecy—the time traveling spell. You alone are the key to igniting it."

"What?"

He nodded. "You don't know this, but I just returned to the night before your father left for Spanish Point twenty-seven years ago."

I gave myself a hard shake. "Wait, are you saying that you just traveled back in time?"

"Yes. This was a test, but also a necessity," Max said. "I needed to return to that one dreadful moment when Davin decided *not* to go to Spanish Point and retrieve the firestone, and all was lost."

"Okay, you lost me."

"That manipulative fiancée of his, Laticia Bertram, convinced Davin to return to London with her that next day to push up their wedding date."

"More, please."

"Which meant that your parents didn't meet, didn't locate the firestone, and didn't get together to have you three girls," Max added irritably, as if I was too slow on the uptake. "I suspected for a long while that she was working with someone outside the coven, but never found out who, no matter how close I got to her this past year. I almost convinced her to divulge this information when your sister Amelia went and killed the vampire witch. I'll never forgive her for that."

"That doesn't make any sense though. I'm here. My sisters are here. It all happened."

"Because I just traveled back in time and corrected that mishap," Max said. "I broke in on Laticia's play, then convinced Davin he should go to Spanish Point and locate the firestone in order to save his father and coven. Since you are here and the portal to the Dark Dimension remains unopened by the dark mage trying to do so now, I succeeded. Obviously."

I frowned. "But if Davin didn't go the first time, I wouldn't be here to be the key to send you back in time."

"It's quite a paradox, I'll admit, you being the key to your own existence."

"Whoa, this whole thing makes my head ache," I groaned.

"It's probably best if you don't think about it too hard. It can be quite vexing."

That was putting it mildly.

"So you knew they would fall in love with each other then?" I asked.

"I did watch their movements through my crystal, yes," he admitted. "I needed to make certain they were protected against this dark mage's machinations."

"But you didn't zap some attraction spell on them yourself? Please say you didn't."

Max eyed me with annoyance. "Please give me some credit, Jillian. You know it's forbidden, not to mention impossible, to manipulate any person's freewill. If they fell in love, it was of their own doing. I was merely an observer to the event."

That didn't exactly answer my question. I was mature enough to know that physical attraction and casual flings didn't always necessitate love.

"So you *didn't* use *any* of your magic to get them together?" I questioned harder. "Tell me the truth."

He lifted a shoulder. "Maybe a touch of an attraction spell on Davin. He is my son after all, and I wanted him to at least recognize the woman he was meant to be with."

"Yeah, you're a regular yenta," I stated dryly.

"Not much was needed, in any case," Max assured me. "They were destined to be together. I'm certain they sensed this when they met. I just gave them a nudge in the right direction."

"Back to the matter at hand though," he added. "Time travel has now been successfully accomplished, and now history and the future are back on the correct course."

"That much is good, I suppose," I remarked.

"Quite so. As I suspected, the spell itself has a short timespan, however. Twenty minutes at best, and then you're pulled back into your present time."

"That explains a lot," I muttered.

"Explains what exactly?" Max questioned.

I shook my head. "So we need geodes to do this then?"

Max picked up the broken half. "Only these particular rocks with the magical qualities inside them. It took me decades to locate just these four near a volcano in the Congo, so we will have to be selective with their use until I'm able to locate more."

"So what makes these so special?" I asked.

"The amount of natural luminaries they carry," he explained, setting it down again. "They act like flint to ignite your particular spark to the travel spell itself."

"You mean like my crystal conductor," I reasoned.

"That's a fair description," Max said.

"Great! Now we can send Marc back in time to wake me from my sleep-curse."

"So he was your mysterious mage visitor who did so then," Max remarked.

I gaped at the mage. He caught me. Then again, now that he knew time travel existed, I figured that I might as well tell him the rest.

He didn't appear surprised when I finished the new paradox.

"So you have to send him back, or I'll never wake up and be here right now to send you back in time. God, this gets more complicated by the minute."

Max shook his head. "I can't send him back yet. We still don't know the mage who cast the spell, so I can't find a spell to counteract it. Every mage has their own fingerprint. It's like needing to identify a specific poison before a cure can be diagnosed and dispensed."

"That sounds reasonable, I suppose. Still, I have to tell Marc about this ability to time travel, so that he's ready to act when you are."

Max touched my shoulder. "You can't tell anyone about this, Jillian. Not even Marc. If word of this ability got out for any reason, the mage council will confiscate the geodes, imprison me for breaking their antiquated law, and might even send you to the Dark Dimension just to safeguard the ability to time travel. And without you joining with your sisters at the appointed time, the Red Moon Prophecy cannot be fulfilled, and this world will be lost to darkness forever."

Another disastrous paradox. So yes, Max had a strong point. But I didn't like keeping such vital information from Marc either.

"We can trust him though," I said.

"We can, to a point," he said. "I know my apprentice well, Jillian, and Zander loves you and will do or say anything in order to protect you. It wouldn't take the enemy any more than threatening your life for him to divulge this information."

"Okay. Yes, you're right. I'll keep this under wraps then, even from Marc. For now."

Max nodded. "I'll send you back to your hotel before you're missed. I'm sure Zander is on his way there now."

"Now? No, I told him that I wanted to be alone tonight."

He quirked a smile. "As I said, I know my apprentice well. He loves you and can't stay away from you for very long. Not even by your own choice. Say nothing to him about this."

I frowned at him, thinking of something else. "Hey, you didn't manipulate *us* to get together, did you? I mean, did you even guess about us?"

Max lifted his chin, but I swore I saw a tiny corner of his lip curl upwards. "You'll never know, will you? I suppose there are some things you will just have to take on faith. Sweet dreams, Jillian. And find those text fragments. Time is running out."

Suddenly I found myself back inside my hotel room. Just as there was a quiet knock on the door.

CRYSTAL MOON

CHAPTER 16

"I'm so glad you called, Jillian," Brenna said warmly.

"It's not too late there, is it? Or too early? I forget how the time works between here and California."

Marc was in the shower. This was the end of the first week of true work. Helene was thrilled with the various deposits found so far, but I wasn't. None of the geodes we uncovered contained text fragments.

"Anytime is fine, if it's you," Brenna said. "How's the trip going?"

I scrunched my nose. "Fine for the official dig itself. Not as well for the other purpose we're here though."

"No other parchment pieces then?"

I shook my head. "Nope. Just a bunch of rainbow quartz that really shouldn't be here, enough to keep the professors happily distracted and the project itself going for a while longer."

"Have you kids thought about striking out on your own?" she suggested.

"Not sure if it would help. We're all looking for these geodes. Me and the sisters are just looking for pieces of the prophecy text inside them. I'm so afraid this whole thing might end up a bust."

And the world itself fall into utter darkness because of our failure.

There was a pause.

"Brenna?"

"I'm here," she said.

"Good, I thought we'd lost connection."

"I was thinking," she added. "What if the rest of the original text wasn't torn and distributed into various geodes? What if it's still intact, at least mostly, and the first piece was only meant to draw you all there to find it?"

I straightened in my chair. "Actually, I never considered that angle."

Marc exited the steaming bathroom wet with a towel wrapped around his lean hips, hotly distracting my thoughts for a moment.

"Jillian?"

I startled back to the conversation. "Sorry, I'm here."

"Oh good. For a moment I thought that *I* had lost connection with *you*."

"No, just distracted a second," I said, narrowing my stare at Marc.

He cracked a wicked, half-smile, then arched a brow. I flushed and turned away from him in order to finish this very important conversation.

"Anyhow, even if you're right about the rest of the text being intact, we still have no idea where the blasted thing is."

"I would imagine near the first geode," Brenna said. "The Ancient Ones might have used it as a sort of landmark. At least you're in the general vicinity of where you need to be."

"Maybe." I absently tapped a ballpoint pen on top of a hotel brochure, considering different angles of the problem. "The old fortress ruins that led you and Davin Laith to the firestone was located off Spanish Point, right?"

"Yes, about five miles."

"What if the text itself is down there somewhere?" I ventured. "Do you remember any place of interest where you think they could have hidden it."

There was a pause before Brenna came back on the line and said, "The Prophet Seat possibly."

"Prophet Seat?"

"That's what Davin and I believed it to be anyhow," she added. "It was a large anteroom towards the end of our search. It was like a throne room or gathering place of some sort and had writing all across the walls etched in gold paneling. It must have been something in its time. I don't know though. There didn't seem to be anywhere to hide much of anything, which is why we moved on. But that's the only place I can think of."

"How did you get inside this structure again?"

"Through an old watchtower," she said. "Outwardly it looked like some tall natural rock half-buried under the ground. We would have missed it entirely if it hadn't been for Davin's keen eye. We worked to crack an opening and found it to be hollow inside. It was mage-protected though. Only when we broke the blood magic seal did the flooring drop out and we climbed down to the fortress itself."

"Then what happened?" I prodded, feeling as if I was on the cusp of finding the answer.

"We repelled down twenty or thirty feet to the bottom, then walked forever down one corridor after another. It was like some confusing maze. A couple of places weren't even passable, so we had to backtrack and try another route to keep moving forward.

"Wait! No, first we needed the oxygen masks that Davin thought to buy along with the climbing equipment the day before. There was no air down there for a long time, not until we reached the Prophet Seat itself."

"How did you open up the tower's hatch in the first place?" I asked.

I had learned enough now to know that even as a half-mage, Brenna wouldn't have been able to break the blood seal. It would take a full-blooded mage to crack something that powerfully guarded, and for good reason, I imagined.

"I couldn't at first," Brenna said. "Davin used his strength to force it harder onto the runes inside."

"He held your hand down on it?"

"Yes. Then it worked, and half the tower door dropped away."

Of course! Brenna may have only been half-mage, but so was Davin. Together they made a whole.

We needed to find that tower. The sooner, the better.

"Brenna, what are you doing the next couple of days?"

* * *

In the passenger's seat of our rental car, I turned around to Brenna sitting behind me. Nervously she smiled, twisting a hotel brochure in her lap until it was practically shredded.

"Ready to finally meet your third daughter?" I asked.

As agreed, I had Marc teleport her from her secured manor in the forested hills of Santa Barbara to my hotel room just an hour ago. I was getting better at the skill, but wasn't confident enough yet to send her clear across the country and Atlantic Ocean, afraid I might inadvertently land her on some passing cargo ship or iceberg.

Brenna's main purpose in coming was to lead us all to the original ruins site where she and Davin had discovered the firestone. With any luck, the cavern itself was still open, and she could guide us through the confusing maze to the large anteroom where she thought the original text of the Ancient Ones might be hidden.

She winced, looking at the medical tent at the end of the camp. "This might not be such a good idea. I never wanted to force myself on Amelia. I know what she thinks of me and how she feels about what I did to all of you, and especially to Davin."

I grunted. "Her perceptions were false from the start. I've tried to explain what I could without breaking my promise to you, and I think it just made things worse. It's time you woman-up and tell her the whole story yourself, whether she likes it or not."

"If she'll give me the chance," Brenna muttered, setting the twisted hotel brochure aside.

"Even if she doesn't now, you'll have a captured audience when we finally get down into the tunnels. Come on, let's go."

All three of us walked to the medical tent. Inside, Amelia was assisting Ethan apply a plaster cast around a girl's fractured wrist. Another echoed memory flashed just then of being rushed to the local infirmary myself in a small Argentina town.

The recall flashes were coming fast and frequent this past week, as if the walls of my jammed memory were finally crumbling apart. It made me hopeful that I would soon remember all of my past.

"Looks like we have another patient," Ethan remarked when seeing us while smoothing down the moistened plaster strip on the volunteer's casted forearm. "Amelia, you want to check her out? I'll just finish up here, then be right with you."

"Will do, doctor."

She handed him another strip, then peeled off her latex gloves and disposed of them, replacing them with a fresh pair before walking up to us.

"Bringing in patients from the outside now?" Amelia remarked with a chuckle. "Don't think we're busy enough?"

I braced myself for the upcoming storm, touching Brenna's arm. "No injury. I'd just like you to meet someone."

"Glad to." Amelia smiled wide, extending her hand. "Hi, I'm Amelia Laith-Valter. Nice to meet any of Jillian's friends."

"Amelia," Brenna said shakily. "It's so nice to finally meet you."

"You too," she said. "So how do you know Jillian? From the college?"

"No. Not college."

Something in the crack of Brenna's voice made Amelia tilt her head and study her harder. Slowly the friendly smile melted off her face.

"Wait, I know you from somewhere. I could swear…Last fall! You came into the E.R. at Everett Memorial."

Brenna bit her bottom lip. "Yes, I was there. I…needed to see you."

"See me? I don't understand. Who did you say you were again?"

At the long silence, I knew I would have to be the one to come right out with it.

"Amy, this is Brenna Callaghan."

There was a stunned five-second delay before Amelia's gaped, then turned a stormy look of betrayal to me. "You arranged this?"

"Yes. Sorry, but we need Brenna's help with our personal quest. She has a good idea where the whole thing is, and she plans to lead us to it. And I thought that since she was here anyhow, it was long past time you two met."

"*You* thought? Since when were you appointed the person to decide what we all do? The stunt you pulled with Rosalyn last weekend was bad enough, but this?"

She shook her head and was about to storm away, but I barred her exit around me. "Just wait until you hear what she has to say. You owe her that."

 Amelia narrowed her eyes at me. "I owe her nothing. She made her choice to drop all association with us from the time we were born, so she can live with that same choice now that we're grown. And if you still feel that I'm wrong, then maybe I should stop my association with you as well."

I didn't react, ignoring the injury her harsh words dug into me. She did have a right to be angry. Furious, even. This was the second time I had blindsided her, but I couldn't see any other way to make peace between us all, and time was fast running out.

"This isn't your sister's fault," Brenna desperately cut in.

Amelia shot her a lethal glare. "No, it's yours! It always has been yours, hasn't it, *mother*?"

"We should all talk this out," I suggested, seeing the anxious looks on the few people observing us.

Marc exchanged a pointed look to Ethan saying, "Maybe we should give them all some privacy."

Ethan turned to Amelia who nodded, then aided his patient off the exam table and guided her out of the tent.

"Amy, I told you that a lot of what you believed was misinformation," I began when we were alone. "It's time you heard what really happened."

She folded her arms and leaned against the exam table. "I'm listening."

I let go of a huge breath and turned to Brenna. "You're up. Tell her everything."

So Brenna did, from beginning to end, this time leaving nothing out, including the fact that the priceless knowledge stone everyone assumed she stole out of personal greed was nothing more than a semi-precious garnet gem, and nothing more.

"You're saying that you lied and left Davin and split us all up and gave us to other couples in order to save our lives from some unknown enemy? Is that right?" Amelia remarked after Brenna finished the story.

"It is," she said quietly.

Amelia grunted, not entirely convinced.

"Okay, so she told you," I said to her. "It's done now."

"So done," Amelia grumbled.

"Look, Amy, whether you believe it or not, it's the truth. So please put your prejudices aside for now, and let's all focus on the true purpose of this trip. Brenna's here now at my invitation to help us find the missing text to the prophecy, and she has a good idea where it is."

Amelia shifted a hostile stare from me to her. "Where is it then?"

"I don't know for sure," Brenna answered, wincing. "I only have a strong guess that it's in the anteroom of the castle ruins Davin and I discovered years ago. It looked to be of some great importance. There were writings on the walls."

"She plans to lead us all down there tomorrow night after we talk with Rosalyn and Brian about this," I added.

"They don't know?" Amelia questioned.

"Not yet. No one knows about this. Not even Max."

She snorted. "He knows. I'm sure the nosy old codger is probably watching all of us right now through his evil crystal ball." Amelia looked around and shouted, "Got all that, grandpa?"

Frowning, Brenna leaned into me whispering, "Did she just say 'grandpa'?"

"Yeah, there's something else you should probably know."

* * *

The next night, we all packed up and headed to our vehicles with the other workers done for the day. However, we forked off as Helene and the other team members headed for the small town of Clare. We were the lead car as Brenna guided us down several unmarked roads that she remembered led to the castle ruins.

"There, up ahead," she said pointing to the right in the darkness. "Park at the end of this dirt road."

"Are you sure?" I said, craning my neck to see what she could apparently see with her supernatural wolf night vision. "I can't see a blasted thing."

"I'm sure," Brenna confirmed. "The ruins and rock tower that the old professor told Davin about should be another half mile walk down this hill. Or I suppose it was really Max Valerian in disguise who told Davin. Who is really his son." She shook her head. "So many deceptions for so many years."

"Uh, looks like we're not the only ones who found this place," I remarked, seeing the dark BMW a hundred yards ahead parked along the end of the field. "It's a little late for sightseeing the Irish countryside, isn't it?"

"It is," Marc confirmed, shutting off the ignition. "I'll check it out. Stay in the car."

"Nope," I said, opening the door.

"Dammit, Jillian. At least stay behind me then."

I twitched my lips at his protectiveness. Possessing my own magic, I could easily take care of any possible attacker. Not to mention that I had a few werewolves and a couple of vampires at my disposal to help out, if needed as well.

Still, it was a sweet gesture, so I did as requested.

The others got out of their respective vehicles, then grouped together, everyone braced for attack. That's when the driver stepped out of his own car and walked towards us.

"Davin?" I gasped when his face came into view of the headlights. I turned to Amelia. "You told him about our search here tonight?"

"Of course," she said. "He has as much right to know about this as Brenna. Besides, he can just as easily help us find our way to this secret cave of yours too."

That wasn't the point. It obviously alluded my sister that this would be the very first time in twenty-seven years that our parents faced each other after their heartbreaking separation at the Dublin airport.

I looked at Davin, then Brenna, watching breathlessly as they stared at each other, shocked and silent.

"I…how are you, Davin?" she nervously rasped.

"How do you think I am?" he stated through gritted teeth.

"Furious and upset. And you deserve to be."

"Glad to meet with your approval."

There was a long pause before Brenna broke the tense silence saying, "I'm sorry, I probably shouldn't have come. Jillian called me and…I just wanted to help the girls."

His stare narrowed at her. "Like you did when you sent them out to the four winds as infants, never to know their true heritage? Never to know me? Or you?"

"It was for their own protection," she desperately reasoned. "And yours."

"So you claim," Davin stated hard, stepping closer to her. "Why, Brenna? Tell me at least that much. Didn't you trust me enough to care for you, all of you?"

"It wasn't about you! Or me."

"Bullshit. This has always been about us and the love and life we *should* have had together that you alone decided to throw away."

I was about to intervene, but Marc barred my approach with his arm, shaking his head at me to let them talk.

He was right. This was something between my parents alone, a conversation long overdue.

Tears flowed down Brenna's cheeks when she said, "I had no choice. It was the firestone."

"Really? That's your excuse—the firestone made you do it? Made you steal it from me, manipulate me, lie to me, leave me, *keep our children from me?* Well, I hope that cursed rock has given you everything you've always desired, Brenna Callaghan, because it's the only thing of value you have now. I hope it was worth it. Goodbye."

"Is that what you believe?" She yanked something from her jeans pocket and pushed it at him as he was about to leave. "Here it is then, you stupid, stubborn vampire. Take it and good riddance! I don't want it. I never wanted it. It's been nothing more to me than a cruel reminder of what I lost, everything we both lost."

Davin held out his palm, and I saw the large garnet sitting there. He frowned at it, then at her. "I don't understand."

It started to rain, but Brenna didn't move, only hugged herself tightly as Davin stared at her with decades worth of injury and betrayal and longing and loss.

"Don't you get it yet, even after all these years?" she said with a sardonic laugh. "This gem is worthless. The moment I took hold it in that sea cave, *I* became the firestone!"

"You?"

She nodded. "All of its knowledge placed inside of it by the Ancient Ones flowed into me. I saw what would happen to our girls if we stayed together, if they stayed together as they grew up. I saw what would happen to you once this dark mage discovered our connection to them. He would mercilessly torture you to find the girls before they came of age and into their own power. I loved you too much to let that happen."

Rain dripped off Davin's face as he processed everything.

I gripped Marc's bicep and didn't let go of the breath I was holding as I watched them. My heart sped up at the softening of my father's expression.

It was happening. It was finally happening!

"Why didn't you tell me this, Brenna?" he questioned. "At least find a way to get a message to me. Something."

"I couldn't take that chance," she told him. "The knowledge stone only gave me a certain amount of information, and no more. I don't even know the identity of this dark mage wanting to kill our girls. Splitting everyone up, hiding everyone, was the only answer."

"All these years, I thought you didn't…"

She shook her head, hitched a sob. "No, Davin. It wasn't an act just to get the firestone. I loved you, really loved you. I've never stopped loving you. I never will, no matter how you feel about me now."

"My God."

Romantic that I was, I fully expected them to crash into each other and maddeningly kiss the lonely years away. So yes, I was hugely disappointed when they both remained standing in place, sharing sad, awkward smiles.

Marc slipped an arm around my waist and gave a little tug in understanding and consolation. He knew me much too well.

Well, at least the full truth had finally come to light, and peace had taken place between my birthparents now. Maybe that's more than anyone could reasonably hope for anyhow. At least at this point.

"Ahem, I hate to interrupt this happy reunion," Rosalyn said. "But the weather's turning rather grim, so we should either get on with this hunt for the old text, or call it a night and do it another time."

Davin broke his stare from Brenna and turned to us, saying, "Climbing and digging equipment will be needed. And oxygen masks. The air is practically nonexistent down in those tunnels."

"I told them everything," Brenna said. "We're prepared."

He nodded with resolve. "Then let's do this now and be done with it. According to Max, we have less than one week to solve this puzzle and stop the dark mage from ushering in something we'll all live to regret. If any of us lives at all."

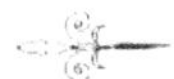

CRYSTAL MOON

CHAPTER 17

The rain stopped just after the men unloaded the needed spelunking equipment.

Davin pointed to a place out in the dark distance. "It's down there at the bottom of this ravine, hopefully still undisturbed by humans. It wasn't of interest to the locals even then. You'll see what I mean."

I and Marc didn't see anything. That was the problem. While the others forged down the grassy knoll surefooted in the black night, we switched on our flashlights and carefully picked and stumbled our way down behind the others. I hoped it wasn't going to be like this the entire way.

"There! I see it," Brenna said, pointing to a set of craggy rocks in the distance, then poured on the werewolf speed and was down there beside them in the blink of an eye.

She was touching the side of one tall, mossy boulder with amazement when the rest of us caught up with her. "It's still here."

"Where else would it go?" Davin remarked, looking up to its twenty-foot top. He pressed his palms here and there, then squatted and examined a crumbled area at its base. "The opening we made has been closed by the elements. We'll have to make another way inside."

"I can help with that," I remarked.

I called up all my magic to puncture the boulder that indeed proved to be hollow, then laser cut a five-foot hole for easier access.

"Ta da!" I announced, gesturing proudly to the opening.

Marc gave me a chiding look. Okay, so maybe I was showing off for my new parents and siblings a bit.

"Isn't she amazing?" Brenna quietly remarked to Davin.

"Very impressive. She must get her talent from your side of the family."

"Both our sides."

"Yes, right," Davin muttered angrily. "Max confessed his relation to me after he told the girls. It explains a lot in my life now."

Brenna laid a hand on his arm. "It doesn't change who you are. Or that you are still Samuel Laith's son."

"Not by blood."

"No, but by heart. That's all that really counts, isn't it?"

He smiled at her. "I suppose you're right. Thank you for that."

Brian stepped up and peered inside the dark cavern. "I don't know. It doesn't look very big inside, and the ground is solid. Are you sure this is the way into the castle itself?"

"It gets larger. And deeper," Davin said. "Jillian, you'll need to diffuse the mage magic sealing the opening."

"I'm sorry, I can't." I turned to Marc, explaining, "I figured out that it's probably guarded by blood magic."

He cursed, dragging a rough hand down his stubbled jaw. "Which means we need a full blood mage to break the spell. Damn."

Which counted both of us out, since even together we were biologically only three-quarters mage.

I turned back to Brenna and Davin. "Marc and I can't do this. There's not enough mage blood between us. Only you both have the ability to break the seal, you both together."

"Of course," Davin said, then touched Brenna's shoulder. "That's why it worked the first time. And in the cave that hid the firestone."

She grimaced at the enlarged hole in the rock. "Okay, let's try."

Brenna ducked inside, and Davin followed.

"Just like you did before," I instructed them, scanning my light beam around the cramped, cylindrical room. "There, those runes. Press both your hands on them."

At first nothing happened. Seconds later, I heard and felt the mild rumble and the blast of cold, dank air as the right half of the floor disintegrated and fell away.

"We're in!" I turned and called to the others. "Grab the oxygen masks."

I passed two to Davin and Brenna. Marc nudged me to one side to examined the newly opened cavern and frowned.

"You both repelled down the first time?" he asked.

Davin nodded. "It was about thirty-five meters down, in my estimation."

"If the flooring hasn't given way since then," Marc added. "I think we'd better nix the ropes and kick it old school magic to be on the safe side. Jillian and I can levitate everyone down, but individually. I want to conserve our energy for more urgent needs that arise."

"Agreed," Davin said. "Take me down first, so we know what to expect."

One by one we levitated everyone down into the black depths. First Davin and Brenna, then the others. Finally Marc lowered me down, then I returned the favor.

Now all together we were down in the belly of whatever ancient fortress this must have been thousands of years ago. Brenna had described it in vivid detail when she first told me the story, but it was much more disturbing and sinister than I imagined.

"Where do we go from here?" I asked, noticing several different passageways, none of them looked inviting.

Brenna checked around, then winced at Davin. "Didn't we take that corridor to the left?"

"Yes, left," Davin said. "Stay close."

"And let's hope we don't have any visitors like the last time," she murmured.

He grunted his agreement, stepping cautiously forward, Brenna bringing up his rear. I gripped Marc's belt determined that he wasn't taking one step without me, and we all trailed after them, trusting their recollection of this black, mossy, airless cavern.

Whatever happened now, at least we were all together. I only hoped that we would find our way to this anteroom, and that the elements didn't cave in any of the passageway before we reached it.

And especially after we did.

* * *

We took a few wrong turns here and there, Davin and Brenna debating a few times over their remembered direction. Frankly every vegetation riddled corridor and tunnel began to look the same to me. I would have gratefully given up this underground hike and returned to the surface, but according to the electronic directional unit Ethan carried, we were far passed the halfway mark of where they found this alleged Prophet Seat anteroom.

Davin took off his oxygen mask and tested the air, then nodded to us. "It's relatively good now. I remembered a natural ventilation system down in the anteroom, but I didn't think to test anywhere before that."

"Thank you," Rosalyn muttered, slipping off her mask with the rest of us.

"This right hallway, I think," Brenna said when we reached yet another fork in our journey.

Davin looked at both, then nodded. "You're right. We'll know for sure, because I remembered that it dipped down a few hundred feet further. Watch your step."

It did indeed drop down dramatically. The way forward was also blocked by a minor cave-in.

"Drat," I grumbled. "Now what?"

"Now, we dig," Ethan said, handing Amelia his electronic device. "Brian, Davin, want to give me a hand?"

"I can help," Marc offered as the other men began to dig and haul rocks and debris to the side.

"No, son," Davin instructed as he worked. "We have the natural strength of our species to cut the time and effort in half. I need you to conserve your energy and magic for emergencies."

By Marc's rigid nod, I saw that he accepted my father's instruction, but his male ego still took a hard hit at not being included.

Davin was right though. In fifteen minutes, they had cleared enough away for us each to squeeze our way through the new opening and continued forward.

Up and down and around we trudged. The fatigue of the day and now the night was catching up to me as I dragged my feet every new exhausting step of the way, making me sorely regret suggesting coming down here to begin with.

Marc slowed up to me and slipped his hand around my waist. "Shouldn't be much further, love. Hanging in there?"

"Oh, sure. Nothing like a casual midnight stroll with the fam."

He kissed my temple, giving my ribs a squeeze. "You're doing great."

"Yeah? Tell that to my barking feet. God, it's like a freezer down here too. Didn't the Ancient One believe in central air and heat?"

He chuckled. "Let's pick up the pace. We're lagging behind the others."

"Just a couple of ultra-slow humans. Well, mages."

"Come on, pokey."

They had in fact pulled ahead several hundred yards and had turned a corner, leaving us relatively by ourselves. I even started to enjoy the bit of solitude from the others.

Until I heard Amelia yelp and the snarling growl that proceeded it.

"Brenna, Davin!" I yelled.

Marc and I ran and turned the corner.

Then halted at the sight of an incredibly opulent, golden and ruby room, the colors reflecting off the wings and armor and swords of the shining warriors lined against the far wall and its other exit.

"Fey!" Marc yelled, shoving me behind him.

I processed the scene in a millisecond—the shredded clothes and discarded equipment, the three very large snarling wolves, the other three terrifying vampires with glowing eyes and wicked long, sharp teeth and claws, all facing off against this stacked army of beautiful beings.

Marc raised his hands to cast. I jumped to his side, ready to follow his lead.

Then as one the fey raised their gleaming broadswords.

And charged.

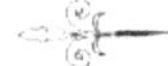

CRYSTAL MOON

CHAPTER 18

Marc cast a fireball at the center of the fey army, knocking one down. I did the same, grazing one on its shoulder. Fireball after fireball, we both shot in rapid fire motion.

The others were fighting more fey in hand-to-hand combat. One wolf caught a broadsword by the haunches, sending it wailing across the room. Another wolf was busy scratching and biting another, while the third was attacking two other fey at the same time.

The vampires weren't fairing much better. Amelia was on the back of one, going for its jugular when she was knocked off by another fey warrior. Ethan attacked it, his natural strength, picking it up and throwing it across the room to explode against the golden metallic wall.

Davin had managed to get one of the fey broadswords and was swinging back and forth with the strength, precision and expertise of one who had used this in combat before. Considering his extensive age and the multitude of wars he must have seen through the centuries, perhaps he did too.

"Marc, look!" I shouted, pointing to the far exit.

Because as many fey as we successfully eliminated, more were magically appearing to replace them. I didn't know anything about fey beings, but I didn't think they could magically appear out of nowhere.

"Mage magic," Marc said, reading my thoughts.

"What do we do?"

"Do you remember the *illuminatae tricanter* spell I taught you?" I nodded, hoping I remembered all of the words memorized. "On the count of three."

"Three," I said, not wanting to waste anymore time.

Together we raised and pointed our fingers at the glowing army, murmuring the ancient words in the language developed and recited by mage alone.

One by one, the fey began to lose steam and dim in their appearance, until every one of them at last disappeared.

"What happened to them?" Amelia said, huffing hard, some of the lethal cuts and scrapes across her face and hands already healing and disappearing.

Marc looked at me, and I shook my head at the rest of them explaining, "They weren't really here. They were just conjured images."

"They felt real to me," she said. "Ow."

Ethan took her bloodied arm and licked it, instantly healing it.

"Thanks, hon," she said.

The wolves were now in the process of shifting back to their human forms, and I magically clothed them during the process.

"Okay, let's not do that again," I suggested tiredly. "Let's just find what we're looking for in here, then get the hell out of Dodge."

The other readily agreed.

With the fey defeated, I now had a good look at this large room with gold metallic paneling, a long dais, and a high domed ceiling with ruby colored glass, dirty and cracked with age and the elements, vegetation stringing from several of the rafters.

Over at the south wall, Brenna studied what looked to me to be a cross between Egyptian hieroglyphs and ancient Nordic writing engraved into the metal panels.

"I remember these," she said, touching them gingerly. "Davin, do you remember?"

He moved beside her, studying them with a nod. "I do. I recreated what I could for Max a few months later. He confirmed that it's the language of the Ancient Ones." He looked all around, adding, "At least we're in the right place to begin our search."

Ethan checked around with shaking head. "There are no shelves or pockets in the wall for them to hide any items. I don't see how this helps us much."

I didn't either. Aside from the writing itself, I couldn't see any place that could have been made to hide anything at all.

Disappointment hit me as I looked at the picture and symbol laden walls. We had come so far and had even fought an entire army of supernatural fey warriors. We couldn't go home emptyhanded now. It just wasn't fair.

"I hate to say it, folks, but I think this was a waste," Amelia said after searching around and behind the long dais for anything of significance.

"No. We can't give up now. It's here. I know it," I said, stubbornly holding on to any morsel of hope.

"She's probably right, Jillian," Rosalyn said, laying a hand on my shoulder as I furiously studied the metallic wall.

She was, but I still refused to give up. Not until I studied every stick figure and ancient letter…

My fingers halted at the starburst type letter next to a rough looking eagle and more stick writing. Quickly I pulled my cellphone out and powered it on.

"Calling for a pizza?" Rosalyn said, chuckling tiredly. "Meat lovers for me."

"I'm not making a call," I said, then pulled up the snapshot I made of the original parchment I had taken in Helene's lab that first day.

Bingo.

"Look! Here's the same symbol or letter or whatever it is that Helene found in the geode she first cracked open," I said, pointing to the engraved symbol on the wall.

Marc and the others came up behind me and checked the photo, then the wall.

"It just represents something, Jillian," he said.

"Yeah. Us," I said. "Can you find if there are more of these starbursts around the room?"

Everyone began to quickly search the engraved symbols on the walls.

"Found one!" Rosalyn called from the western side.

"Here's another one," Ethan called from the opposite end where he and Amelia were searching.

Standing behind the dais with Brenna, Davin shook his head. "I don't see it anywhere else."

"I didn't think you would," I said. "Rosalyn, Amelia, press your palm against the starburst symbol that you're next to. Three, two, one—now!"

Simultaneously we palmed our respective symbol, and the areas around our hands glowed, and a drawer at the base of the dais itself popped open.

"Ta, da!" I said proudly.

"How did you guess?" Brenna said with amazement, while Davin the men dashed over to retrieve the rolled parchment from its hidden compartment.

"Everything else, all the writing was duplicated again and again, just like any other writing would typically be. All but this one symbol, the one found in the geode. The parchment Helene found wasn't a piece from the original text. It was a lead, a key, to help us find where the true text was hidden. And Max called us the three keys."

"Genius," Rosalyn said, giving me a high-five.

"Good. Now let's get out of here," Marc said. "The mage that sent those fey to stop us obviously knows we're down here, and I'd rather not go for a round two."

* * *

After backtracking through the cavern, thankfully with no more mishaps or unwanted supernatural attackers, we all climbed out of the turret opening and headed to our cars.

With scrolled parchment in hand, Davin said, "Let's all meet back at my hotel room in Clare. I have the largest one, and it's away from your friends from the campsite."

He then sent a slight smile to Brenna adding, "Care to come with me?"

I gripped Marc's arm, holding my breath when she nodded shyly and walked with him to his BMW. He patted my hand in understanding, then opened the passenger's door to our own car.

"Do you think my parents will get back together?" I asked as we drove the dark highway.

"Don't get your hopes up, Jillian. I know you'd like to see them back together, but it's their lives and a lot of time has passed."

"I know."

"Do you?"

"I do." I let go of a long breath, easing tiredly back in the seat. "It's a good step though, don't you think? They're talking now."

He gave me a tired half-smile. "Yes, it's a good step. Still awake?"

"Hmm? Yeah, I'm…"

I yawned large enough to feel the crack of my jaw.

Then startled awake at the gentle shake of Marc's hand on my shoulder.

I instantly straightened in my seat to see that we were now parked in a hotel parking lot.

"What happened?" I asked, checking around.

"You drifted off a few minutes. We're here now."

I followed Marc and the others up to Davin's hotel room suite. Once we were all together, Marc contacted Max who then appeared in the midst of all of us, turning an interested eye to see us all together.

"A nice family gathering, I see," he remarked, then turned to Davin and greeted, "Son, nice to see you again."

Davin snarled. "Don't ever call me that."

"Too soon?"

"It will always be too soon, you manipulative, lying bastard. The only reason you're not flying through this wall right now is that I'd rather not have my daughters believe me to be a violent man. You're only here as an interpreter and nothing more."

"Very well then," Max said with a bored expression. His gaze then traveled to the parchment laid out on the dining table held in place by several small paperweights. "I see you found what you were searching for."

"Jillian figured out the puzzle," Davin said.

"I knew she would," Max said. "Well done, my dear. I couldn't be more pleased, if you had been my own apprentice."

I glared at him, not impressed by his praise. "Can you translate it or not, Max?"

He meandered over to the dining table, then studied the writing for a long moment. I eased only slightly when Max nodded, then turned back to Davin.

"It's a rough translation at best, you understand," he began. "The language hasn't been spoken in more than eighteen hundred years, and I'm a bit rusty."

"Yes, go on," Davin said.

"First, it confirms the Red Moon Prophecy itself," Max said, then recited, *"When the Red Moon aligns with the Sun, and Mars draws his fiery sword. Then Venus will join with Jupiter, and three stars will steer the Earth."*

"Yes, I've heard this prophecy half my life," Davin said. "Please tell me that we risked our lives for more than just this common recital."

"Actually, it gives a better translation that is most helpful," Max said. "To begin with, everyone, including myself, naturally assumed that the Red Moon in the prophecy itself meant a full super blood moon, which happens during a lunar eclipse at night."

"Go on."

"But this translation gives an indication that it will take place during the middle of the day. In fact, the moon covers the sun for a total solar eclipse. But in this very rare, once in history instance, the sun will not turn black as the moon passes over it, but dark red."

"A *red* solar eclipse?" Marc repeated.

"But another solar eclipse isn't scheduled until next fall," I reminded. "We have the timing all wrong then."

Max shook his head. "This will be an unprecedented event, because a portal to the Dark Dimension will be opened, throwing everything, including our own cosmos out of order. We have, in fact, only a few more days before this is to take place, according to the added text."

"What added text?" I repeated.

"Oh, goody," Rosalyn grumbled. "I was hoping there would be more worldwide calamity and bedlam."

I arched a brow in agreement to her sarcasm. Maybe we didn't want to know. Ignorance sometimes was bliss.

"*Mars*, of course, refers to our unknown dark mage who has somehow developed the ability to open this portal to the Dark Dimension," Max continued. "Venus refers to Brenna, and Jupiter to Davin, who then created you three lovely stars."

"We know that much, Max," I said.

"The text reads that you three young women will 'steer' the earth's direction," he said, unperturbed with my interruption. "But it would be better translated as 'stop'."

Okay, now he lost me once again. I frowned at the others who all looked shook their heads in confusion as well.

Max sent us all withered stares. "No one? Really? What is this next generation coming to?"

"Max," I spat low and lethal.

"It obviously means, dear one, that you three together will be able to stop Mr. Mars from opening that portal to begin with, thus stopping the darkness that will encompass the future here. No universal disaster, no unscheduled red solar eclipse, and all will be well with no one on the earth the wiser. It will be as if the Red Moon

Prophecy was just another unfounded myth. Which happens more frequently than you can guess. Disturbing thought, I know."

I waited for more, but apparently I wasn't going to get anything.

"Does the text also say how we can accomplish this?" I asked.

"Excellent question, my dear."

"I'm glad you think so. What's the answer?"

"Find the dark mage," he said. "Once you find out who he is, then you will discover his weakness."

"Good advice. You wouldn't by chance happen to know where we might look for him."

"That's the wrong question, I'm afraid," Max answered. "You should be asking yourselves where the portal itself is hidden."

"You must know, since you're a master mage able to send others there," Amelia said.

I turned to her, knowing the answer to this one. "He's not speaking of the slight hole the mage council uses to send others there to mete out justice against our kind. Max is suggesting that there is another portal that none of the mages know about, one large enough that those sent to the Dark Dimension, as well as other monsters living there now, can come through into this world."

"Excellent, Jillian," Max said, smiling wide at my astute conclusion.

"This mage must have stumbled onto it by accident somehow," I added, then turned to Marc. "Aren't all dimensional portals underground? Do you think it's back there at the Prophet Seat?"

Marc frowned. "I doubt it. You and I would have felt something. It's vibration. Even a protection spell."

I turned back to Max. "What more does the text read?"

He turned back to it and read, "'Darkness hides in the den of the talking wolf.' Then it says something about how all three of you need to combine your abilities to bring back the light, or something to that effect."

"The talking wolf?" I repeated. "That doesn't make sense. Wild wolves have been extinct here in Ireland for over two hundred years."

"It's a metaphor perhaps," Amelia suggested. "Like we're the stars. Maybe the wolf means some kind of greedy, evil person."

"Hey, don't appreciate the comparison," Rosalyn stated.

"Sorry, I didn't mean…Actually, I have no idea what I mean."

This was getting us nowhere. If we didn't figure this last puzzle out fast, the entire world was going to suffer for our incompetence.

"What if it's a literal description," Brenna suggested, then looked to Rosalyn whose eyes grew wide. "We do talk after all."

"Werewolves," she said.

Brenna nodded. "Folklore of our kind have been around for centuries. Sometimes it's the only way normal human beings can make sense of our species when they accidently come across one of us in full or partial shift."

"Then the den of the talking wolf means *your* home," Davin said to her. "Castle Callaghan."

"Or what's left of it," she agreed. "I haven't been back there since, well, the massacre. I'm not even sure of what's left."

"Then I suggest we all take a trip across the country here and find out," I said.

Marc nodded. "I'll leave a message for Helene that we're needed elsewhere for a few days."

CRYSTAL MOON

CHAPTER 19

Marc and I were the first to arrive at the Callaghan Castle ruins. We could have, of course, just teleported ourselves and everyone there, but I sensed that all of us needed a short reprieve to collect ourselves from our previous, near deadly hunt, take a breath, and think things through. Several hours of sleep, then another six hour cross-country drive through the beautiful, green hills and valleys of Ireland had been sorely needed.

"Four more kilometers," he announced, checking the GPS.

"I wonder what we'll find there," I remarked.

"Guess we'll find out."

We drove off the main highway and continued down a winding hillside. The road was paved, but cracked and rutted with disuse and lack of maintenance over the years. Roughly rounding one final hill, the old castle finally came into view.

"Wow, there it is," I said.

Less than half of the entire structure remained. A small sadness washed over me as we passed what was left of the stone wall that surrounded the entire place and parked in front of the what would have been the entrance to the castle.

"Looks like we're the first ones," Marc said.

I stepped out and surveyed the building and structure in one wide sweep, trying to get a sense of the place. Hanging in Brenna's library, there was a painting of the castle as it would have been in its heyday, an incredible five-story structure that was now razed down to less than three stories of burnt oak and crumbling harled stone.

Amazing to think that my mother actually grew up in this place. More incredible to think that I could have been born and lived here too, if circumstances had been different. Every little girl dreams of being some fairytale princess, but I could have actually been one.

"So what do you think?" Marc asked, surveying the area.

"I'm...not sure."

There was a sense of loss at the heritage I could have experienced, one that had been stolen from me before birth. I was glad to now have my birthparents and sisters, of course, but there were still more extended family members I wished I could have known, gone now, never to even know I existed to pass down their legacy.

"Not much left," Marc commented as he walked around the immediate area, loose stones and gravel crunching beneath his shoes.

"A shame," I said with a sigh, gazing up at the dusty, split remains of the large oak door. "I wonder what it was like to grow up here."

"Brenna could answer that, I'm sure. Shall we go see more of it?"

Together we carefully picked our way around the castle ruins. I tried to imagine the people who lived and worked here, visualizing the kitchen staff bustling in and out with deliveries of food and drink, the groundskeepers carrying new flowers and tree saplings from the maintenance building to be planted.

I peered into what looked to be the old stable that had been converted into a garage for the cars and vehicles that would have replaced the horse and carriages through the centuries.

Strange, but even though the Laith estate was much larger and more grand, it was only two centuries old and had been constantly retrofitted and remodeled to modern times, tastes and conveniences. This castle fortress was older yet by three centuries and had clung to its ancient roots and character with a vengeance.

Even though it was mostly razed to the ground from the night of my family's massacre and the elements of three decades attempted to destroy the rest, still this proud, fierce castle stood as a testament to its tenacious refusal to die out completely. I felt a fierce pride flow through me at the thought.

"There's Rosalyn and Brian driving up the road," Marc said when we circled back to the front. "Looks like Brenna's with them."

They parked and stepped out of the car. The afternoon sun was still high in the cloudless sky, so the vampires were most likely keeping out of daylight somewhere else.

"Where are the others?" I asked Brenna.

"Holing up in a hotel room in town until the sun goes down," she said. "I told them we could all wait to check out the Keep after dark, but Davin reminded me that yours and Marc's night vision isn't as acute as ours, and it's probably safer for you both to explore the place when it's still daylight."

"Right. Sorry," I remarked.

"Nothing to be sorry about," she said. "Never be sorry for who and what you are, Jillian."

Brenna gazed up at the castle, then scanned the entire area with shaking head and a long sigh.

"A little different than the last time you saw it, huh?" I remarked.

"Not the very last time, actually. But yes, I get your meaning. And yes, it has sadly changed so much from its original grandeur. It was such a busy, vibrant place, and now it's nothing more than an abandoned relic and memorial."

"Shall we get to this then?" Marc prodded. "The sun will be setting shortly."

Together we explored the exterior, then finally ventured inside the castle itself, Brenna leading the way since she was familiar with its rooms and corridors.

"Careful," Marc hissed through his teeth when a rotting wood plank broke under my foot as I climbed up steps leading to the second floor. He had reflexively grabbed my waist, breaking my plummet ten feet below. "You won't do me, your family, or anyone else any good by breaking your neck."

I continued my climb behind the others to the first level of this wing which was still somewhat intact. Like many of the other areas, the floors and walls were made of brick or stone, the reason they still stood after the original fire, but were crumbling and not altogether trustworthy from age.

"That was my room," Brenna said quietly, touching an arched opening, its oak door broken and burnt.

We all walked inside after her. The ceiling was gone, as was one of the walls. What was left of any furnishings had been looted or destroyed in the fire and the ash blown away with time.

I saw the distraught look on Brenna's face as she surveyed the room with glistening eyes and gently touched her shoulder. She offered me a sad smile, and patted my hand.

"I'm sorry," I said quietly.

She shook her head. "It's just a shock to see this place again after so long. And its destruction." She pointed to the eastern wall that was no longer there. "It's gone now, but there used to be a window on the opposite side that had a magnificent view of the lake. Those trees directly below made it easier to jump down and hide from my father's guards and sneak away."

I chuckled. "You naughty rebel, you."

She grinned at me. "Yes, I tried my father's great patience more than once. He and my brother both. Although Jimmy was more understanding and sympathetic to a wolf princess locked away in a turret tower all the time and once in a great while covered for me. He even helped me escape once."

"Really? What happened?"

She smiled at the half-destroyed wall, gazing out at hillside beyond. "I had just turned sixteen. There was a local dance that I wanted to go to. A modern school dance with others my age, not the traditional town gathering. Dad didn't approve, of course, and forbade me to go.

"Knowing I would find a way anyhow, Jimmy thought it best that I do so safely under his guidance. So in the presence of my father and others who could hear and witness, he asked that I join him in his room for a game of chess."

"Chess?"

Brenna chuckled. "It was the longest game he could think of. Together we left the castle through a secret passage in his bedroom suite, and he drove me to the dance, then picked me up exactly two hours later."

"Go, mom," Rosalyn remarked, joining us. "Just two hours though?"

"That's all he was able to cover my absence. Or so he claimed. Now, I just think he didn't trust the local boys enough to have his baby sister stay longer."

"Did your dad ever figure it out?" Rosalyn asked, joining us.

Brenna shook her head. "No. At least I don't believe so. Although he did make a remark one time two months later about hearing of a girl looking very similar to me being seen in town that night, and I wouldn't know who she might be, would I?"

She laughed, adding, "My face went white as a sheet. I swear, if he had any doubts then, I had surely given myself away."

"But he never said anything?"

"No. I think Dad knew his young colts needed to kick their heels a bit from time to time. As long as he still put doubt and the fear of God into us, we would mind ourselves properly. I did after that, let me tell you. I never dared leave the castle without his knowledge again. Not until that last night, of course."

"Yes, you said you got out by some back passage in your brother's room."

"Yes, his suite was next to mine. You can't see it now, the wall itself is half gone, but that's where I got through without being detected. It took me hours, but I had scratched my way through the rock and mortar to slip inside Jimmy's room next door. My own was being guarded by order of my father."

"Why did he order that?" I asked.

"My brother's friend, Dudley, along with a few other local pack sources told me about the newly discovered Laith vampire compound,"

Brenna explained. "The race of vampires had just come out of the proverbial shadows amongst the supernaturals, you understand, so none of us trusted them. We all knew very little about their species, just the brutal folklore and myths, and assumed the worst. So I approached my father to go spy on them and discover why they were suddenly here in Ireland. Were they going to try and wipe us out and claim the territory?"

She shook her head. "My father was a diplomat first and a warrior second. He had already met with Samuel Laith, sire of the U.K. vampire coven, and tried to broker peace between our people.

"Neither I, nor Jimmy believed any vampires would abide any treaty. As the direct heir, he couldn't disobey our father and had to stand in solidarity with him. That left me alone to find out the truth. So I approached my father, and he gave me a direct order to stay put and planted a guard in front of my bedroom door to make certain I did."

"That's why you made your way into your brother's room, to leave the castle from the secret passageway."

Brenna nodded. "The castle itself was built in the seventeenth century. At that time, enemies were everywhere, especially with werewolf packs, the reason for the secured Keep itself to begin with. As such, the original High Alpha, Seamus Callaghan, built two passageways for emergency escape. One you can access from the master suite where our parents slept. The second, in the direct heir's room."

"Incredible," I remarked.

A medieval castle with secret tunnels and exits were definitely on my interest radar. Although I had to admit that it wasn't quite fair to the other members of the household not to have their own emergency escape routes in case of torch and pitchfork wielding villagers.

"So where is this famous escape route?" I asked.

Brenna picked her way carefully around the large suite of rooms, trying to visualize the old room in all of its modern opulence to the half-destroyed rock and ruins that remained. She stopped when rounding a remaining wall and pointed to the six-foot opening just beyond it.

"There, that's it," she said, eyeing it with wonder. "It was hidden behind paneling and a tapestry at the time, which I'm sure were burnt in the fire. You wouldn't even know that it was there."

"Which was its purpose, of course," I added.

"Yes," she confirmed. "I remember that it leads downstairs and through a tunnel that opens back up outside the castle walls."

"Genius," Rosalyn remarked, peering into the dark depths.

"A necessity when this place was built," Brenna remarked. "Not that it didn't have its advantages in modern times."

"Especially for young teenage girls bent on going to a local dance against her father's expressed wishes," I chuckled.

Brenna smiled wide, nodding.

"So let's go down," Rosalyn said. "I always wanted to go into some secret passage."

I looked to Marc who just shrugged. "Sure, why not? Brenna, you want to lead the way?"

"Watch your step," she said, walking towards it. "I'm not sure how damaged the…"

Brenna abruptly halted at the door. Raised her hand to touch the air.

"What's wrong?" I asked.

"It's…I don't know, I can't move forward. It's like there's some invisible wall…"

I shot a wide look to Marc who frowned as well.

"Let me try," I said.

Brenna stepped aside, and I started to walk through the opened doorway, immediately brought up short by the same invisible field that stopped her. I raised my palm and pressed it forward. I fully expected to feel a vibrating field barring us. Instead, there was a painful shock that made me yelp and shake out my hand.

"Ow!"

"What is it?" Marc asked.

"The blasted thing bit me."

"Mage protected then?" he ventured.

"Feels like it, but I don't see how. Or why. Unless…"

Unless we were closer to the hidden portal to the Dark Dimension than we thought.

I closed my eyes and called up my magic, then pressed both hands on the invisible wall, forcing myself to handle the sparking burns it was giving me. Ten seconds, and it gave way and nudged forward. A little more, and the spell completely dissolved, exposing a draft of dank, musty air.

"There we go," I breathed with relief, again shaking out my hands. "Hope we don't encounter too many more of those."

"It was mage-locked then," Marc commented. "I'm not sure if I like that."

"Neither do I, but it's a good sign we're heading in the right direction. Let's go."

He barred my step forward, saying, "Let me at least take the lead."

"No arguments from me. Lead on."

Marc pulled the flashlight from his back pocket and switched it on, then proceeded forward into the darkness. Swallowing hard, I gripped the back of his belt and kept close as we cautiously descended the circular stone stairs.

"The end of this is not far down," Brenna quietly reassured us from behind. "Just one level. Then it leads through a very short underground tunnel that resurfaces just outside the castle walls. Or what's left of them anyhow."

We hit the ground floor, and Marc shined his light beam to the tunnel still in its place. I was more interested in the closed oak door beside it.

"What's behind this?" I asked.

"Probably a storage room of some kind," Brenna said.

"You don't know?"

"I never had the inclination to find out," she said. "The last two times I was down here, I was more concerned on getting away."

There strangely wasn't any handle or knob to open it with. I pressed my palms on the thick planks and felt static vibrations.

"I think this is mage-locked, too."

Marc shined his beam at the door, then came up and pressed his own palm. "I don't feel anything."

Brenna walked up and felt the door. "Actually, I feel it, too."

I pressed my palm against it, definitely feeling the stabbing crackle. Rosalyn joined us and nodded as well.

There a gut-dropping click that made us all jump back.

And the door opened.

"Whoa," I muttered, stepping beside Marc. "Now *I'm* getting a bad feeling about this."

"Maybe we should leave," Brenna suggested.

Marc nudged in front of us. "Let's see what's in there first."

"Hey, didn't anyone ever tell you never to go down into the dark, scary basement?" I nervously remarked.

He cracked a half-smile at me. "Chicken?"

"Buk, buk, buk."

He chuckled, shining the flashlight into the room. "Stay out here then."

I groaned, knowing he knew me too well. "Nothing doing. You jump, I jump, Jack."

"Stay behind me anyhow."

"Gladly."

All of us cautiously entered the long room. I was just making out the odd furnishings of the room when Marc's flashlight blinked out, throwing us all into utter blackness. I yelped and grabbed his belt as he pounded the flashlight. Giving up normal human methods, he snapped his fingers and the room was suddenly lit with candles and electric lanterns.

"Okay, this was unexpected," I remarked as I gazed around the large dungeon room.

It looked very reminiscent of Max's working lab, but more ancient than modern. By the various books and scrolls and paraphernalia, this was definitely a place where magic was experimented with. I pressed against one of the stone walls and felt the protection spells inside of them.

"Brenna, when Rhiona was your pack's sorceress ambassador, did she have a special place where she practiced her magic?" I asked.

She nodded, frowning at the place. "Yes, but not here. She never lived in the castle, but kept her own place in the Wicklow Mountains. Besides, Rhiona is a naturalist, and the forest gave her inspiration. This…no, she wouldn't have come down here, much less worked down here. It would have creeped her out."

If not her, then who?

I hugged myself tightly as I wandered the room. Something seemed…off.

"Hey, does anyone else notice that this place isn't dirty," I remarked.

Not a single cobweb or dusty book or anything to say that it had been closed off for twenty-six years or more.

Brian's police detective instincts were moving him to examine everything with precision. He picked up a local newspaper and showed it to everyone. It was dated less than three weeks ago.

"Someone's been down here. Recently," he stated.

"And whoever this belonged to, knew your family personally," Marc commented.

He held up a photograph that was sitting on a shelf.

Brenna walked up to him and took it, nodding. I joined them and saw the colored photograph of her between two blond men.

And my stomach dropped.

"Me, my father and brother," she explained.

My head spun in stunning horror. "Your brother, Jimmy."

"Yes," she said.

"James Nolan."

"Yes. How did you know his second name?" she asked.

That hard fact triggered something inside my logjammed brain, and like a volcanic eruption, all of my memories exploded at once. Suddenly I remembered everything about my past—every year, every person, every moment that led up to the night of the car accident that stole my memories and nearly took my life.

But didn't.

Causing my uncle, James Nolan Callaghan, to cast me into a permanent sleep-curse so that I wouldn't interfere with his plans to open up his newly discovered portal to the Dark Dimension and unleash unholy hell onto this unsuspecting world.

CRYSTAL MOON

CHAPTER 20

"It's here then. The hidden portal," I remarked with horror.

The others looked around the room with morbid fascination. None being active mages themselves, they had only an inkling of the nightmare this signified. Marc and I did, especially now that I had all of my memories back.

A huge part of me cringed at the idea of my unwilling involvement in aiding Jim Callaghan's plot to open this black portal. He accidentally discovered his magical abilities inherited from his mother's mage genetics and lusted after much greater power than merely becoming the future High Alpha of his werewolf pack.

Jim then sought out an ambitious mage who agreed to train him covertly for his own greedy purposes. Until the apprentice became the ruthless master and successfully sent his unwitting pawn mentor to the Dark Dimension through the hidden portal that he discovered below their very castle home.

"I remember now," I said. "Jim told me that he studied the old texts and the Red Moon Prophecy in specific. He wanted to be the one who opened the portal fully and ruled the earth with an iron rod and an army of demons under his control."

But his father Quinn Callaghan nearly squashed his plans by brokering peace with the Laith vampire coven.

Jim interpreted the texts correctly that the three stars would consist of mage, werewolf and vampire blood, but as long as vampires and wolves remained enemies, the "three stars" would never be conceived.

"He was the one who orchestrated the massacre of your own pack," I said to Brenna, "then laid the blame on the Laith vampire coven. He fanned the hate flames, even with you. Only he didn't count on you remembering the secret exit from his room and escape the castle during the slaughter by his controlled vampires."

"My God, you're right," she said. "I discovered another sorceress posing as Rhiona trying to stop my efforts in locating the firestone, but Rhiona always believed she was working for someone else even more powerful."

"A master mage," I added. "Jim Callaghan, your brother."

But Jim Callaghan's plan backfired. His little sister didn't die with the rest of his pack during the massacre. She instead escaped the castle before the attack in order to seek out and kill the Laith true blood heir in revenge. And in the process learned his coven had nothing to do with the massacre and became his trusted partner in seeking their common enemy.

Then trust evolved into love, which gave birth to the three stars with equal portions of mage, vampire and werewolf blood.

"Then Jim didn't die that night with everyone else," Brenna said, still wrapping her mind around this.

"I can verify myself that he's alive and well," I stated viciously. "He tried to manipulate me to become one of his mindless minions."

When Rhiona's memory loss spell dissolved on our twenty-fifth birthday, the frequencies were clear enough for a master mage like Jim Callaghan to see that the three stars of the Red Moon Prophecy were the unknown daughters of his own sister and Davin Laith.

A brilliant statistician, he decided an even more effective plan would be to gain one of those daughters' complete loyalty. It took just a drop of his own familial blood and gaze into his own crystals to hone in onto his niece whose flash magic had just come into fruition.

But instead of approaching me to apprentice himself, he sent one of his own protégés, Doug Hayden, to do the work, thus keeping his own identity safe. Until Jim decided it was time he approached and convinced me to join him.

"I knew his plan was dark and ugly and wrong when he explained it to me in whole," I continued. "I wanted to covertly go to the mage council and tell them everything."

"Why didn't you?" Marc asked.

"I was going to," I said to him. "But I made the mistake of trying to convince Doug on the way home one night to go with me, to back up my unbelievable story. That's when his attraction spell over me dissolved, and I learned the full truth of what was happening."

I rubbed my forehead roughly. "He vanished from the driver's seat and let the oncoming diesel truck hit me head-on. If not for the protection spell Rhiona cast on us as babies, I probably would have been killed then and there. But I survived. So Jim himself put me under a death-sleep curse, hoping I would at least stay under until the time of the Red Moon Prophecy passed, and it would be too late."

Still thinking it over, it must have shocked and infuriated Jim that I had woken from his curse. It was only sheer luck for him that I woke with no memories of our connection. So he contrived to create a false narrative that Doug and I were happily engaged and living together in his hometown. They must have done a massive group cast over the entire neighborhood to back up their story when I finally came home.

And their plan to keep me ignorantly in the dark might have worked, if it hadn't been for Marc coming back to me from the future to wake me and launch me off on my quest for the truth.

"Where is Hayden now?" Marc stated through his teeth.

I shook my head. "It doesn't matter. The damage has already been done."

"He's very dead when I catch up with him," he stated with clenched fists.

"Right now, we have more important things to do," I said. "You and I need to go back to Max's lab, or all of this is over anyhow."

"Why? What do you mean?"

"You have to go back and wake me from my sleep curse, or none of this will matter. Jim will win just by waiting out the clock. But now that I know who cast the curse, Max will be able to find a counter spell."

"Okay, you're still not making any sense, Jillian."

"Max discovered the ability to time travel. And that I'm the key to sending you back."

***

I starkly felt Marc's accusing glare on me after looking at the geodes lined against the wall of Max's work lab.

"And you kept this from me," he stated after I explained everything.

"For your own protection."

God, I sounded like my mother now.

But I understood her precarious position a little better now, too. Keeping anything from Marc, the one I loved most, had eaten and gnawed away at me for days. I couldn't imagine how Brenna lived with her own betrayal and lies to Davin for years, decades.

He shot a narrowed stare at Max adding, "I'll never forgive you for putting her in this position, old man."

Max hiked his brows. "It's her destiny, Zander. You of all people know we can't keep it from her. She was born to do this."

"The hell she is!"

Marc launched himself with fists at the mage who merely held up his hand. Marc's fists then slammed into an invisible shield, breaking his knuckles.

"Max, stop it!" I yelled, running up to them.

He arched a brow at me. "He started it."

"Very mature," I grumbled, then waved my hand over Marc's hand, instantly healing it.

"That's one, Valerian," Marc growled, shaking out his stiff fingers.

"You watch your temper," I chided him. "Besides, he's right. I still don't know how to stop Jim Callaghan from opening up that portal, or even where it is. But I can't do anything, if you don't go back in time to wake me up and convince me to find you in the first place."

"Are you sure he even went back in time, Jillian? He's well known for his smoke and mirrors and could have tricked you into believing he did."

Max hiked his brows, twitching a slight smile.

It then occurred to me that Marc might be right, that Max had deceived me into thinking he went back in time. It's not like I had proof that he did, other than his own word.

I probably never could know the truth, but I did know without doubt that Marc himself had come back to save me. Even if that's all I had to go on, it was still enough to grant me that bit of faith.

"I know it's a big risk, but do you love me enough to do it anyhow?"

Marc cupped my cheek with his hand. "I would cross time and dimensions for you, Jillian Azure. I love you with my entire being, now and forever."

"Then please go back in time and wake me up and convince me of this timeless love we share. You're the only one who can."

Marc kissed me softly, thoroughly, then heaved a long breath and turned to Max. "Did you figure out the counter spell?"

"Yes," he said, handing Marc a written slip of parchment. "It's a simple, but drawn out one. Memorize it. You only have fifteen to twenty minutes with each trip."

"Each trip?" Marc echoed turning to me.

"Yes," I said. "Three. The first one is to wake me up. The second is to keep me awake, because Jim tries to put me under again."

"The bastard. Okay, and what do I do on the third trip?"

I snapped my fingers and handed him my original pink rose quartz crystal stick that I rediscovered my magical abilities with. "Give this to me and tell me to find you. Tell me to 'follow the bread crumbs.'"

"What does that mean?" he asked.

"I'll know. Or I'll figure it out. I'll need to figure all of this out on my own, or I can't come to this place of full knowledge now. I know, it's a paradox. Please do it anyhow."

He memorized the parchment and handed it back to Max. Then he cupped the back of my head and kissed me again, this time hard and desperately.

"I love you, Jillian Azure. See you soon."

"Make sure you come back to me, Magic Man."

"I promise," he said, then gave a nod to Max.

Max handed him the geode. "I'll recite the incantation. Jillian, you just concentrate on the place where he needs to be sent."

I placed my hands beneath Marc's on the rock, closed my eyes, then concentrated with all of my strength, envisioning that day in the hospital when I opened my eyes to a frightening and unfamiliar world. Until Marc Zander had entered it.

Max murmured the same ancient words I heard him utter before during the first test.

The geode vibrated, cracked.

And Marc disappeared in a vapor of blue smoke.

The emptiness I felt without him in this present time period was overwhelming. I nearly lost my breath when raw fear of our failure. What if we had just sent Marc to the wrong time, the wrong place, maybe even into some eternal oblivion?

How was I to know?

"Don't worry, my dear" Max said, laying a hand on my shoulder. "Time doesn't pass at the same length where he's sent. If Zander is successful, he will be back here in approximately…" He checked his gold watch. "Three more minutes."

"And if I didn't send him to the right place or time?"

Max's jaw muscles bunched as he remained silent.

Right. Marc wouldn't reappear at all. Ever again.

"Steady," he said as the seconds slowly ticked by.

"Easy for you to say."

"Probably."

He glanced at his watch, then up at me again. I couldn't swear, but thought I saw a flash of concern…

There was a vacuumed pop, and Marc suddenly appeared in front of us, staggering a bit. Both Max and I let go of a breath of relief.

Marc scooped me into his arms and kissed me hard. Relieved, I held him tightly against me for a long moment, until Max cleared his throat and we broke apart.

"We don't have all the time in the world, if you forgive the pun. Were you successful, Zander?"

Marc nodded. "She's awake. Damn, if I wasn't tempted to go strangle both your uncle and his disciple with my bare hands when I saw them in the hospital corridor."

"They didn't see you though, did they?"

Marc shook his head. "I was careful."

"Good. Time for round two then."

As before, he handed Marc the second geode, and I took hold of it and concentrated on the right time and place to send the love of my life to bring me back from the dead-sleep, while Max murmured the incantation.

Again, the geode vibrated and cracked, and Marc disappeared into a puff of smoke.

"Only three minutes?" I remarked to Max.

He twisted a sympathetic smile. "Four, total. This time should be easier."

"But not shorter."

Funny how eternally long four minutes could be when waiting to find out whether the love of your life was alive and would come back to you, or be lost in the utter void of the universe forever.

God, I hated time travel.

"No wonder Marty McFly destroyed his DeLorean," I muttered.

"Who's Marty McFly?" Max asked.

I shook my head, not in the mood to explain modern pop culture to a two-millennial.

Marc reappeared after another vacuumed pop, and everything within me relaxed again. He nodded to Max of the success of his trip, then turned to me.

"One last time, then you should be well on your way to regaining your life and achieving your goals, Jillian," he said.

"Let's make this last geode count. There aren't any more." I clasped my hands in Marc's and kissed them. "Remember, you have to do anything you can to convince me to find you. Tell me to go to the university, to 'follow the bread crumbs.'"

"I will." He kissed me, holding my cheek in his hand. "I'll be right back."

Max started to hand me the last whole geode, then jumped back when there was another vacuum pop, and yet another Marc Zander staggered in front of us.

"Wow, I swear I almost didn't make it that time," he said. "Let's hope the next..."

I jumped back, looking from one Marc to the other. "W-what's going on?"

The first Marc shoved me behind him protectively, raising his hand like a weapon, ready to cast. "A glamor, I suspect. Stay behind me."

"Whoa! Wait!" the other said, holding both his hands up. "Jillian, it's me. He's the phony."

"Yeah, nice try, Callaghan," my Marc said, keeping me behind him as he backed up. "Keep back, or I'll blast you to Antarctica."

I didn't know who to believe, which one was the real Marc Zander. Until I looked down at his back jeans pocket.

I whipped a pointed stare to Max. He narrowed his eyes and gave an imperceptible nod.

Then tossed the geode to the other Marc.

He caught it with both hands, and I shoved the false Marc to the ground and dashed towards the real Marc Zander, the one who had my crystal still in his pocket.

"Now, Jillian!" Max yelled.

The glamor fell off the false Marc to reveal Doug Hayden who yelled and launched himself at us. Max pointed his hand and zapped Doug, who reflexively defended himself by zapping back, hitting Max between the eyes—a mage death blow.

"Max!" I yelled as he collapsed to the ground.

I ran over to him, bent down, pressed a healing hand on his forehead, but I could feel the lifeforce slipping from him fast.

"Stay with me, grandpa. Please."

"Lair. Not…den. In his…"

Max's body went limp. His eyes glassy and staring vacantly.

"Noooo!"

"Jillian, now! Send me back now!" Marc yelled.

Weeping, I jumped up and ran to Marc still holding the geode, then pressed my palms to the craggy rock. Closing my watery eyes, I did my best to recall and recite the correct incantation, then used every last ounce of strength I had left and blasted it into the geode.

It vibrated, cracked.

Marc disappeared.

And I was left alone inside my mage grandfather's workroom, facing a furious, magical ex-fiancé.

CRYSTAL MOON

<u>CHAPTER 21</u>

"God, the hours and hours I wasted on you," Doug said, as we side-stepped each other, both of us with hands raised to cast. "Training you. Teaching you. And this is thanks I get? You turn on our master at the first opportunity."

"Callaghan may be your master, but he's definitely not mine, Hayden," I said, trying to figure a way out of this.

He tsked. "Hayden, is it now? I remember a time when you called me 'master'. Particularly in bed. And on the couch. And the kitchen table. Yes, you were quite submissive to my thorough training then. Remember, dear heart?"

I did then, cringing at the sudden memories. Yes, there had been times, lots of them.

"It was just the attraction spell you cast," I remarked. "I'd never be with such a revolting man like you under my own power."

But those spells are tricky and have a limited lifespan, days at best. He must have continued casting it, again and again, keeping me chained to him like some caged animal.

Doug grinned. "Very good, Jillian. Sorry, had to do it. It was Jim Callaghan's wishes that I train you, and you weren't warming up to my advances in any natural way."

"You are one sick pervert."

"Oh, not at all," he went on. "Personally, I didn't want to have anything to do with you, but for some reason he insisted, and I couldn't disobey my holy master. Honestly, I don't see why he bothered trying to turn you to our side. You weren't anything special, just some freak girl with a drop of mage blood."

He shrugged as we continued to circle each other. "You know, Master Callaghan was still willing to give you a second chance when you woke from the sleep-curse. I would have guessed that he had a thing for you, but he asked me to pose as your fiancé, so I have no idea why now. A shame. You could have ruled with us in the dark age to come, Jillian. You could have had it all, but you just thew it away."

"I'll happily do it again too, you sick bastard!"

"Fine by me. Glad to be rid of you myself. You've been a pain my ass from the very first."

I was losing time fast. Two more minutes, and Marc would pop back into our presence. I had no doubt that Doug planned to take him out on reentry as well.

"Goodnight, sweetheart," he said, then cast a death ray at me.

I threw up a shield, and the red laser bounced off the invisible wall and exploded up through the ceiling.

"Not bad, not bad," Doug said, eyeing me speculatively. "I did train you well after all. But how about this one, dear heart? Watch your step now."

He zapped the floor, and the tiles around my feet gave out, and I dropped into an endless void. I fell into blackness and continued falling and falling. Gathering my wits, I poured on my own magic that stopped my descent, then rocketed my body back up and onto the room's solid floor.

Just as Marc popped back into the room as well.

"Watch out!" I screamed at him.

But Marc had been ready to fight and cast on his reentry and honed in on Doug, zapping and knocking him across the room. Doug jumped up and cast his own laser beam at Marc who deflected it, rolling on his side and jumping back up to shoot another bolt of lightning at him.

On and on it went, back and forth, both casting and deflecting in some bizarre, magical western shootout, everything around the room exploding with every hit. Their movements were so fast and precise that I didn't dare intervene, fearing I would cast and hit the wrong person at the wrong moment.

Frantically I searched around, trying to think of something, anything that would help. The sunlight caught and glittered the burgundy amethyst crystal inside half of a cracked geode. Max said these were special, and apparently they were, if they successfully helped Marc travel back in time.

But their natural power was spent now, so they weren't of any use. Unless…

Unless their elemental power *wasn't* completely spent.

Both men distracted with their own battle, I launched myself at the closest geode half and pointed it at Doug. Pouring all of my furious power into it, with a warrior's yell, I cast my own white laser light at my false fiancé.

The lightning bolt hit him upside the head, knocking him to the side, allowing Marc's own electrical bolt to hit him in the chest.

"Quick, Jillian! Bind him! Now!" Marc yelled.

I twirled my hand and bound Doug with glowing electrical ropes from neck to ankle as he cursed and squirmed against them like a caterpillar trying to fight its way out of a cocoon. Marc then levitated his struggling body high into the air.

"Here's for trying to kill the woman I love and reason for my existence," Marc stated through clenched teeth.

With a growl, he shoved his arms forward, the force of his magic crashing Doug's frame out the glass window and into the azure blue sky. I ran up to see the still squirming, bound body hover above the glittering Mediterranean ocean in the far distance, then drop like a rocket down into its depths.

"Don't worry," Marc said. "He won't break those bonds until he speaks to the fishes for the very last time."

I threw my arms around Marc's neck and wept. He just held me tightly.

Suddenly remembering, I sucked in a sharp breath and ran over to Max, bending down to his collapsed form and felt for a pulse. Finding none.

"He's dead," I announced with a hitched sob.

There was a part of me that grieved his death deeply. He was after all my grandfather, and the one who was indirectly responsible for my birth, for my protection, and for helping me discover my greatest gifts. He loved me in his own way. And I would miss him.

"I'm sorry, love," Marc said, standing beside me. "Max said he would die before all this was over."

"You knew this would happen?" I jumped to my feet, furious. "You knew and didn't tell me that my own grandfather was going to be killed?"

Rescuing me.

In the end, Maximum Valerian had done the honorable thing and sacrificed his own life for mine. And maybe for the rest of his family, now and in the future.

"Sorry, Jillian. He made me swear not to tell. It was for your own protection."

Ironic. I hoped there would come a time when none of us felt this need anymore.

I swiped at my wet cheeks. "Come on. We need to get back to the others. I know where the portal is. More importantly, I think I know how to stop my uncle from opening it."

* * *

Marc and I popped back onto the grounds of Castle Callaghan. Davin, Amelia and Ethan had arrived prior to this and were with the others. As one, they all rushed up to us. Brenna desperately embraced me, Davin embracing us both and kissing my head.

"I thought I lost you again," Davin rushed out.

"Hi mom and dad," I said breathlessly, breaking from their hold. "Love the warm family hugs, but this is going to have to wait 'til later. Jim Callaghan knows we know about him now, so I expect he'll be showing up here at any moment."

"Where should we go?" Brenna asked me.

"And what's our next step?" Davin added.

The others waited for my answer too. It was nice their confidence leadership was so strong, but I wasn't so sanguine.

"We stay here," I said. "The portal to the Dark Dimension is right here in Uncle Jim's underground hideaway. At least I think so."

"But we already checked there," Rosalyn remarked.

I shook my head. "Not every place. I believe Max was trying to tell me that before he…"

I choked on the words, unable to voice them. Strange that a man I hadn't known most of my life could make a huge impact in such a short amount of time. I would miss the arrogant old mage.

"Honey, what is it?" Brenna asked, gripping my arm.

I turned to Davin with blurring eyes. "Max is…gone. He saved my life, all of ours in the process, if that counts for anything."

Davin's expression darkened as his jaw muscles bunched. He merely nodded at the news, refraining from saying anything.

I turned back to the matter at hand. "We need to get back down to Jim's workroom and find that portal. It's somewhere inside there, I know it."

"Then what?" Amelia asked as we all headed around the corner of the ruins.

"I'm not sure. Guess we'll figure that part out next."

At least I hoped so.

* * *

Brenna showed me the opened tunnel door a quarter mile from the outer castle wall. It was partially hidden behind vines and bracken.

"Here's where the escape passage leads out," she explained. "The tunnel itself is the same one I showed you next to Jim's secret workroom. Some of the area is caved in slightly, but it's still clear enough to get through."

"It'll do. Let's go," I said.

Marc and I could have popped us all inside the underground workroom, of course, but I was tiring and he suggested I rest my magic until it was truly needed. The power behind our magic wasn't inexhaustible, and I was still relatively new at this, so I didn't argue his logic. I would need all the energy and magic I could muster for the critical event to come.

Walking through the dark, stone encased tunnel was too reminiscent of our cavern expedition back at Spanish Point. Nervously I kept close to Marc, his arm banding me against him as we walked behind the others.

It wasn't a long hike, and soon we were standing in the same place we teleported from. The workroom door was closed again.

"Why did you close the door?" I asked.

Brenna frowned at others, then shook her head at me. "We didn't. It was open when we left."

I shot a look to Marc who read my expression. Tentatively I pressed my palms to the thick oak planks.

Then was violently thrown backwards, my hands burning with the massive shock they received.

"He knows," Rosalyn said ominously.

I frowned, picking myself up. "He's here."

"Then the portal is inside, or Callaghan wouldn't be guarding it," Marc said, hovering his hand around the door. "I can definitely feel the mage magic burning through it. He's just waiting out the clock until the portal itself opens."

"What do we do now then?" Amelia asked.

Brenna looked at me for the answer. So did my sisters.

Why did everyone assume I had all the answers? If I did, I wouldn't have been deceived by my evil uncle and his sick minion in the first…

"God, why didn't I remember?" I remarked, then fixed my stare with Marc's. "Max's last words to me was to tell me something about how to counteract Jim's power. Whatever it is, it's in his *lair*, not his den."

"Which he's sealed up tight," Marc reminded.

I shook my head, gesturing with my hands. "No, I never knew about this place, because I had never been here to begin with. This isn't where Jim Callaghan practices his true black magic, his real lair. I know, because Doug took me there to meet him for the very first time when I finally passed his mage training.

"It was there Jim explained his plans for the future and offered me a place to rule beside him in his future dark world."

"Can you get us all there?" Marc asked.

I shook my head. "Maybe you and me at best. My powers have been greatly depleted from our last bout."

"Let's go then."

Brenna hugged me again, whispering, "Please be careful. I can't lose you again."

"I will, Mom. See you in a bit."

I waved to the others, then nodded to Marc. He slipped his arm around me, then flicked his other hand, popping us out of the Castle Callaghan's basement.

CRYSTAL MOON

<u>CHAPTER 22</u>

And into a very modern laboratory that would make the scientists at JPL envious.

"He has all the latest and greatest equipment, I'll grant him that," Marc commented as he picked up and put down various devices.

"We have to find something here to defeat his own mage magic," I said, rifling through books on the various shelves, both new and ancient. "There has to be a spell or relic that will keep him from opening the portal to begin with."

"And if there isn't?" he remarked as he helped me search, flipping through old leatherbound grimoires and opening scrolls.

"There has to be something. You told me when we were training that no matter how much magic a mage knows, there is always someone out there who knows more."

"In this case, that one person would be Max Valerian, but he can't exactly help us now."

"He did, though. Max said for us to look here for the answer to Callaghan's ability to open the portal. Maybe we could find its chinks, his weakness, something to counter it."

"Keep looking then. We're running out of time."

"Yeah, yeah. God, I hate the 'T' word. Never say it to me again."

I frowned, moving to a work desk in the corner, rummaging through a stack of papers by the computer terminal. I noticed two handmade ceramic wolves and picked one up, seeing the childish scrawl reading Brenna's name. They both sat next to the framed photograph of Jim and Brenna as young teenagers, his arm lounging across her shoulders as they smiled for the camera.

"That's it," I whispered.

Jim Callaghan's true weakness—family.

He may have had mage blood, but he was still half-werewolf. Raised as the alpha heir to his pack, he could never get away from his genetics or upbringing or primal instincts that a wolf valued his family above everything else. Having killed his father and entire pack and chased his only sister into hiding, Jim suffered the overwhelming loneliness of being an Omega—a lone wolf. For almost three decades.

Until he discovered me—his niece, his family.

Like him, I was part-mage, part-wolf. Just like the sister he loved and lost, I could fully understand him. And he was no longer alone.

That's why he wouldn't let Doug Hayden kill me, instead training me, offering me to rule beside him instead of his own apprentice, his minion.

I was his ultimate weakness.

Now I knew what I was searching for—the counter to Jim's mage blood spell that would open the portal. As his family, it would probably take all three of us, his nieces to ignite it. That's why we were the three keys. Not to unlock—but to lock the portal back up.

"We need to find something referring to the original prophecy itself," I rushed out.

Both of us frantically flipped through page after page and book after book of the ancient texts. Marc cursed and dragged a hand roughly through his mussed hair after tossing the last book across the room.

"Maybe what we're looking for is back at the other workroom," I suggested.

He shook his head. "If this is Callaghan's main lab, he would keep his most valuable and secret documents here for safeguarding. The only reason we were able to break in here now is that you and he share the same blood."

"Right. So where would I hide the ancient secrets of the universe, if I were him?" I remarked.

"Not here. We searched everything."

Yes, we did. Then where?

Biting my bottom lip, I surveyed the entire room, considering the possibility of him creating a secret compartment like the Ancient Ones did with the parchment we found recording the prophecy.

Of course, we weren't living in the second century now.

And Jim Callaghan was a modern man not much older than my own mother.

"Oh God, right under our noses," I muttered.

I dashed back to the desk and powered on the computer. It was password protected, but an easy hack for someone with computer skills like myself, along with a touch of blood magic. I keyed a few entries, touched the screen, and cracked the code.

"Okay, we're in," I said. "Not sure where to go from here."

"My turn."

Marc nudged me aside touched the screen, and data flickered and rolled across the screen at lightning speed until it finally stopped at the heading of *Red Eclipse*.

It was a scan of the original text in its mage language. Jim had definitely studied it then, adding his own notes and calculations.

What was more disturbing as Marc scrolled down the document was the attached dossiers on Rosalyn, Amelia, and myself. All were very detailed, including the DNA reports on each of us, linking us together and with Brenna and Davin.

He knew we were all equally vampire, mage and werewolf then, identifying us as the three stars, the keys to opening his portal to the Dark Dimension.

No, not opening—*closing*.

And locking for good.

"Here it is," Marc pointed to a place he scrolled to. "It's the incantation to opening the portal."

"We can't stop him from opening it," I remarked with dread. "So how do we close it?"

"The counter to any spell is just the original said backwards," Marc explained. "Sort of an undo or refresh button, along with your familial blood. We need to you get back to the castle now and find that portal before your uncle returns to find you missing."

CRYSTAL MOON

CHAPTER 23

"Any luck?" Davin said when Marc and I popped back inside the castle passage beside the others.

"Some. But you don't want to know what," I remarked.

"We need to get this door open, Jillian," Marc said. "You and your sisters can't do anything until we get inside and locate the portal opening."

Cautiously I approached the door again, slowly raising my palms to it. Even a foot away I could feel the electrostatic vibrations reaching out to shock me backwards.

"No good," I said, lowering my hands. "If we're to get inside, it has to be by another route."

"I don't remember any other door or window the last time we checked," Rosalyn said.

I turned to Brenna. "Are there any other secret passages inside the castle? Any unusual exits at all?"

"The other one from the master suite, of course," she said. "But that would have been from the top floor which has been leveled."

"Your father's and brother's were the only two then? Are you sure there were no other emergency exits?"

"Not that I remember." Brenna thought, then her expression widened. "Wait, I did stumble upon a strange entryway once when I was helping the kitchen staff with a holiday dinner. There was an odd looking door through a thin cut-through inside the pantry room. The whole thing was mostly blocked by crates of food at the time, and I was too busy to care about where it led. I have no idea if it was anything at all, or if it's still even there."

"Show me."

We all raced back up the circular stone staircase, then down again to the first floor, following Brenna as she jaunted through several rooms into the kitchen area.

"The pantry and storage room were back here behind the ovens," she said, dodging several half-walls, making her way around other obstacles and debris.

"Through there, if you can even get through," she said, pointing at the extremely narrow hallway.

There was indeed a small door at the far end of the thin, brick passage. Why it was there was a question in itself. It would be difficult enough for one person to slide through to even get to it.

This might be something all right. Trying to picture myself as a seventeenth century lord consulting his architect in the construction of his castle, I wouldn't have relied solely on one escape route in and out. Not in my own suite, or my heir's.

"This could connect to Jim's passage, through his workroom," I suggested. "We might be able to get inside through there."

"Wouldn't this be mage protected too?" Amelia remarked.

I shook my head. "Not if Jim didn't know about it. Brenna didn't. The knowledge of the secondary escape route may have been lost with the generations."

"Worth a shot," Rosalyn remarked, then looked at me and Amelia. "I'll go. No offense, but I'm skinnier than either of you, and a lot stronger too."

"Debatable," Amelia said snidely. "But go ahead."

Rosalyn squeezed herself through the thin passageway until she reached the end. Then with a heavy, huffing shove with her shoulder, the thick oak door gave way and opened to yet another dark corridor.

"It's open," she called back. "Looks like this other tunnel leads to someplace anyhow."

One by one we all squeezed our way through the narrow cut-through and gathered into the much wider stone corridor. All together we walked its descending floor around several bends until reaching nothing but a stone wall.

"Well, that was a bust," Rosalyn remarked. "What now?"

I studied the wall, touched the rocks. I felt no electrical vibrations, but I was still convinced that I was right.

"There wasn't another doorway into Jim's workroom," Marc reminded me.

"It could've been hidden or camouflaged with a glamor."

"Possibly."

I studied the solid rock and mortar wall, damp and dusty with time and the elements. I felt so sure that I was right, that we had been onto something. Why build a tunnel behind a door from the kitchen area if you didn't mean for it to lead anywhere?

I turned to Marc saying, "What if this does lead to the other workroom, but the passageway was never completed? That's why there's no door here, and it's not mage protected. Jim doesn't know that it's even here!"

"A big stretch, Jillian," he said.

"Doesn't matter either way," Brian remarked. "We can't get through to find out what's on the other side."

Marc and I smiled at each other.

"I'll do the honors," he said. "I want you to conserve your energy for the real need to come."

"Blast away," I said.

He pointed his right hand to the wall and a red laser streamed from his fingers, effectively cutting a nice sized hole for each of us to climb through.

Straight into Jim Callaghan's personal home workroom.

* * *

"It's empty," I said looking in all directions. "Where is he, the sneaky rat? Are you hiding somewhere here, uncle dearest?"

Marc felt the air in various places, shaking his head. "He's definitely not here, not even in disguise."

"Then we're good," Rosalyn said, brightening. "We've caught the little weasel before he opened the portal. What should we do now?"

I shook my head, whispering, "I don't know. This doesn't feel right. Knowing this man and his determination, there's no way he would make things this simple for us."

"Maybe we just got lucky," Rosalyn said.

"No, your sister's right," Brenna said, nervously looking around. "You don't know the lengths Jimmy would go to in order to get what he wants. I've known him to do some very unsavory things."

"While we're waiting for the scumbag, don't you think we should be looking for the actual portal?" Amelia suggested.

I nodded. "Right. It has to be inside the walls here somewhere. Maybe hidden behind something else. You and Rosalyn press against the walls. Jim is using blood magic, so you should feel something."

"What exactly?" Rosalyn asked, feeling her way along the western wall next to the other closed door.

"I'm don't know exactly. Static, or something extraordinarily cold. Or hot. Anything different."

"That helps a whole lot," she muttered.

"Can I help?" Brenna asked. "He's my brother, so I should be able to feel something too."

I shook my head. "It's meant to keep the three keys out, so only us three will be able to feel the spell. I think."

"You think? So what do you *know*?" Amelia asked, pressing her hands here and there along the wall.

"I know how to counter his spell if or when he casts it," I said, feeling along my own wall, pulling down charts and notes as I went. "It's going to take all three of us combining our blood on the portal itself as I recite the incantation."

"And that will close it," Rosalyn said.

"Yes. In theory." I flushed at her glare. "Just keep searching."

Amelia gasped and jumped back. "I feel something."

"So do I," Rosalyn said from her end of the room.

I did, too. But it wasn't the opening of any portal. It was the vacuum suction of a someone teleporting themselves from a great distance.

"Watch out!" I shouted, whirling around, ready to cast my deadliest lightning bolt.

White light shot from my fingers, exploding against the door, still held in place by mage magic.

"Hey, watch your aim, girl!" Rhiona said, popping into the room, dodging my cast in the nick of time.

"Rhiona!" Brenna rasped. "What are you doing here?"

Our aunt sent her a disapproving glare. "The real question is, why didn't you contact me with what you were dealing with in the first place? I'm here to help.

"By the way, I contacted the mage council and told them what was going on. As usual they'll evaluate the situation and send their special forces if they deem necessary." She snorted. "We should see them next Christmas sometime if the world is still intact, the anal old goats."

She moved next to me, asking, "What do you need from me, niece?"

"Be ready to cast," I warned. "Jim Callaghan will be showing up any moment. It's almost high noon, a perfect time for a solar eclipse."

"*Solar* eclipse?"

"Jim Callaghan is Mars, the dark mage of the Red Moon Prophecy," Rosalyn explained to her. "He's going to try and open a hidden portal to the Dark Dimension."

"My stars in heaven," she breathed heavily. "That boy was always too ambitious for his own good. Quinn always thought that was a good trait for a future High Alpha. I disagreed. So where is this portal you found?"

"We haven't yet," I said. "It should be somewhere here in his workroom, but we can't find hide nor hair of it."

"What makes you think it's here?" Rhiona questioned.

"Max Valerian interpreted more of the original text to read that we'll be able to find it in the wolf's den."

"Here?" She scrunched her lined face as she looked around, shaking her head. "I can't feel his presence anywhere here within the last few hours."

Everyone turned wide eyes to her.

"Hours?" I questioned.

My stomach dropped, remembering Max's warning, figuring out why Jim Callaghan wasn't here.

And where he was now.

"God, this was a stupid decoy!" I ground out, turning to Marc. "He played us. All of us."

I whipped my head to Rhiona. "You have to teleport all of us to Jim's laboratory in the States. I have to conserve my energy."

"Where exactly?" she asked.

"The town of Oakwood, Colorado."

I gave her the address to the house I had allegedly shared with my false fiancé. That's why I was able to instinctively transport Marc and myself the first time.

Jim's true lab was hidden underneath the house.

And he chose this location, because that's where the unknown portal to the Dark Dimension was hidden.

And where he was this very minute.

CRYSTAL MOON

CHAPTER 24

I clung to Marc, and immediately we were teleported to the front lawn of the Oakwood house. It brought back the memory of me standing alone here in the misty night, and Marc time traveling back to convince me to find the truth and him, everything now full circle.

"What the hell is that?" Rosalyn shouted.

We all turned and looked up just as a screeching black dragon with a thirty-foot wingspan flew by. The thing somersaulted and circled back around towards us, then pulled back its long, thin scaly neck and breathed a white hot fireball at us.

"Look out!" someone yelled as Marc reflexively knocked me to the ground, covering me with his body.

The fireball hit the ground a few hundred yards away, exploding and shaking the ground beneath us.

Humans rushed out of their houses, screaming and pointing at the flying monster who was circling us and getting ready to take another shot. Two cars driving by crashed into each other, the people jumping out and running for cover.

"We're too late. The portal must be open," I said to Marc, still protectively laying on top of me. "That must have come from the Dark Dimension."

"Not necessarily," he said, watching it circle us. "There are dragon shifters out there."

"There are?" I remarked.

"Yeah, but none who'd want to kill us," Rosalyn said, both her and Brian ducking behind a tree.

Brenna and Davin agreed. So this wasn't a typical dragon shifter. And chances were that it wouldn't be the only one.

"You need to bubble the entire town," I told Marc. "We have to contain the area."

He nodded, then slid off of me. "Go to Rosalyn and Brian. Now!"

Marc jumped up, and I dashed to the tree hiding my sister. He stood up and shot a laser beam at the flying beast, knocking it out of the sky. It screeched with the hit, then crashed through the roof of the house across the street.

"Nice shootin', Tex," Rosalyn said.

Marc grinned and winked, then drew his arms up and murmured a covering spell. In seconds, the entire town was enclosed inside an invisible bubble.

"Are we safe now?" Amelia asked, her and Ethan plastered to the side of the house, along with Brenna and Davin.

Her question was immediately answered when the front door of the house blew out against the tornado force wind. The twirling black stream shot upwards and hit the ceiling of the bubbled shield, spreading outward and down, filling the sky with dark, menacing smoke.

Trees were uprooted, and cars and roofs and people blew across the roadway. Roaring, growling demons, serpents and dragons exploded from the house from the doors and windows.

That was when I looked up at the break in the smoky thunderheads and saw the moon moving across the sun, darkening it to an eerie blood red.

It was happening.

We hadn't arrived in time, hadn't stopped our uncle from opening the portal to the Dark Dimension, spewing out its monstrous inhabitants.

But we could close it now.

"We're too late!" Rosalyn yelled above the ear-splitting mayhem.

"Not yet," I determined fiercely. "Rosalyn, Amelia, we have to do this together."

"What? Storm the castle and conquer the villain?"

"In a manner of speaking, yes," I told her. "Follow me. Callaghan's lab is in the basement, and so is the portal. I know a way in."

Marc gripped me by the shoulders. "I'm not leaving you."

I kissed him, pulling his hands away. "You and the others have to stay here and destroy the demons that have already come through. Me and my sisters have to close the portal before anymore get out. Your shield around this town won't last forever. I feel the threads of the spell already unweaving against the darkness. We have to do this now, or we are all toast."

"Jillian!"

I kissed him again. One last time. "I love you."

One particularly nasty looking green dragon hovered and landed on the roof of the house, searching for us. I waited until its head was turned, then nodded to Amelia and Rosalyn who crouched and ran with me around the other side of the house, ducking into the bushes.

"The main basement access is inside the house," I whispered to them. "But there's another way in through the outside storm door just around this corner."

"Then what?" Amelia asked.

"With the portal open now, we won't have to guess where it is. But we will have to close it by using our combined blood and my reciting the counter spell."

"Gotcha," Rosalyn said. She looked up to where a dragon's tail swung from the rooftop. "Guess we're going in cowboy style then?"

"On the count of three," I said, then held up one finger, two fingers, then three.

Together we jumped up and ran around the corner of the house to the closed and locked basement doors. I cast and broke the lock, then opened the right side, and together we sneaked down the stairs and into the basement itself.

Which was dark, silent and empty.

"You were wrong," Amelia said.

"Maybe it's upstairs," Rosalyn posed.

Cautiously I switched on the light and looked around, frowning at the typical suburban house basement with worn garage sell furnishings, laundry facilities and electrical and plumbing pipes.

Something was definitely wrong. Not that I remembered coming down to the basement the one day I had allegedly lived here. This hadn't really been my home with my fiancé after all. This had been just a ruse.

All of it.

"Of course," I whispered.

Pulling up my magic, I waved my hand, and the glamor of this room fell away to reveal a very modern looking laboratory. The same one Marc and I discovered just a few hours ago.

"Very good, niece," Jim Callaghan said standing in the far corner. "I should have known you would be the one to figure it all out. There's still time to join me, my dear. We could rule this new dark world together, you and I."

"Jillian, the portal!" Amelia said, pointing at the invisible shimmer in the corner.

"It's too late," Jim said to me. "It's already open and the breach between this dimension and the other is already broken. There's nothing you can do now. Last chance, Jillian. Join me, or die with all the others."

I frowned, noticing something else, something wrong.

Nothing else was coming through.

"You opened the portal, but only so far," I figured out. "That's why you really wanted me all along. You can't open it all the way with only your half-mage blood. You need mine as well."

That's why I was his true weakness, and the real reason he wanted, needed me to join his plan. I was the one sister who took on the mage side of our trifecta, the one whose blood could supercharge his own.

His startled, furious expression told me that I was right.

"Sorry, uncle. Guess I'm not as ambitious as you are. Amelia! Rosalyn!"

I flicked my fingers, making a penknife appear in Rosalyn's palm. She sliced her hand, then tossed the knife to Amelia who cut hers, then tossed it to me. I sliced my palm, drawing a thin line of blood, waiting for my sisters to swipe theirs against the shimmering portal before I smeared my own over theirs.

We clasped hands, and I recited the memorized incantation in reverse.

Cursing, Callaghan launched himself at us, but some invisible hand yanked him away, tossing him across the room. He hit the wall with incredible force, knocking him unconscious.

Seconds later, the shimmering portal dimmed until there was a loud vacuum pop that knocked us all on our backsides.

Suddenly everything stilled.

The noise and wind outside silenced. Dawn broke and brightened from the open basement access door.

"Did we close it?" Amelia asked, standing.

"We did," I confirmed, smiling wide.

Marc and the others burst through the door above the inside stairs and scrambled down to us.

"The portal?" he rushed out.

"Closed," I said. "And Uncle Jim is resting comfortably in the corner there."

Rhiona and an eclectic group of people I didn't recognize, our mage special forces unit I would later learn, all glared down at him.

"Let's bind and take him to the council, Finnlee," Rhiona said to the elegant looking black woman. "I'm sure they'll have no issue with sending him to the very place he tried to bring to us here."

"Sounds like an excellent plan." The woman turned to the older hippy-dressed woman and the young, Asian computer geek next to her saying, "Loralee, Daniel, handle this gentleman, if you please."

"Sure thing, Finn," the young man said, then whipped out an amethyst conductor and whirled invisible chains around my uncle, then all three popped out of the room.

Rhiona nodded her thanks to the woman. "Perfect timing as always, Finnlee. I owe your team big time, again."

The black woman waved her manicured hand. "We're all just doing our job in keeping this world spinning. Speaking of which, after we clean up the mess outside, I'll have the elders reset the sun and moon back into their proper orbit. I hope the old prophecy rings true from this point on about a new age of peace coming up. I could use a nice vacation."

"You and me both, sister," Rhiona said. "So I'll see you at the next council meeting?"

"I'll be there. Oh, and don't forget to bring your niece. I'm sure the others will be very interested in talking with her."

"Will do."

The woman, Finnlee, gave me a wink, then disappeared.

I collapsed into Marc's arms, grateful that this horrible nightmare was indeed over. I dreaded seeing the destruction up top, and I hoped I had enough strength and power left to clean up the neighborhood. Several memory-loss spells would have to be cast, too.

"Well, gang, we still have a lot to do. Let's get to it," I said.

* * *

"We still have a lot of incredibly rare specimens to take home, even though no more surprise easter egg parchments inside the geodes," Helene remarked as the last were crated.

She gripped the small of her back and arched back with a groan. "I love these field trips, but it'll be nice to get back home again. Hey, maybe we can all detour on our way back and hit a fossil dig in Montana the bone guys are going to. It'll be fun."

I tiredly leaned against Marc, his arm banding me against him. "Thanks, I'll pass. This trip really took it out of me."

"Lightweight," she complained. "You've been away from this too long."

"Probably right. I'll be better on the next one."

"I'll hold you to it," Helene said.

I watched the volunteers take down and load up the last of the equipment. Last night, Ethan and Amelia had closed up their medical tent and left for their estate in England, along with Davin. Rosalyn, Brian and Brenna were boarding their own flight bound for California right about now.

Marc and I had decided to stay behind and help button down the dig, then spend a day or two in Dublin just to decompress from the entire grueling trip. Thankfully alone this time.

"Sure I can't convince you guys to come with us to Montana?" Helene said.

I smiled and shook my head. "Another time. After all, there will be plenty of others now that I'm going to be teaching alongside you and Marc at USC next fall."

"Okay, then." Helene gave me an enthusiastic bearhug, then pointed a warning finger at Marc. "Take care of my bestie, Magic Man, or I'll personally cast a nasty spell on you."

He grinned, holding up his hands in surrender. "You have my word."

"See you both back at the ranch then," she said, waving as she got into the van filled with volunteers.

Marc and I were the last to leave, only our rental car parked beside the rural road. I was about to head to it when he touched my arm to stop me.

"Not so fast, Professor Azure. There's still one last thing to take care of here before we leave."

Frowning, I surveyed the work area in one wide sweep. On every dig, the team would make sure to repair any damage to the natural landscape, and I had personally inspected the work to make sure the place was as good and green as when we arrived.

I shook my head. "I don't think so. Everything looks perfect."

"Not yet, but it will be," he said. "At least I hope so."

"What are you talking about?"

Marc turned me to face him and fixed his emerald green stare with mine. "Jillian Azure…"

I gasped. "Oh, crap."

He cracked a sexy, half-smile, adding, "I love you. Now. In the past. In the future. In fact, I don't want to live one day without you, no matter when that is."

"Oh, God."

"Jillian Azure, will you do me the extraordinary honor of becoming my wife?"

I blinked hard, completely dumbfounded. "But I thought mages don't get married or have families."

"There's always a first," he said. "And I hope we're it. So will you?"

"Will I..?"

"Marry me," Marc added for me. "Please."

"Yes."

He grinned. "That easy, huh? And here I thought I was going to have to debate long and hard with you on the subject. Maybe even have to do a few magic tricks to impress you too."

I slid my arms around his neck and drew him down for a very long and thorough kiss. "Idiot. I said yes to you the very first day I opened my eyes and saw you standing beside my hospital bed. No magic needed."

"How about this then?"

Marc snapped his fingers, then presented me with a long-stemmed lavender colored rose, and a diamond ring tied to a white ribbon around it.

I untied the ring and allowed him to slip it onto my finger. "Now that's impressive."

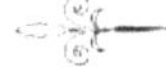

CRYSTAL MOON

EPILOGUE

The sun was setting over the restless, windy ocean as Brenna Callaghan walked along the shores off Spanish Point, Ireland.

It was a nice relaxing holiday after settling everyone into their new respective roles. It had had been a big job transferring the position as High Alpha to Rosalyn, but with Brian Lochlan by her side, along with the other family members, the American Callaghan wolf pack would be in excellent hands. Rhiona had promised to stay and help out as sorceress ambassador, and as always, Brenna knew she could fully trust her aunt to take care of anything needed.

That done, Brenna hopped a flight to Dublin with the plan to locate any other Callaghan pack remnants to join them in the States. Or she could help them form a new pack here in Ireland. Maybe she would be the one to successfully reintroduce the wild wolves back to her homeland, at least the talking ones.

"Not to sound too cliché, but at last we meet. Again."

Brenna whirled around to face Davin suddenly standing there. His incredible vampiric speed never ceased to amaze and impress her. As well as his insight and instinct and strength and compassion and...

"What are you doing here?" she asked, trying to pull back the welling tears.

"Where else would I be?" he remarked with that slight, sexy smile of his.

"Back at your Cambridge estate with our daughter and her husband, for one."

Davin shook his head. "Amelia is quite capable of managing the estate, the business, and the entire coven without me. Now that I've officially retired."

"You've stepped down as sire?"

"Yes. She's quite perturbed with me about it, too."

"I would imagine so. Why did you do it?"

He lifted a shoulder as they strolled along the dark beach. "Necessity. Whim. Frankly, I'm just tired of living my life for others and need a bit of a break. You?"

"The same. How did you know that I stepped down as High Alpha?"

"We have daughters who talk to each other now," he chuckled. "I hear Jillian wants to push up their wedding date to next month before the new semester at the university begins."

"Yes, she mentioned that. I hoped to see you then."

"You're seeing me now," he said. "Not disappointed, I hope."

"Not at all." Brenna breathed in the cool, salty air. "Lord, it's good to be back home again. I've missed this."

"I've missed you. For so many years. All of my life."

Brenna halted. Davin turned and faced her.

"We can't," she said, tears welling in her quicksilver eyes.

"We can," he disagreed.

"We shouldn't then. It's been too long."

"What is time when it comes to real and lasting love?" he remarked, cupping his hand on her cheek. "Silly, beautiful wolf. Don't you know yet that I could never stopped loving you no matter the amount of years that passed?"

"Davin, I—"

"No, let me finish," he interrupted. "Brenna, I've been lost to you since the moment I first met you, my personal angel in wolf's clothing. My love for you has only grown stronger with every day, year and decade that has gone by, and it will continue to grow stronger through the centuries and on into eternity."

Davin pulled a garnet ring set in gold and surrounded with tiny sparkling diamonds. It was the same stone they hunted for a lifetime ago, one that she had kept always on her mantle to look at every day since then.

"Our duties are done now, Brenna Callaghan," he said. "We have passed the crowns to our heirs. It's time you and I enjoy the happiness we have fought so long and hard for all of these long, lonely years. Marry me. Be my life-mate. I've wasted too many decades without you. Please don't make me face the endless centuries to come alone."

Brenna smiled and allowed him to slip the ring onto her finger. Then she threw her arms around his neck and kissed him with all the passion she held in restraint since they parted at the Dublin airport twenty-seven years ago.

"Now we have the difficult decision on where we both will live," she said, laughing with disbelief and utter joy.

"Anywhere you wish, my love," Davin said, his eyes narrowing playfully as his eyeteeth began to lengthen and nibble on her exposed neck. "But first, let's go back to your seaside cottage and pick up where we left off three decades ago. I believe there's a certain something wild that you promised to show me."

"If we have time," she reminded.

"Oh, I think I can spare as much as you'll need. And then some."

END